THE 20th VICTIM

BOOKS BY JAMES PATTERSON FEATURING THE WOMEN'S MURDER CLUB

A complete list of books by James Patterson is at the back of this book. For previews of upcoming books and information about the author, visit JamesPatterson.com, or find him on Facebook.

THE 20th VICTIM

JAMES PATTERSON

AND MAXINE PAETRO

Little, Brown and Company

New York Boston London

Copyright © 2020 by James Patterson
Excerpt from *WMC 21* copyright © 2020 by James Patterson

Hachette Book Group supports the right to free expression and the value of copyright. The purpose of copyright is to encourage writers and artists to produce creative works that enrich our culture.

The scanning, uploading, and distribution of this book without permission is a theft of the author's intellectual property. If you would like permission to use material from the book (other than for review purposes), please contact permissions@hbgusa.com. Thank you for your support of the author's rights.

Little, Brown and Company
Hachette Book Group
1290 Avenue of the Americas, New York, NY 10104
littlebrown.com

First edition: May 2020

Little, Brown and Company is a division of Hachette Book Group, Inc. The Little, Brown name and logo are trademarks of Hachette Book Group, Inc. Women's Murder Club is a trademark of JPB Business, LLC.

The publisher is not responsible for websites (or their content) that are not owned by the publisher.

The Hachette Speakers Bureau provides a wide range of authors for speaking events. To find out more, go to hachettespeakersbureau.com or call (866) 376-6591.

ISBN 978-0-316-42028-0 (hc) / 978-0-316-49494-6 (large print)
LCCN 2020931931

10 9 8 7 6 5 4 3 2 1

LSC-H

Printed in the United States of America

*Dedicated to law enforcement officers throughout
the United States who put themselves in harm's
way to protect the rest of us.*

THE 20th VICTIM

CHAPTER 1

CINDY THOMAS WAS tuned in to her police scanner as she drove through the Friday-morning rush to her job at the *San Francisco Chronicle.*

For the last fifteen minutes there'd been nothing but routine calls back and forth between dispatch and patrol cars. Then something happened.

The Whistler TRX-1 scanner went crazy with static and cross talk. It was as though a main switch had been thrown wide open. Codes in the four hundreds jammed the channel. She knew them all: 406, officer needs emergency help; 408, send ambulance; 410, requested assistance responding.

Cindy was an investigative journalist, top dog on the crime beat. Her assistance was definitely not requested, but she was responding anyway. Tips didn't get hotter than ones that came right off the scanner.

The location of the reported shooting was a Taco King

1

on Duboce Avenue. Cindy took a right off Otis Street and headed toward the Duboce Triangle, near the center of San Francisco between the Mission, the Castro, and the Lower Haight.

With the sirens from the patrol cars ahead and the ambulance wailing and honking from behind, she sure didn't need the street number. She pulled over to the side of the road, and once the emergency medical bus had passed her, she drafted behind it, pedal to the floor and never mind the speed limit.

The ambulance braked at the entrance to the Taco King at the intersection of Duboce Avenue and Guerrero Street. Cruisers had blocked off three lanes of the four-lane street, and uniformed officers were already detouring traffic. People were running away from the scene, screaming, terrified.

Cindy left her Honda at the curb and jogged a half block, reaching the Taco King in time to see two paramedics loading a stretcher into the back of the bus. She tried to get the attention of one of them, but he elbowed her out of his way.

"Step aside, miss."

Cindy watched through the open rear doors. The paramedic ripped open the victim's shirt, yelled, "Clear," and applied the paddles. The body jumped and then doors slammed and the ambulance tore off south on Guerrero, toward Metro Hospital.

Police tape had been stretched across three of the four lanes, keeping bystanders from entering the parking lot and the restaurant. At the tape stood a uniformed cop—Kay Kendall—a friend of Cindy's live-in love, homicide inspector Rich Conklin.

She walked up to Kendall with her notebook in hand, greeted her, and said, "Kay, what the hell happened here?"

"Oh, hey, Cindy. If you hang on, someone will come out and make an announcement to the press."

She growled at her.

Kendall laughed.

"I heard you were a pit bull, but you don't look the part." She wore blond curls, with a rhinestone-studded clip to discipline them, and had determination in her big blue eyes. That was how she looked, no manipulation intended. Still.

"Kay. Look. I'm only asking for what everyone inside and outside the Taco King saw and heard. Gotta be forty witnesses, right? Just confirm that and give me a detail or two, okay? I'll write, 'Anonymous police source told this reporter.' Like that."

"I'll tell you this much," Kendall said. "A guy was shot through the windshield of that SUV over there."

Kendall pointed to a silver late-model Porsche Cayenne.

"His wife was sitting next to him. I heard she's pregnant. She wasn't hit and didn't see the shooter. That's unverified, Cindy. Wife's inside the squad car that's moving out of the lot over there. And now you owe me. Big time. Give me a minute to think so I don't blow my three wishes."

Cindy didn't give her the minute, instead asking, "The victim's name? Did *anyone* see the shooter?"

"You're pushing it, Cindy."

"Well. My pit-bull reputation is at stake."

Kay grinned at her, then said, "Can you see the SUV?"

"I see it."

"Take a picture of the SUV's back window."

"All right, Kay. I sure will."

Kendall said, "Here's your scoop: the victim is almost famous. If he dies, it's going to be big news."

CHAPTER 2

KENDALL SHOOK HER finger at Cindy, a friendly warning.

Cindy mouthed, "Thank you," and before she could get chased away, she ducked the tape, got within fifty feet of the SUV's rear window, and snapped the picture. She was back over the line, blowing up the shot, when Jeb McGowan appeared out of the crowd and sidled up to her. McGowan looked like a young genius with his slicked-back hair and cool glasses with two-tone frames. He played the part of journo elite, having worked crime in his last job at the *LA Sun Times.* He had a daily column—as she had—and had done some interviews on cable news after he reported on the Marina Slasher two years ago.

Back then McGowan had implied that San Francisco was small-time and provincial.

"Why are you here?" she'd asked.

"My lady friend has family in Frisco. She needs to see them more. So whaddaya gonna do?"

Cindy had thought, *For starters, don't call it Frisco.*

Now McGowan was in her face.

"Cindy. Hey."

That was another thing. McGowan was pushy. Okay, the same had been said of her. But in Cindy's opinion, McSmarty was no team player and would love to shove her under a speeding bus and snatch the top spot. Or maybe he'd just stick around, like gum under her shoe, and simply annoy her to death.

"Hiya, Jeb."

She turned away, as if shielding her phone's screen from the morning sun, but he kept talking.

"I had a few words with a customer before she fled. I have her name and good quotes about the mayhem after the shooting. Here's an idea, Cindy. We should write this story together."

"You've got the name of the victim?"

"I will have it."

"I've already got my angle," she said. "See you, Jeb."

Cindy walked away from McGowan, and when she'd left him behind, she enlarged the image of the Porsche's back window. A word had been finger-painted in the dust.

Was it *Rehearsal?*

She sucked in her breath and punched up the shot until *Rehearsal* was clear. It was a good image for the front page, and for a change, no friend of hers at the SFPD was saying, "That's off the record."

As she walked to her car, Cindy wondered, *Rehearsal for what?* Was it a teaser? Whatever the shooter's motive for shooting the victim, he was signaling that there would be another shooting to come.

Cindy phoned Henry Tyler, the *Chronicle*'s publisher and editor in chief, and left him a message detailing that her anonymous source was a cop and she was still digging into the victim's identity.

Back in her car, she listened to the police scanner, hoping to catch the name of the victim. And she called Rich to tell him what she'd just seen.

He might already know the victim's name.

CHAPTER 3

YUKI CASTELLANO LOCKED her bag in her desk drawer, left her office, and headed to the elevator.

A San Francisco assistant district attorney, Yuki was prosecuting an eighteen-year-old high school dropout who'd had the bad luck to sign on as wheelman for an unidentified drug dealer.

Two months ago there'd been a routine traffic stop.

The vehicle in question had a busted turn-signal light and stolen plates. The cop who'd pulled over the vehicle was approaching on foot when the passenger got out of the offending vehicle and shot him.

The cop's partner returned fire, missed, and fired on the vehicle as it took off on Highway 1 South. The cop called for assistance and stayed with the dying man.

A few miles and a few minutes later the squad cars in pursuit forced the getaway car off the far-right lane and road-blocked it. The police found that the passenger had ditched, leaving the teenage driver, Clay Warren, and a sizable package of fentanyl inside the car.

The patrolman who'd been shot died at the scene.

Clay Warren was held on a number of charges. The drugs were valued at a million, as is, and impounded. Warren and the car were identified by the dead cop's partner, and Forensics had found hundreds of old and new prints in the vehicle, but none that matched to a known felon.

Bastard had worn gloves or never touched the dash, or this was his first job and he wasn't in the system.

Yuki doubted that.

So in lieu of the killer dealer, the wheelman was left holding the bag.

The DA was prosecuting Clay Warren for running drugs in a stolen car and acting as accomplice to murder of a police officer, but largely for being the patsy. Yuki had hoped that Warren would give up the missing dealer, but he hadn't done so and gave no sign that he would.

Using the inside of the stainless-steel elevator door as a mirror, she applied her lipstick and arranged her hair, then exited on the seventh floor and approached Sergeant Bubbleen Waters at the desk.

"Hi, B. I have a meeting with prisoner Clay Warren and his attorney."

"They're waiting for you, Yuki. Hang on a sec."

She picked up the desk phone, punched a button, and said, "Randall. Gate, please."

A guard appeared, metal doors clanked open, and locks shut behind them. The guard escorted Yuki to a small cinder-block room with a table and chairs, two of the chairs already occupied. Clay Warren wore a classic orange prison jumpsuit and silver cuffs. His attorney, Zac Jordan, had long hair and was wearing a pink polo shirt, a khaki blazer, jeans, and a gold stud in his left ear.

Zac gave Yuki a warm smile and stood to shake her hand with both of his.

"Good to see you, Yuki. Sorry to say, I'm not getting anywhere fast. Maybe Clay will listen to you."

CHAPTER 4

ZAC JORDAN WAS a defense lawyer who worked pro bono for the Defense League, a group that represented the poor and hopeless.

During a brief break from her job with the DA, Yuki had worked for Zac Jordan and could say that he was one of the good guys and that his client was lucky to have him.

In this case, his client was facing major prison time for being in the wrong car at the wrong time.

Yuki sat down and asked, "How's it going, Clay?"

He said, "Just wonderful."

Clay Warren looked younger than his age. He was small and blond haired, with a button nose, but when he glanced up, his gray eyes were hard. After his quick appraisal of Yuki, he lowered his gaze to his hands, the cuffs linked to a metal loop in the middle of the table. He looked resigned.

"Clay," she said, "as we discussed before, a police officer is dead. You know who shot him. I'm asking you again to help us by telling us who did that. Otherwise, I can't help you, and you'll be charged as an accomplice to murder and for possession of narcotics with intent, and tried as an adult. You're looking at life in prison."

"For driving the car," he said.

"Do you understand me?" Yuki asked. "You're an accomplice to the murder of a *cop*. If you help us get the shooter, the DA might help you out. The charges could be lowered significantly, Clay."

"I don't know anything. I was driving. I heard the siren. I pull over and get charged with all of this bullshit. It's wrong. All wrong. I was speeding. Period."

"And the drugs inside the car? Where'd you get a million dollars' worth of fentanyl?"

Yuki knew that there was a tentative ID on the dealer. The cop who'd watched his partner die on the street had reviewed photos of likely suspects, big-time drug dealers, and thought the shooter might be Antoine Castro, but he wasn't entirely sure.

Yuki said, "Why are you taking the weight for scum like Antoine Castro?"

The kid shook his head no.

Castro was on the FBI's Most Wanted list. By now, Yuki was willing to bet, he'd left the country and assumed a new identity.

Zac said, "Lying isn't helping you, son. I know ADA Castellano. I'll negotiate for you."

"For God's sake," Warren shouted. *"Leave me alone."*

Yuki imagined that if the killer dealer was Castro, he'd gotten word to the kid. Warned him.

You talk. You die.

Clay Warren wasn't going to talk. Yuki stood up.

"I'm sorry, Zac."

"You tried," he said.

She went to the door and the guard opened it for her. She left Zac Jordan alone with his client, a scared kid who was going to die in prison, just a matter of when.

CHAPTER 5

FRIDAY MORNING AT 9 a.m., give or take a few minutes, homicide lieutenant and acting police chief Jackson Brady strode down the center aisle of the bullpen.

The night shift was punching out, day shift straggling in, calling out, "Hey, boss," "Yo, Brady." He nodded to Chi, Lemke, Samuels, Wang, kept going.

At the front of the room there were two desks pushed together face-to-face. Boxer and Conklin's real estate. Brady had partnered with both of them when he first came to the SFPD as a switch-hitter. Stood with them with bullets flying more than once. He counted on them. Would do anything for them.

Brady slid into Boxer's desk chair. He looked at Conklin over Lindsay's small junkyard of personal space, swung the head of the gooseneck lamp aside, moved a stack of files and a mug to make space for his elbows.

Conklin looked up, said, "You okay, Lieu?"

Brady knew that he looked like shit. Too many hours

here. Too much junk food. Too little sleep. Worried eighteen hours a day. His collar was tight. He loosened his tie. Undid the top shirt button.

"So the way I understand it," Brady said, "Boxer had a doctor's appointment yesterday afternoon. A checkup. She calls to say, 'I'm fine, boss. Doctor said I need to start taking me time.'"

Conklin said, "She told me the same."

Brady thought about when Boxer had been very sick. Took off a couple of months and came back. Said she felt perfect. So now what was she saying?

"You think she's all right?" said Brady.

Conklin said, "She's fine. Doctor told her she shouldn't run herself into the ground like she does. So her sister has the wild child, and Lindsay and Joe took off to parts unknown for the weekend, maybe another day or two. You know, Brady. Most people take weekends off."

"Oh, really? I don't know many."

Brady gathered up loose pens and pencils and put them into a ceramic mug.

Conklin said, "What worries me is how *you* look."

"Don't rub it in."

Brady had been working two jobs since Chief Warren Jacobi had been retired out. Filling Jacobi's old chair on the fifth floor as well as running the Homicide squad room felt like having his head slammed in a car door.

The mayor was pressuring him; choose one job or the other, but decide.

Brady had talked it over with Yuki, who'd offered measured wifely advice, not pushing or pulling, just laying it out as a lawyer would.

"I can make a case for taking on more responsibility while working fewer hours per day. I can also give you reasons why Homicide is where your strengths lie. And you love it. But you have to make a decision PDQ, or the mayor is going to make it for you."

Conklin was saying, "I can work with Chi and McNeil until Boxer is back."

"Yeah. Do that."

Brady left Conklin and the bullpen, took the fire stairs one flight up to five. When he got to his office, his assistant, Katie, said, "Lieu, I was just about to look for you. Check this out."

He took a seat behind the desk. Katie leaned over his shoulder and brought up the *Chronicle* online, paused on the front page, and read the headline, "'Roger Jennings Shot at Taco King,'" then added the takeaway, "He's in critical condition."

Jennings was a baseball player, a catcher nearing the end of his professional career.

Why would anyone want to kill him?

CHAPTER 6

I'D CALLED JOE as soon as I left my doctor's office and told him what Doc Arpino had said: "Lindsay. Live a little. Get out of town for a few days. Go to a spa."

My dear husband had said, "Leave this to me."

I'd left word with Brady and Conklin: "I'm off duty."

Words to that effect.

Now, with our phones locked inside the trunk, Joe and I were heading north, breezing across the Golden Gate Bridge, sailboats flying below us across the sparkling bay.

Joe was at the wheel and I was sitting beside him, saying, "I did not."

"You did, too. You came to the airport. You said, 'I want you. And I want the jet.'"

I laughed out loud. "You're crazy."

"You remember the company plane?"

"Oh. Yes."

"Louder, dear."

"Oh, YES."

We both laughed.

Joe and I had met on the job, heads of a cop and DHS joint task force charged with shutting down a terrorist who was armed with a deadly poison and a plan to take down members of the G8 meeting in San Francisco. He killed a lot of people, including one very close to me, before we nailed the bastard and took him down.

I blocked thoughts about all of that and said, "You remember when we broke away from the G8 case for the investigation in Portland?"

"Do I ever," said Joe. "Inside that conference room with a dozen people working a national-security murder and you saying, 'If you keep looking at me like that, Deputy Director Molinari, I can't work.'"

I laughed and said, "I told you that afterward. I didn't say that out loud."

I was sure I was right, but it was also true that working with Joe under so much adrenalized fear and pressure had unleashed some pretty amazing magic between us. And before we'd left Portland for San Francisco, we'd fallen in love. Hard.

Was it perfect from then on?

Hell no. We lived on opposite sides of the country, and so we rode the long-distance relationship roller coaster for a while, cured loneliness and longing with adventures for a few days a month until Joe gave up his job and moved to the City by the Bay.

About a year after our wedding, I gave birth to Julie Anne Molinari while home alone on a dark and stormy night with electric lines down across the city. While I panted and pushed and screamed, surrounded by firemen, Joe was thirty-five thousand feet overhead, unaware.

He'd made it up to me and our baby girl when he finally reached home. Joe Molinari, intelligence agency consultant and Mr. Mom.

He asked now, "Where are you, Lindsay?"

"I'm right here."

I leaned over, gave him a kiss, and said, "I was remembering. Where are *you*, Joe?"

He put his hand on my thigh.

"I'm here, Blondie, thinking about what a good mom you are, and how much I love you."

I told him, "I sure do love you, too."

This weekend Julie was staying at the beach with her aunt Cat, two cousins, and Martha, our best doggy in the world, while Joe and I got to be two fortysomething kids in love.

Joe turned on the radio and found the perfect station.

We were cruising. The weather was sunny with a side of sailboats, and we were singing along with the oldies: "Free to do what I want any old time."

When we reached our first destination, Joe and I were in a honeymoon state of mind.

CHAPTER 7

JOE SLOWED THE car and parked us in front of a modest-looking two-story building made of river stones and timbers, surrounded by greenery.

I recognized it from photos of where to go in Napa Valley. This was reportedly one of the best restaurants in the world, as it had been for the last twenty years.

Yes, best in the *world*.

I shouted, "The French Laundry? Seriously?"

I'd read about how hard it was to get into this place, revered by foodies all over and winner of Michelin's top ranking, three stars. A two-month waiting period for a lunch reservation was *typical*.

"You didn't pull this off overnight."

"I have a connection," Joe said, giving me a twinkly grin.

Wow. After the burger-and-coffee diet that went with being on the Job, I wondered if I could even appreciate fine dining. But now I knew why Joe had said to wear a dress—and surprise, surprise, I had one on. It was a navy-blue-and-white print, and I'd matched it with a blue cashmere cardigan. I pulled the band from my sandy-blond ponytail, flipped down the visor, and looked at myself in the mirror.

I fluffed up my hair a little and pinched my cheeks.

I looked nice.

The restaurant's farm garden was across the street, and it was open to visitors, a lovely place for a Friday stroll. I told Joe I was going to need my phone after all so I could take pictures. He got out of the car, and the trunk lid went up.

That's when a panel van pulled up to the rear of the car and buzzed down its passenger-side window. I couldn't see the driver, but I heard him yell, "Joeeey."

Joe called back, "Dave, you crazy SOB."

I watched him go over to the van, open the door, lean in, and hug the driver. Then he came back to me and said, "You're finally going to meet Dave."

When Joe spoke of David Channing, it was always with love and sadness. Dave had been Joe's college roommate at Fordham back east in the Bronx. I'd seen pictures of them on the field. Dave was a quarterback and Joe played flanker. He'd shown me pictures of the team, whooping, high on victory, both Joe and Dave tall, brawny, handsome, and so young.

Joe had told me that after a day like that, a win against Holy Cross, there'd been a sudden cold snap and a snowstorm had blown in from the west. Dave had been driving his girlfriend, Rebecca, home to Croton-on-Hudson, about forty-five minutes up the Taconic, a lovely twisting road with a parklike median strip and beautiful views.

But, as Joe had told me, on that late afternoon the snow had melted into a coating of black ice on the road. Dave had taken a turn where a rocky outcropping blocked his view of a vehicle that had spun out of control and stopped across both lanes. Dave had braked, skidding into the disabled car, while another, fast-moving car had rear-ended him.

Before it was over, thirty-two cars had crashed in a horrific pileup. Rebecca had been killed. Dave's spine had been crushed, and the young man who was being scouted by NFL teams had been paralyzed from the waist down.

His parents, Ray and Nancy, had brought Dave home to their little winery just outside Napa, and there'd been years of painful rehab. During those years, Joe had said, Dave had walled himself off from his friends and pretty much the whole world. Lately, he kept the company books, ran a support group for paraplegics, and mourned his mother's death from lymphoma. That was all Joe knew.

Joe opened my door, offered me his hand, and helped me out, saying, "I've been waiting a long time for this, Linds. Come and meet Dave."

CHAPTER 8

DAVID CHANNING DID some show-off wheelies, pushed his chair wheels to fade back, and told Joe to go long.

He tossed an imaginary football, and Joe made a big show of snatching it out of the air, running across an invisible goal line, and spiking the ball in the end zone.

Dave laughed as Joe did a victory dance. Then he grinned shyly and held out his hand to shake mine, and I turned it into a hug.

"It's trite but true," he said. "Joe has told me so much about you."

"Back at you, Dave. He can really riff on you, too."

Joe squeezed his friend's shoulder, said, "Shall we?"

Dave said, "I'd love to join you, Joe, but I'm just here to finally meet Lindsay, and now I've got to get back."

Joe said, "*Hell no, you don't.* I haven't seen you in three years. We're having lunch together. All of us. It's on me."

Dave protested. He said that this was our weekend, lunch

was all set for us, he didn't want to be a third wheel—but he didn't have a chance versus Joe.

I heard him mutter "You're still tough, old man" as Joe, steering us toward the restaurant and holding open the shiny blue-painted door, ushered us inside. We were greeted by the maître d', who called Dave "Davy," and we were shown to a table, seated so that I was between Dave and Joe, Dave saying, "These folks are customers of ours."

Joe said, "I think we'll be having the Channing Winery Cab."

Sounded good to me.

Claire Washburn, my BFF, had been here for her anniversary last year and had given me the CliffsNotes, saying, "A meal at the French Laundry changes your life."

I didn't doubt my friend. In fact, I couldn't remember a time when she'd been wrong about anything. But I wasn't sure that a single meal could change my life, even for a day. Joe's lasagna was a high bar and possibly my favorite dish—in the *world*.

I looked around and immediately warmed to the restaurant; the main room was comfortable and homey, with sand-colored walls, a dozen round tables, a coved ceiling, and sconces between the casement windows.

Our menus arrived and Dave said, "I recommend the tasting menu. Today's version will never be served exactly the same way again."

Lisette, our server, concurred. A quick look at the menu laid out a journey of nine little courses of classic French cuisine with a three-star spin. And along the way there would be wine to taste.

I'm no math whiz, but it was easy to see that lunch for three was going to come in at over a thousand dollars.

Possibly *well over* a thousand.

Joe put his arm around the back of my chair and pulled me closer to him.

Dave apologized for not making it to our wedding, and I told him that we'd felt him there nonetheless.

"Love the wedding present, Dave."

He laughed, said, "Not everyone loves an antique gun safe."

Joe and I said it together.

"We do!"

CHAPTER 9

BEFORE THE FIRST dish arrived, the two old friends started catching up on who'd married, who'd gone into politics, who had passed away.

The salmon tartare was served in a little cone. Adorable. My taste buds maxed out but rallied in time to taste what Lisette said was one of the French Laundry's signature dishes: two oysters on the half shell with pearl tapioca and Regiis Ova caviar, served in a small white bowl. I dipped a fork into the oyster shell and brought the creamy, buttery, salty aphrodisiac of foods to my mouth.

It was good. Very good. I was still thinking about the unusual textures and flavors when the next in a procession of beautifully plated delicacies arrived.

I didn't quite get the creamed English peas and pork jowl, the marinated nectarines, the soft-boiled red hen egg in the shell that looked as though it were made of porcelain. But from the ecstatic expressions at my table and surrounding ones, I understood why the French Laundry was the gold standard for people with sophisticated taste.

Three hours later, when we were sipping our coffee and sampling the wondrous variety of sweets, we convinced Dave to talk about himself.

"Joey knows this, Lindsay, but my mom passed away just before you two got married. My dad and I were always close. But working together has really given us a—I don't know what else to call it—a deep friendship."

Dave sighed.

Joe put his hand on Dave's arm and asked him what was wrong.

Dave said, "Dad's sick, in the hospital, and I'm very worried."

"Why? What happened?" Joe asked.

"He has a thoracic aortic aneurysm brought on by high blood pressure. It's grown to the size that might require surgery. His doctor prescribed him beta-blockers but says he's got age-related system breakdown. But I'm not buying it. He's seventy-two. He's never been sick before."

Joe said, "I'm sorry to hear this, Dave."

"If you have any time, Joe, I know he'd like to see you. He was our biggest fan."

Joe looked down at the table. I'm pretty sure he was flashing back on those college football years, their families screaming from the stands.

Joe lifted his eyes, looked at his friend, and asked, "When would be a good time to see him?"

CHAPTER 10

AS WE PULLED out of the parking lot, I told Joe, "He's great, Joe. I feel bad for him."

"It was good to see him. Hey, you're sure it's okay?"

"Of course. You go see his dad and I'll go to the spa."

Joe nodded, said, "I'll be back in time for dinner."

"Perfect," I said. I was thinking of a massage, some kind of exotic wrap. Freak out the guys at work by getting a manicure. I could almost hear Brady saying, "What happened to you, Boxer?"

I grinned, but when I turned to share my joke with Joe, he was in deep thought.

He saw me out of the corner of his eye and said, "I can't help but think about what his life might have been but for that bad turn in the road." And then, "I think that a lot of guys who play pro ball have broken lives. Not just physically, but the fame and money and disappointments, all of that. I'm just glad he's the Dave I know."

I nodded my agreement.

He said, "And you, sweetie? How was your lunch?"

"It was fabulous, the best meal I've ever had, and you know why? Because you thought of it, Joe. You made this great plan in a split second. You called Dave and got it done. You spent a bundle on *lunch*."

"What about the food? You didn't mention the food."

"Well, may I be honest? I'm sure that I'm crazy and I should have loved the farm lamb and that steak thing and the green-pea puree and the whatever, but you know what I liked the best?"

"Let me guess," Joe said. "That little glazed donut at the end. Like a mini Krispy Kreme."

"Come on. How'd you know?"

"One, you're a cop. And two, you were making some very sexy noises."

"Huh. Maybe I was thinking about you."

"You were not."

"And since I'm going to the spa, I should be very relaxed and dreamy and smelling like flowers when you get back."

"Hold that thought," said Joe.

CHAPTER 11

THE MILLIKEN CREEK Inn is perched on a terraced hillside with views of the Napa River.

I came back from the spa to our room with its balcony view of the river, its fireplace, and its huge bed with a novel feeling. I felt no stress whatsoever. No rush. No hurry. No worry. Nowhere to go and nothing to do—but rest.

I dressed in a white robe and a pair of socks, then climbed aboard the California king with its down comforter and regal headboard. I woke up to Joe calling my name, flipping on the lights in the darkening room.

"Sorry, Linds. Didn't mean to wake you."

"What time is it?"

"Seven something. Seven twenty. When we came back from seeing Ray, Dave and I got into a pile of yearbooks and photo albums, and then, of course, I told him everything Julie has said and done since she was born."

I said, "Oh, man. All caught up now?"

Joe laughed, asked, "Do you want to go to the restaurant for dinner?"

I shook my head no. I was so comfortable.

"Me neither. I want to clean up and get into bed. But wait," he said.

He sat on the side of the bed and phoned room service, ordered cheese and fruit for two, basket of bread, bottle of Channing Winery Sauvignon Blanc, concluding with, "You got some candles? Good. Twenty minutes would be great."

He hung up the phone, shucked his jacket, came back to the bed, and kissed me.

"God," he said. "You *do* smell like flowers."

I showed him my newly polished fingers and toes, and he kissed me again, lifted a few strands of my hair away from my eyes.

"I'll be back," he said.

I fluffed my pillow, gazed out through the sliding doors to the balcony as the glow left the sky, and listened to Joe singing an old rock-and-roll hit in the shower. That oldies station we'd driven to must have gotten stuck in his head.

"'Do you *love* me? *Do* you love me?'"

He burst out of the bathroom in a robe singing the chorus.

"'Now…that I…can *dance*.'"

I laughed and opened my arms to him, and he got into bed.

I put my arm across his chest. He drew me close, and I tipped my head up and kissed him again, this time putting a little heat into it.

He said, "Look at us. Two oysters in white. No caviar required."

"Call your daughter," I said, "before it gets too late."

Joe got up, found his phone in his jacket pocket, and came back to bed. Together we FaceTimed my sister, her two shrieking little girls fighting over who should tell Uncle Joe about their day. And then we shared a sweet conversation with a sleepy Julie, who I could see was in bed with Martha. Julie said, "Mommy, say 'woof.'"

I did it.

"Nooooo. Say it to Martha!"

Cat cackled in the background as Julie took the phone to my old dog. I woofed on command. Then Joe and I kissed Julie through the screen of the phone and told her to sleep tight.

When we were alone again, Joe told me that Ray Channing looked terrible, but that he couldn't suppress his happiness at seeing Joe again after so many years.

"Told me I hadn't changed a bit."

We both laughed, and room service knocked and delivered.

Joe and I sipped wine. We nibbled. We talked, and then Joe put the candle in its little glass globe on the dresser before rolling the cart outside and locking the door.

He took off his robe and tossed it over a chair, came back to bed, and helped me out of mine.

"I have a confession," I said.

"Now? You wish my chest wasn't hairy?"

"I love your hairy chest. The lobster mac and cheese. That was my favorite course."

"It beat out the mini donut?"

"It was the best thing I've ever eaten."

Joe laughed. "Mac and cheese."

"With lobster."

"Got it. I think there's a recipe for that."

By eight thirty or so we were making love by enough candlelight for each of us to see into the other's eyes.

Joe asked me, "What did you say, Blondie?"

"I'm so lucky."

"Lucky me, too."

CHAPTER 12

TWENTY MINUTES AFTER kissing my child, my husband, and my border collie good-bye, I parked my Explorer under the overpass on Harriet Street.

It was only a half block to the medical examiner's office. I wanted to see my best friend, and I thought coffee with Claire would be a nice, soft entry to my Monday-morning return to work.

I pulled on the heavy glass doors, said "Hey" to Patrick, Claire's new receptionist, who told me, "Dr. Washburn said go into her office. She'll be there in a second."

Five minutes later Claire and Cindy came through the office door, Claire looking harried, Cindy wearing her deep-in-a-story face. I stood up and put my arms around them both and gave them a group hug.

"Your hair smells wonderful," Claire said.

"I got a hair mask. Me! What's going on, you two? What'd I miss?"

Cindy said, "The day you left, did you hear about it? Roger Jennings gets shot in his car leaving the Taco King on Duboce Avenue."

"I missed it."

"Okay, well, he survives the shooting for a few days, unconscious, never says a word before he passes away late last night. You know who he is? Roger Jennings?"

"Sure. He was a catcher. Released by the A's and picked up by the Giants, what—about a year ago? Was the shooter caught?"

Cindy filled me in. "No one saw the shooter, not even Jennings's pregnant wife, who was in the seat beside him."

Claire said, "The bullet entered through the center of the victim's neck, severing multiple vertebrae and arteries, before exiting through the left side of his neck."

Cindy said, "And someone, the shooter or an accomplice maybe, uses the chaos as cover to write the word *Rehearsal* on the back window of his Porsche Cayenne."

"Rehearsal," I said, thinking out loud. "The shooting was a trial run. Could be that Jennings was a random person in the wrong place."

"Maybe," said Cindy. "But I've been digging into Roger Jennings. I'm thinking he was lining up his next career. A little more dangerous than baseball."

"How so?"

"He was dealing," she said.

I said, "That's a fact?"

"Trusted sources tell me that Jennings was selling MDMA

to his teammates. There may be others. Chi and McNeil are on it. And now," said Cindy, "I've got to get back and file the story."

She blew kisses.

Then she was gone.

CHAPTER 13

AS CINDY FLEW out the door, Yuki blew in.

"I hope there's coffee in here somewhere."

Claire pointed to the coffeemaker, and when we were all topped off, arrayed around Claire's desk, we started catching up. Claire had been working all weekend, trying to organize the cremains of five bodies recovered from a crack house fire in the Tenderloin.

"This is the worst," she said. "Cause of death could be overdose, smoke inhalation, gunshot, all of the above, or none of the above. I doubt I'm going to ID even one of those bodies."

Yuki said to me, "Arson is suspected, but it could have been a crack pipe falling onto a pile of newspapers, everyone too whacked out to notice."

Claire got up from her desk, saying, "Be right back."

I asked Yuki how her case was going, and she said, "This defendant, Clay Warren. When I was working with Zac, I would have been fighting to get this kid released. I would have argued that he was a victim of circumstance. He didn't know about the drugs. I'd have gotten him to give up the puke who left him literally holding the bag. Now I'm gonna send him to prison for the rest of his dumb-ass life. Talk about cognitive dissonance," Yuki said.

She asked about Julie, and I told her that Joe and I were exhausted last night, but Julie didn't want to sleep. At all. "We compromised, let Julie and Martha into our bed, and our snoring finally knocked them out. Next thing I hear, 'Mommy! I'm gonna be late for school.'"

Yuki was laughing when Claire came back and reseated herself in her chair. She took a swig of coffee, sighed deeply.

I asked, "You okay?"

"Sure," she said. "I splashed cold water on my face. I want to sign off on these fire victims before I go home tonight. So tell me. You went to the French Laundry?"

Claire's receptionist knocked, poked his head in, and said, "Sorry to interrupt. Sergeant, Inspector Conklin just called. He said he needs you to come upstairs."

We broke up our little party and hugged Claire good-bye. Yuki and I power walked up the long breezeway that connects the medical examiner's office to the Hall of Justice.

An elevator was waiting and we boarded it, Yuki getting out on three. I exited on the fourth floor and found my partner at the entrance to the squad room, putting on his jacket.

"Good. You're here, Boxer," Rich Conklin said. "Double homicide in Saint Francis Wood. We're catching."

CHAPTER 14

CONKLIN AND I jogged down the fire stairs and through the lobby to the main exit on Bryant.

He briefed me as we checked out a squad car.

"The victims are Paul and Ramona Baron."

"The record producer?"

"That's the one."

I pictured Baron. Dark haired. Midforties. Small guy with a Vegas personality. The picture in my mind was of him recently celebrating a movie deal with a big crowd at the club Monroe.

Rich was telling me, "Their housekeeper, Gretchen Linder, found their bodies when she came to work about a half hour ago. The wife was still breathing, then she died while Linder was calling it in. She's at the scene now."

Conklin got behind the wheel, and while I buckled up and flipped on the sirens, he floored it, the car shooting away from the curb. I held on to the armrest as we sped southwest toward Saint Francis Wood, an affluent old-money enclave, one of those neighborhoods where nothing much ever happened—until it did.

Apart from a few expletives when jackass drivers failed to give way, Conklin and I didn't speak again until we arrived at the murder house.

Three patrol cars were in front of a beautiful old home, about four thousand square feet taking up a double-corner lot. The lawn was mown, shrubbery shorn. The property was as tidy as a freshly made bed.

We parked between the CSI van and an ambulance, got out of the car.

I spent a moment taking in the big picture: the multimillion-dollar old homes as far as I could see, ancient trees lining the street. There were two cars parked in the Barons' driveway, a late-model Mercedes and an Audi, both gleaming. A well-used Honda was parked at the curb along with the three black-and-whites, CSI's van, and an ambulance. Incongruent crackles and screeching of car radios, dogs barking, horns honking, underscored that shit had happened.

CSIs waited at their vehicle for a go-ahead. Uniforms taped off the walkway to the house and set up a secondary perimeter, kept traffic moving. The front door of the house at 181 San Anselmo Avenue opened, and Charles Clapper, the CSI director, stepped out and waved us in.

Conklin and I started up the walk—but were stopped by high-pitched *screams*. Two young children, a girl of about four and a boy of maybe six, both in pajamas, tore out of the backyard and crossed the lawn toward the street. Conklin and I captured them, while a pretty woman in a pink, bloodstained tunic over jeans called out, "Christopher. DeeDee. Come to Gretchen right now."

DeeDee had wrapped herself around my knees. I picked up the little girl and she hugged my neck, hard. Rich held on to her bawling bigger brother until their nanny, also crying, disentangled them and gathered them to her.

Conklin introduced the nanny, Gretchen Linder, who was distraught. Very.

"We're not *allowed*—that man told us to sit outside and wait. This is—*oh, my God*. Their *parents*. These poor *kids*. I saw Ramona *die*. I saw…I'm in charge of them. I don't know what to do," she said. "Should I take them to my place?"

It was kind of her to want to take the children home. But that wouldn't happen.

Richie said, "We need to take your statement. See that gray Ford next to the ambulance? What do you say I take you all to the police station? We'll figure out what's best for the kids, short term. And you can help us figure out what happened here."

Linder nodded. She put her hands over her eyes and sobbed, then wiped her face with her sleeve.

With Richie right behind her, she shepherded the children to the squad car.

CHAPTER 15

I'VE NEVER SEEN a room like this inside a *house*," I said to Clapper.

Clapper and I stood together in the foyer of the Barons' house, staring into a screening room that took up most of the ground floor. Wall fixtures threw soft light on a half dozen sectionals arranged in a horseshoe angled toward the wall of large TV screens. Photos of Paul Baron with entertainers he'd produced hung over the back bar.

I said, "It feels corporate."

"Like a first-class airport lounge."

At the far end of the screening room, two pairs of wide-open French doors revealed an open-space family/kitchen/dining room, remains of breakfast still on the table.

I asked, "Where was the point of entry?"

Clapper shook his head and said, "The doors and windows were all secured, except the front door. The nanny opened that and shut off the alarm."

"What, then? An inside job?"

Charlie Clapper is not only a former homicide investigator, but he's a meticulous CSI. He said, "Here's what I know so far.

"The basement level is the recording studio, accessed by the elevator over there," he said, pointing to the door under the rising staircase, "and the stairs at the back of the kitchen."

He continued, "The studio is like a big, soundproof safe with professional recording equipment. No windows. A fire door with a bar lock leads to the outside. Air comes through vents from up here. There's no way to get into that room from the outside unless someone opens the door for you."

"So you're thinking someone let the killer in?"

"Patience, Boxer. Let's go upstairs. Four bedrooms and baths, and the Barons had an office off the master. That's where they were shot dead, one bullet each."

"Murder-suicide?"

"Crossed my mind, but there's no weapon in the room."

"A locked-room murder mystery in real life?"

Clapper grinned. "Hello, Agatha Christie. But I don't think so. You met Gretchen Linder?"

"Conklin's taking her and the kids back to the Hall."

Clapper said, "Here's what she told me. That she came to work this morning, quarter to nine on the dot as always. Front door was locked. She used her key and disarmed the alarm. Called out, 'Hellooooo.' No answer. She didn't see the kids, or anyone, so she went upstairs. Ramona was still breathing. Gretchen called 911. By the time we arrived, Ramona had expired. I kept the EMTs from destroying the scene. From the temperature of Paul's body, I'd say he was shot at around eight thirty, give or take. Likely the shooter knew when the nanny was due to arrive."

I said, "How about giving me the tour?"

Together Clapper and I climbed a winding staircase, walked down a long hallway, passing open doors to the kids' rooms, bedrooms, and baths.

Clapper paused at the entrance to an open room at the end of the floor.

"Grab the walls and stay with me," he said.

CHAPTER 16

CLAPPER AND I paused at the threshold to the Barons' office.

At the center of the room was a sturdy, antique partners desk, made for two people to work facing each other. Behind the desk was a wall of casement windows. There was art on the opposite wall, a large TV screen, an exercise bike, and a water cooler, but my eyes turned quickly to the deceased.

Clapper said, "Paul Baron took a shot to the back of his head." The dark-haired man in plaid and jeans had fallen across his desk, facing the doorway. He had bled copiously over the desk and everything on it. Coffee and blood mixed together and dripped onto the carpet.

Continuing, Clapper said, "Looks to me like Ramona saw her husband fall toward her. She stood up, and that gave the shooter a good clean shot to her chest."

I followed his line of reasoning.

Ramona had dropped and toppled out of her chair, and was lying faceup on the carpet with her eyes open, blood spilling across her chest. I stooped down to get a closer look. She was wearing tights, a pink V-neck sweater, several diamond rings, diamond stud earrings, and a gold chain with a ruby cabochon pendant hanging just above the neat bullet hole through her sternum.

As with Ramona's husband, it looked like one shot had taken her out. The shooter had to have been trusted and standing only feet away. Did he or she have a house key? Know the alarm code? Had Gretchen—had she done this?

It didn't matter how many times I'd seen murder victims, it always hurt. What plans had this couple made? What would happen to their children? How had it come to be that this was their day to die?

I was staring at the small, bloody handprint on Ramona's cheek—looked like it belonged to DeeDee, who was about my own daughter's age—when I heard Clapper say, "Boxer. *Boxer.* Look at me."

I looked up. He was holding up two fingers of his right hand. He moved his hand back and forth until I focused, then he pointed to the multipaned windows beyond the desk, kept pointing until I saw two bullet holes surrounded by crazed tempered glass. On the floor beneath was a spray of tiny shards.

"There. See that?"

This time I couldn't miss it. The two shots must have come through the windows. But we were on the *second floor.* How the hell had the shooter managed two perfect kill shots from outside the house?

I "grabbed the wall," meaning I walked carefully around the murder tableau and looked out through the windows.

There was a pretty brick patio below but no ledge outside the window, no purchase for a shooter to stand and take his shots.

Could the shots have been fired from a neighboring house? Or, more likely, from the top of San Anselmo, two streets over?

I turned back to Clapper. "A sniper," I said. "A damned good one."

Clapper was on to the next. He said, "Look over here, Boxer. I'd like to get into that closet."

CHAPTER 17

CLAPPER AND I didn't need a search warrant to collect evidence in plain sight.

But incriminating evidence found inside a closed room, or drawer or anything with a lid, would be inadmissible in court if, say, a Baron friend or associate was suspected of having committed a crime. So a closed door was off-limits without a search warrant.

However, there was a loophole: "exigent circumstances."

If we had reason to believe that another shooter, or possibly an injured person, was hiding in that closet, we had to check it out. It was reasonable, and I felt duty-bound to clear this room of an armed individual before the CSIs entered it.

I pulled my gun, said to Clapper, "On the count of three. One."

Clapper pulled his gun.

"Two."

I stood to one side of the door as he said, "Three," then

flipped on the light switch and jerked open the door, using it as a shield.

My heart was pounding hard and fast as, leading with my weapon, I took in all four walls of the closet. I saw nothing but shelves and cubbyholes stuffed with padded envelopes.

"Clear," I said. "Thank God." I put my gun away. We gloved up and went in.

A metal cabinet about five feet tall by three feet wide by two feet deep stood at the back of the closet with the doors open. Inside were more padded mailers, some loose glassine envelopes with white powder inside.

Clapper stood beside me. He said, "If they were running a mailbox fentanyl business, we're talking about big money here."

I felt sick with a letdown that was hard to understand, let alone explain. I had been feeling sympathy for the Barons. Now I saw what Clapper saw: an addictive drug, a mailbox business. And if the drug was fentanyl, it was addictive and deadly. If the Barons were dealing, I cared a lot less. Still. I'm a cop. Two people were dead on the floor behind me.

I said, "What the hell, Charlie? Possibly millions in drugs and nothing was stolen. These people were professionally assassinated—but why?"

"What's your theory?" he asked me.

"I see two options. This was a calculated hit, planned and executed by a pro, motive unknown. Or...maybe it was a psycho with a high-powered rifle playing God this morning.

"Either way, shooter braces his rifle on the top of his car, takes a look through the sight. He sees two people he can take out with little to no chance of getting caught. Bang.

Bang. Hit man or thrill killer gets back into his car and takes off."

Clapper said, "And now he's on his couch, waiting for headline news."

I didn't like it either way. Joe would say, "You've been on the case for a half hour, Linds. Take it easy on yourself."

Clapper said, "I've got guys out on the road looking for shell casings, a cigarette butt, something."

"I'll check on that warrant," I said.

CHAPTER 18

CONKLIN TEXTED ME: *Judge Hoffman signed the ticket.*

"We're good, Charlie," I said to Clapper. "We own this place."

I left the Barons' house by the side door as a half dozen CSIs, carrying kits, lights, cameras, and other accessories of their trade, headed up the front walk.

I remembered that I needed a ride back to the Hall and was about to text my partner when the medical examiner's van arrived. I waited to exchange a few words with Claire, but the doctor who climbed down from the van was not a busty black woman with a wry comment about the crispy critters in her cold room. This doc was white, dainty, with streaked blond hair and purple eyeglass frames.

I introduced myself, and the pathologist told me her name, Dr. Mary Ann Dugan, and that she was on loan from Metro Hospital until Dr. Washburn returned.

I asked, "I just saw Claire a couple of hours ago. Do you know what this is about?"

"All I know is that Lieutenant Brady called the hospital asking for a pathologist to sub for Dr. Washburn. And here I am."

It made sense that Claire was probably sacked out at home and would call me when she woke up. I told Dr. Dugan that as soon as she retrieved the slugs from the victims, she should get them to Clapper.

"No problem," said Dugan.

I gave her my card and was looking up the street when I heard my name. There, behind the tape, was Cindy waving to get my attention.

I waved back and ducked under the tape, and Cindy took me by the arm, saying, "Richie said you could use a ride."

I laughed out loud. "What a great guy."

But I knew that by taking Cindy up on this offer, I was essentially giving her a green light to grill me for twenty-five minutes in the car.

She was going to be disappointed.

"Fine, Cindy. Thanks."

An attractive man elbowed his way through the gathering crowd toward me. He was about thirty, was wearing expensive, classic-cut clothes, and had the intensity of a reporter hot on a scoop. He pushed past Cindy, interrupting us to say, "Sergeant, I'm Jeb McGowan from the *Chronicle*. Can you tell us what happened here?"

Cindy looked at me, switched her eyes toward McGowan, and gave off a subzero vibe.

"Mr. McGowan? I can't discuss an investigation in progress."

"Sergeant, it's all right. I'm only asking for a quote."

"Sorry. No can do."

It hadn't taken long for news of the Barons' deaths to get out. A news chopper chattered overhead. An ABC7 News van rolled up the street and stopped at the tape.

Cindy said, "My car's a block away. Follow me."

I followed, got into her car, strapped in, and got ready to keep Cindy at arm's length all the way back to the Hall. In fact, although she huffed and puffed, everything I told Cindy was off the record.

I said that the fatal shootings this morning had added two young orphans to the world, and that we had no suspects or witnesses to the murders. I did not tell her about the probable millions in drugs inside the supply closet. Their value was still to be determined.

My thoughts shifted to what Cindy had told the Women's Murder Club this morning: That a veteran ballplayer had been shot through his windshield while leaving a Taco King last Friday. That the word *Rehearsal* had been scrawled on the rear window of the victim's very expensive vehicle. That anonymous yet reliable sources had reported to Cindy that Jennings had been dealing drugs.

Jennings's execution was similar in style to the Barons' murders. Now I wondered if that drive-through murder had been a rehearsal for the killings this morning. Was there a drug connection between Roger Jennings and the Barons?

There was a lot to do before I would have answers.

But this I knew: my long weekend in Napa Valley with Joe seemed so long ago and far away, it might have occurred in a dream.

CHAPTER 19

CONKLIN AND I waited in the little area outside
Jacobi's former office, now Brady's part-time corner on the
fifth floor.

His door was closed and Katie, his assistant, was at her
desk. She looked up and said, "He'll only be a minute."

Conklin took chairs for us in a row along the wall and
used the time to catch up.

"CPS has the Baron kids, DeeDee and Christopher," he
told me. "Ramona's sister, Bea, is on a cruise. Her ship docks
in Athens in four days, then she'll fly home, pick them
up. Telling her was awful. She refused to believe me, and
when she did, the satellite dropped the call. Awful, terrible,
painful."

"Did Gretchen have any ideas who wanted the Barons
dead?"

"She said that they had friends and haters, and it was hard
to tell the difference."

"Oh. That's great."

Rich took his phone out of his shirt pocket, tapped until his notes came up. He showed me the screen, scrolled down, saying, "Gretchen had a guest list. About a hundred and fifty people attended their movie premiere party last month, not counting the band and the help."

I scoffed. We both knew we could spend weeks checking alibis from the Barons' circle of associates and never get a clue. Or we could get too many clues that went nowhere.

I said, "Maybe we'll get lucky with the neighborhood canvass...."

Brady opened his door, stuck his head and shoulders out. "Come on in," he said. "Sit yourselves down."

The look on his face told me something was up. Conklin and I took seats on the sofa positioned at a right angle to Brady's desk. I was agitated and tried not to show it.

Brady said, "Clapper found a pill presser in the basement of the Baron house. It was still in a crate. He found hazmat suits, scales, glassine envelopes, a few ounces of product still in shipping envelopes addressed to them. The Barons were about to go big-time in the fentanyl business."

He got up from his seat, scrunched up the blinds, and looked out at the traffic on Bryant.

I said, "So what are you thinking, Brady?"

"Boxer, don't worry yourself. You, either, Conklin. The homicide is still your case. I'm worried about the way fentanyl is spreading, mixed into the heroin supply, killing tens of thousands because it's probably fifty to a hundred times more powerful than morphine, and multiple times stronger than heroin, at a fraction of the price. You know how this works?"

He didn't wait for us to say.

"You buy it on the dark web, dead cheap with crypto. Middlemen, that is, folks like the Barons, cut it with lactose or something, press it into pills, and mail out little envelopes through the US Postal Service or a courier service. And the customers? They're caught in the perfect storm between heroin drying up and that nice, cheap opioid high. No needles. Just snort it up and nod off. The more deadly it is, the more they want it."

Brady had been a narc with the Miami PD. This was hitting him personally.

"That's all," Brady said. "Try to get a lead on who killed the Barons. Talk to Chi and McNeil about that baseball guy who got killed last week. See if there's a link."

Before he could say "Keep me posted," his cell phone buzzed. He read the text and said, "Ah, sheet."

He typed a few words, put down his phone, leaned across the big old desk.

"Get this. Guy dropped off his kid at school in LA. Took a shot between his eyes and dropped dead. No other casualties."

I said, "What time?"

Brady said, "I didn't ask. Just before the school bell. Eight thirty?"

I said, "That's the same time the Barons were shot. To the minute."

CHAPTER 20

CLAIRE TEXTED ME as I was driving home.

I stopped at the light on Turk Street and Webster Street and returned the text, asking Claire, *Where are you? Are you ok?*

I'm in my office. Call me.

I pulled over and phoned her. She picked right up.

"Where'd you go, Claire? I got no answer from the mysterious Dr. Dugan."

There was a pause, then, "Where are *you?*"

"Turk and Webster."

"Can you come back, Lindsay? I need to talk to you."

I was about ten minutes out from the Hall. I said so, made a couple of left turns, a right, then a left on Bryant, and found my usual spot on Harriet Street waiting for me.

During those return ten minutes I tried on all kinds of reasons for why Claire needed to see me, and while some were ridiculous, the one that seemed most reasonable and possible was that she'd quit her job.

That crack house–turned–incinerator was a sick night-mare. Claire dealt with death every day, yet this case was singular. The victims were probable longtime addicts, so there was little chance that friends and family members were calling Missing Persons. And even if they did, Claire was at a dead end. No answers to what had happened, how or why, no fingerprints, no way to get those bodies home.

Maybe this fire had been Claire's final straw.

I locked the car, buttoned my coat, and took the short walk to the medical examiner's office. The lights shined through the glass. I saw that the receptionist had gone home, but there were a few people sitting in the waiting room. One of them was a cop I knew. I knocked on the glass and Diaz got up, reached behind the reception desk, and buzzed me in.

A moment later Claire opened the door to reception and leaned out, saying to me, "After I get outta these bloody scrubs and wash up, want to go have a beer?"

I nodded. Good idea.

We went to MacBain's, the bar and grill across Bryant and down the street, named for a valorous homicide captain who'd owned the place and whose portrait hangs over the bar. RIP. At six thirty MacBain's was packed with Hall of Justice workers and one departing pair of lovebirds who'd left an empty table by the jukebox.

We grabbed it.

A sappy pop vocal was on loud, making my teeth vibrate, but at least we had a table. Syd MacBain, our waitress, stopped by and dropped off dinner menus.

Claire said, "Wait a sec," handed back the menus.

"Two Anchor Steams and a bowl of chips," I said.

Syd left, and I imagined a cone of silence dropping over our table so we wouldn't be disturbed. In a way, it worked. The Cheers-like ambiance of the place faded. I asked Claire about the fire victims, a way in for her to say, "This *damned* job is just *too damned much*, Lindsay," but she didn't.

She said, "I've been coughing."

I nodded. I knew that.

"I have lung cancer."

I was sure I was hearing her wrong. I couldn't believe what she had told me. I asked her to say it again, and she did. "I have lung cancer."

I shook my head, *No, no, no.*

"Probably from the disinfectant or the X-rays or whatever fumes I breathe doing autopsies—or all of the above."

"*Claire.* You know this for sure? You've had tests?"

Sydney brought the beer, the chips. We didn't even acknowledge her when she said, "Will there be anything else?"

Claire said, "I had a biopsy. Today I saw my oncologist. It's a carcinoma. It has to come out. I haven't told Edmund. Jesus. I keep thinking about Rosie."

Rosie is their youngest, their beloved change-of-life baby.

Claire coughed into a napkin, then looked at me with water in her eyes. "It's nothing to worry about. I'm a doctor, you know."

Bullshitting herself, lying to me, to Edmund, to people who loved her. That's how scared she was.

"Don't tell anyone," she said.

I reached across the table and grabbed Claire's wrists.

We both burst into tears.

CHAPTER 21

BEFORE CLAIRE TEXTED me, I'd been thinking about how much I wanted to discuss the Baron murders with Joe.

He has decades of experience in intelligence agencies and spent a number of those years as a profiler with the FBI.

I had a new case: a successful record producer and his wife shot dead in their house by a very sophisticated marksman who knew their habits. Possibly knew about their drug business, which was still in a formative stage. The motive was unknown. Suspects, zero.

Joe might see an angle on the case, but my thoughts about the Baron murders had become secondary.

Now I wanted to hold Julie, spend time with her before she fell asleep, read to her first if I could steady my voice and not cry.

I opened the door to our apartment and saw that Joe was across the room in his big leather chair. He lifted a hand in greeting, but I could tell he was deep in conversation.

Martha waggled and shimmied into the foyer, yelping her

joy that I was home. I ruffled her ears and called her pet names. Everything about this old doggy is precious to me. We've been together for so long. I talked to her as I put my gun in the safe that Dave Channing had given us, and she followed along as I went to find Julie.

She was barefoot, still in the school clothes I'd dressed her in this morning, sitting on her bed with a book in her lap. She looked up and said, "Mommy. Martha peed on the floor."

"Oh. Did someone forget to walk her?"

She shrugged, not willing to implicate her dad, too young to do the chore herself.

"Wanna go for a walk?" I asked Martha.

This is every dog's favorite question, and ours responded with a loud, emphatic bark. Yes. Yes, she did want to go for a walk.

We went out to the foyer, where I slipped a collar and leash onto Martha, zipped Julie into a coat, and tied her shoes. I got Joe's attention, and he put his hand to the phone and said, "Just take a quick walk, okay?"

I nodded and the three of us girls took the elevator down to Lake Street. Martha sniffed around the sidewalk, relieved herself for show, and then herded me and Julie together as border collies, even old ones, do.

Back in Julie's room, I found clean pj's and asked her to tell me about her day. She was willing. I brushed the thick, dark curls she'd inherited from her dad, and I thought about Claire. My eyes watered. I heard Julie say, "Mommmmmy, are you listening? That was funny!"

I hadn't heard a word.

"I'm sorry, Julie. Tell me again. Please."

"No," she said.

I asked her if she'd like me to read to her, and she said, "Not yet." She wanted to tell me about a rabbit a classmate had brought to school, and kept talking until Joe came to the doorway and said, "How about a hug good night, Bugs?"

She said, "Dad, Mommy is out to lunch."

"Then, I'll make her some dinner."

We hugged and kissed our little girl, told her it was okay to sleep with Martha for a little while, and shut off her light.

We were crossing the main room when Joe's phone rang.

He picked up and said, "I will, Dave. Of course. I'll call you in the morning. You, too. Good night."

When he'd hung up the phone, we sat together on the sofa. He looked sad. In pain. I asked, "What is it? What's wrong?"

"Ray. Dave's father. He just died."

"Oh, no."

"Dave thinks Ray was murdered."

"What?"

"I have to go back to Napa Valley. I have to be there to help him."

CHAPTER 22

JOE AND I sat together on the sofa, our arms around each other.

Joe spoke haltingly about himself and Dave when they were roommates.

And he told me that he wondered if Dave was in such a bad place that the only way he could accept his father's death was to create a fantasy that Ray had been murdered.

"It doesn't make any sense otherwise," Joe said. "Why would anyone kill Ray Channing inside a hospital?"

I didn't want to break into Joe's thoughts, but I was also grieving. Moments with Claire were flashing through my mind, starting with the look on her face as she told me about the cancer diagnosis, then back to her smiling at me when she painted my toenails the day Joe and I got married. She was Julie's godmother and I was Rosie's. Each of us was the go-to person for the other whenever we needed advice, love, support, and the truth.

I couldn't imagine my life without Claire. And I didn't want her to go.

Joe was holding me, and my body started shaking and I just couldn't stop it. He turned me so that I was looking into his face, gripped my shoulders, and asked me, "Lindsay. What's going on?"

I blurted out, "I said…I wouldn't tell anyone."

My voice cracked. He was alarmed and he tightened his grip on me.

"Tell me," he said.

"Claire has cancer."

I cried. Joe consoled me until he cried, too. Second time I ever saw Joe cry. I was so grateful that Julie was in bed, but Martha felt the sadness, came out of Julie's room, and put her nose on the couch between us.

"Keep talking," Joe said.

"She said it's nothing to worry about, but she was lying."

Joe held me tight. I thought about what Claire must be going through.

"She hasn't told Edmund."

"She will."

"I can't bear this, Joe."

"You can. You will. You'll be strong for Claire."

We went into the bedroom and got in bed, under the blankets, and held hands.

The last time I looked at the clock, it was 3:40 in the morning. The big paw that had once caught footballs enclosed my hand, and when Joe squeezed my fingers, it was gentle. A hug.

I slept hard after that, and when I woke up a short time later, Joe was dressed.

He leaned over and kissed me.

"I made coffee and walked Martha. Julie's still sleeping. Mrs. Rose will take her to the pre-K bus, and she'll pick her up, make her dinner. I'll call you after I see Dave."

I sat up and kissed him again.

He said, "Go back to sleep. I'll call you later."

When the phone rang, I thought it was Joe, but it was Cindy.

CHAPTER 23

CINDY WAS AT her desk at the *San Francisco Chronicle* at 6 a.m.

It was nine o'clock in New York, and news had been breaking across the country all morning. Her scanner was on, transmitting police, paramedic, and fire department radio calls while she booted up her laptop.

First thing, she looked in on the updated SFPD 911 log for calls related to the Baron case. No arrest, no statement, nothing. Next web stop was the *Examiner,* the local competition. Nothing to worry about there. She checked out the major news outlets for any new reporting, found none, and then went back to the updated SFPD 911 log.

There was no hot news at all, so she moved on. Checked her inbox—it was full—and looked to see how much coffee was left in her mug. It was empty.

She watched through the glass walls of her office as reporters, writers, and staff ambled into the city room, navigated the maze of partitioned cubicles to their stations. They stowed their bags, got coffee, then went to work.

It was six fifteen when McGowan came in.

He went to his desk with its clear view of her office. He dropped off his computer bag and waved at her. After opening his laptop, he headed across the city room to suck up to the publisher, who was doing his morning walk-through.

McGowan was the worst kind of phony. A toady. Blech.

Cindy shook off the creeps, turned back to her computer, and opened her crime blog. A lot of people had posted questions about the Baron killings. Sometimes posters had questions for her. But she didn't have anything to tell them, not today, not yet. She blogged that information on the case was pending and she would report to her readers as soon as she could.

Damn it. If Lindsay hadn't blocked her, she could take the action that she and all journalists worked for—breaking the news.

The coffee station, the urn and fixings, were just down the hallway. Cindy brought her mug, and when she returned to her desk, there was an interesting bulletin in the chyron crawling across the bottom of her screen.

A drug dealer had been shot in Chicago yesterday morning. The cops had identified the victim as Albert Roccio but had kept the story quiet for twenty-four hours until the autopsy was completed.

Now the police were asking the public for information on Roccio's death.

Cindy opened her link to the Chicago PD website and read up on the victim. Albert Roccio was fifty-four, a

Chicago native. Owned a smoke shop on North Broadway where he sold papers, smokes, candy, soft drinks. He had an undetermined number of employees, who Cindy guessed were stock boys doubling as drug runners.

Roccio was divorced, no children. He had been exiting his apartment house on his way to work, car keys in hand, when he was shot, one bullet to the forehead.

Roccio's girlfriend, Tonya Patton, forty-eight, and her boy, Vanya, eight, had been walking right behind Albert down the front steps. One bullet had been fired. One only. The woman and child had been spared.

Patton hadn't seen the shooter, was questioned and released. Apart from Patton and Vanya, there had been no witnesses to the shooting, no suspects. Police found a half kilo of heroin taped under the dashboard of Roccio's Subaru Forester.

The news crawl resumed, and this time Cindy read it from the beginning.

Chicago drug dealer shot in execution-style murder at 10:30 a.m. on Monday.

Cindy sat still for a moment and let the connection sink in. Roccio was shot on the same day and at the same time that the Barons had been shot.

She called her boyfriend, Rich Conklin, who she knew was still sleeping.

"Sorry, Richie, but I've got something to tell you. It's hot. Yeah, I'd call it very damned important," Cindy said.

CHAPTER 24

ON DIRECT ORDERS from the man she loved, Cindy waited two excruciating hours, so as not to wake Lindsay, and then she called her.

"Lindsay. It's Cindy."

"Everything okay? I'm trying to get out of here. I still need to press a shirt and dry my hair—"

"What time is it, Linds?"

"You don't know?"

"I'm asking you. What time is it?"

"Uh. Eight thirty."

"That's right, Lindsay. At this time yesterday the Barons were killed, and at this same time yesterday Albert Roccio, smoke shop owner in Chicago, was shot between the eyes. Cops found a hefty bag of heroin taped to the underside of his dash."

Silence on the phone.

"Lindsay? Linds, you there?"

"I hear you."

"Good. Richie told me that I had to tell you that I want to run with this drug dealer–time of death connection, which, as you know, Lindsay, is what the *Chronicle* pays me to do. Chicago dude and Barons, all holding significant drugs for distribution, all shot at the same time, each struck by a single kill shot."

"I gave you information about the Barons in your car and off the record. Do you remember?"

Lindsay's voice was thrumming with badass. She'd seen Cindy make headlines from invisible ink before.

Cindy loved Lindsay and wouldn't betray her, but frankly, she'd just made a connection that spelled more than a coincidence; it was some kind of collusion. TBD. Which was the difference between writing "What to do this weekend in San Francisco" and investigative journalism. She was onto a gangbuster front-page story.

Cindy said, "I *know*. I *know* you told me off the record. Otherwise I wouldn't be asking for your permission."

"Calm down, Cindy."

"You, *too*, Lindsay."

Henry Tyler, the publisher and editor in chief of the *Chronicle* and her "rabbi," knocked on her glass door, then came into her office and sat in the side chair. He held up his hand, mouthed, "I can wait."

Lindsay was saying, "I understand this is some kind of sacrifice, but I'm going to give you another *off-the-record tip* as compensation. Hear me?"

Cindy scoffed. "Yes. What is it?"

"Here's another dot to connect. There was a shooting in LA yesterday, 8:30 a.m. But as of now, nothing about drugs."

Cindy nodded to Tyler, held up a finger, *Just a minute*, and said to Lindsay, "Can you officially confirm that?"

"No. It's an anonymous tip. Find out some other way. You can't quote me or say sources close to the police or anything like that, and do not link that up with the Baron murders—"

"Or what? Roger Jennings was my story, by the way."

"Don't do it, Cindy. I'll give you the go-ahead with a quote soon, but I need to see if there really is a connection before you take it public and warn off the shooters."

"Okay. So no problem with the LA piece?"

"Just don't mention the time of the shooting."

Cindy exhaled her exasperation, said, "Okay. Talk to you later."

She clicked off and said "hi" to Tyler, a kind man who'd backed her wild notions and promoted her to senior reporter on the crime desk.

He said, "Sorry to interrupt. Look. Do me a favor, Cindy. Take McGowan under your wing, will you? He's a good writer, but he's new to us. He could use some help getting into the swing of things around here."

"Sure, Henry," she said.

Tyler thanked her and left her office. He had just left when McGowan stepped in, without knocking, and sat down in the chair.

"So, Cindy. What's the inside scoop on the Baron killings? Tyler wants us to work together on the story."

71

CHAPTER 25

I ARRIVED IN the squad room an hour and a half late that morning.

I was still rattled from the fit Julie had thrown because Joe couldn't take her to the pre-K school bus, and was sick with worry about Claire's heartbreaking news. Cindy's phone call had scrambled whatever cognition I had left after my sleepless night, and a traffic detour on Bryant had made me frustrated and bad tempered.

All I said to Richie was, "Life kneecapped me this morning."

He gave me a long look, pointed at my jacket.

I looked down at the dribble of white down my jacket lapel. Even the toothpaste was out to get me. I shrugged off my jacket, hung it on the back of my chair. I noticed that someone had messed with my desk.

"What happened here?"

"Brady happened," Conklin said. "You were still floating on the wine country afterglow. He's a little compulsive."

"Ya think?"

I sat down, wheeled the chair up to my desk, and started returning articles to where they belonged. Lamp, notepad, picture of Julie and Joe. I stared at my mug, now full of pens, and said, "Any progress on the Barons?"

He said, "Clapper called. The bullets were recovered, but they're soft points. One was deformed by the inside of Paul's skull. The other went through Ramona, smashed into a wall."

"So much for ballistics," I said.

Richie went on. "I spoke to Sergeant Noble, LAPD. They have nothing yet on the Peavey shooting, but they want to work with us. And here's the name of the primary lead detective on the Chicago shooting. I left a message. No call back."

Conklin passed me a sticky note over the narrow gulch separating our desks. It read, "Det. Stanley Richards. Victim, Albert Roccio, smoke shop dude."

It was 11:50 in Chicago. I made the call, was passed around the police department until Detective Richards picked up his phone.

I introduced myself, said that my partner was also on the line, and told the detective that I'd read about Albert Roccio. I said, "We've had a couple of similar shootings here."

Richards said, "What can I do for you?"

I couldn't keep the stress out of my voice as I gave the detective what we had: the "rehearsal" at the Taco King and the Baron shootings. I also told him about Fred Peavey, the LA dealer who'd dropped his kid off at school and taken one through the forehead. Richards was aware of only the Barons, who'd made the national news.

I said, "The Barons and Peavey happened at the same time, 8:30 a.m. Monday morning Pacific Standard Time."

Richards grunted, said, "That's a match. Roccio was offed at ten thirty here." He sounded bored. "Boxer, right? Good luck with your DBs."

He was hanging up.

"Richards."

"Yeah?"

"You got anything on Roccio? A motive? A suspect?"

"Sorry. I can't help you."

Richards was keeping the case to himself, and frankly, I wasn't into pulling teeth from another cop.

I said, "Do I have this right? You're the primary on Roccio, I've got a case that could be its twin, and you're jerking me around? Maybe your captain can give us an assist. I'll give him a call."

Richards said, "Hang on, Boxer. Happy to tell you about our big file of nothing."

Reluctantly he told us much of what we already knew: that Roccio's girlfriend claimed not to have seen the shooter and knew nothing about his drug business. As of now, Chicago PD didn't know if Roccio had enemies.

"Roccio's body is still warm," Richards said, giving me notice that he was done.

We signed off. Richie muttered that Richards was a jerk, and I agreed with him as I typed a note for the file.

Richie said, "Did Cindy catch you this morning?"

"Yep. I promised her an exclusive. I'm guessing I bought us eight hours before she runs a serial killer story."

Conklin flashed his winning smile and said, "Serial killer scores in three places at once."

I said, "Let's hope for a break on the Barons before Cindy turns that into a headline."

CHAPTER 26

IT HAPPENED JUST before Cindy was getting ready to leave work for the day.

McGowan walked to her doorway and held up a copy of the *Examiner* so that she could read the headline from her desk.

SNIPERS HIT DRUG DEALERS IN THREE CITIES.

Hey. What? That was *her* story. She'd been scooped by the *Examiner*—and that meant her world was ending. Her work was now running in the public domain without her byline.

McGowan said, "I told you not to hold the story."

Cindy blew up, like a virtual bomb. She said to McGowan, too loudly, "Listen, you dumb shit. You don't screw with police sources."

He laughed. "Man, that must be a drag for your boyfriend."

Cindy's face burned. "You're disgusting," she said.

"He's a cop, right?" and as McGowan was saying, "Oh, come

onnnnnn. Where's your sense of hu—" Cindy crossed the office and slammed her door in McGowan's grinning face.

Ignoring the shocked faces of her colleagues staring through her glass wall, Cindy went back to her desk and typed the headline into her browser. Then she watched the bad news fill her screen; Google, Bing, *USA Today*, network and cable news, all had the same or similar headlines.

The writer at the *Examiner* had gotten all details of this shooting spree correct, but how?

Cindy stopped scrolling and took a head-pounding minute to think about the four incidents in an attempt to understand how a reporter at the *Examiner* had made the connections.

First, Jennings, whose status as a minor celebrity with a fan following had gotten him ink and on-air mention. But the word *Rehearsal* on the back of Jennings's car had not been released. The press had been kept far from the scene, and if Rich's friend Officer Kendall hadn't pointed it out to her, Cindy wouldn't have seen it.

The Barons' murders had been uncontainable because Paul and Ramona were both celebrities. But *details* of the killings had not been released; not the shooting of the couple through the second-floor window, not the drugs in the supply closet.

In LA, Peavey had gotten ink and air time because the shooting had happened outside his child's school. But Peavey's involvement in the drug trade was not mentioned.

Albert Roccio was a sidebar.

His death had been reported as a one-inch mention in the Chicago papers only. He sold porn and cigarettes. The drugs were sold old-school. Over the counter or by messenger for cash. This was also not mentioned in the article.

The timing of the shootings, that all the victims had been shot by a single, well-aimed bullet, and most especially the drug connection were still an inside cop theory that Cindy alone had known—until the *Examiner*'s exposé.

She read the *Examiner* story again.

It was well written by Galina Moore, a writer whose name Cindy didn't know. A few clicks later Cindy learned that before coming to the *Examiner,* Moore had worked the crime desk at the *LA Sun Times.*

McGowan had worked at that same paper before making his big move to the *Chronicle.*

It was stunningly clear to Cindy.

Her story had been leaked—and she knew who'd sprung the leak.

She called Henry Tyler's extension, told his assistant, Brittney Hall, that she needed a few moments with the chief before he left for the day.

"I'm sorry, Cindy. You just missed him," she said.

CHAPTER 27

CINDY COOKED DINNER, banging the metal spoon on the pot lids for emphasis as she rehearsed what she would say to Tyler.

"Henry." *Bang.* "He's not just a *sneak*." *Bang.* "He's a *spy*." *Bang.* "He *tipped* off a *reporter* at the *Examiner*." *Bang. Bang. Bang.* "He's a danger to *all* of us." *Bang. Bang. Bang.* "This is—"

Richie came up behind her and said, "Hands up, sweetheart. Drop the spoon and step away from the stove. Do it now."

She gave him a look like, *Funny. But I'm not in the mood.* He tapped her on the butt and took over the stove, checked on the chili and the corn, turning to say, "Want to make a salad?"

"I shouldn't handle knives," she said. "Trust me."

Cindy paced in the living room, a dark, narrow space banked with bookshelves and Richie's photographic cityscapes. She brooded over McGowan, couldn't help it. He was a bad guy. She'd run into bad guys before, *criminals*. But this guy had stood outside her office, smiling about handing their news off to the competition. This had never happened to her in her life.

Tyler would believe her. She had 100 percent credibility.

Rich called, "Cindy, put some music on, okay? Something chill."

"I'm eyeball-deep in righteous indignation," she called back, "and I gotta let it work its way out. Which maybe I can do if you come in and *talk* to me."

"Music," said Rich. "I'm bringing beers."

Cindy riffled through the stack of CDs, found one by Metallica that fit her mood. She cued up "Fade to Black," pressed Play, jacked up the sound, and threw herself onto Richie's old blue couch. She put her bare feet up on the coffee table and exhaled.

Rich came in with a couple of bottles of Anchor Steam, saying over the discordant noise, "We don't need a salad. Beans. Corn. Hops. We're good. So tell me from the beginning."

He lowered the volume, sat down next to Cindy, handed her a cold one, and put his arm around her shoulders. She tipped her head back and guzzled half the bottle.

Rich gave her a squeeze. "Speak."

"He told me not to hold up the story—"

"McGowan?"

"Yes. McGowan. I told him it was just a temporary hold. That I would get inside dope from police sources if I just let the cops do their job without warning off the shooters."

"Right thing to say and do," said Rich.

"And because Lindsay asked me to, *I sat on it*. The story leaked. The connection between the hits *was* the story. Somehow I was scooped."

"I hear you, Cindy."

"That's McGowan. A snake. A traitor."

"Okay," said Rich. "I'm going to ask you some questions."

She sighed loudly.

"How do you know it was McGowan who squealed?"

"Because, Richie, a writer who used to be at the *LA Sun Times* broke the story. McGowan worked there until a couple months ago."

"Speculation. What else?"

"No one connected Roccio to the Barons. Or Jennings and Peavey, for that matter."

"You sure? Because I spoke with the primary on the Roccio case this morning, and Lindsay and I linked up the timing of the shootings for him."

"You did?" she said tersely. *"Why?"*

"Seriously? We're working a double homicide. We talk to other cops. Here's my point. You have a suspicion, but you don't have proof."

"Oh, crap."

"We'll try to make it up to you, Cin. Go sit at the table. Take your beer."

Cindy was relieved that she hadn't told Tyler that McGowan had leaked her story. Richie was right. She didn't have actual evidence.

Still, she had a gut feeling that she was right about McGowan. And she was going to harbor that feeling, massage it, and polish it until she could prove it.

CHAPTER 28

JOE WALKED ALONGSIDE Dave, who was pushing his wheelchair through rows of grapevines.

"I work in these fields," Dave Channing told Joe.

"Really? I thought you were Mr. Inside."

"I'm multitalented," Dave said, forcing a smile. Joe recognized that smile, same as when he broke his wrist at practice, same as when Carolyn Kinney broke up with him and he said, "It's not the end of the world."

"I do the books, but I also prune, tie up the vines, harvest the grapes. See the clouds? Mare's tails and mackerel scales. It's going to rain tomorrow. We need the rain."

Joe felt as though his coat were weighed down with stones. Did Dave's belief that Ray had been murdered make any sense at all? Or was that his grief talking? He didn't know how or if he could help his friend.

The two men stopped at the top of the field and looked down at the two stone houses and the winery across a country road from the vineyard.

"Stick with me," said Dave, taking the lead, setting a downhill course for a stone patio outside the winery. Joe took a seat on a bench with a view, and when both he and Dave were settled, Joe said, "Tell me all of it."

Dave took a deep breath and said, "We lived next door to each other for the last twenty-five years. Started our day together with morning coffee and ended with dinner in the restaurant kitchen when we were done for the day. I never got tired of being with my father. He had a big personality, you know? A lot of love."

Joe nodded and said, "Tell me again what happened."

"He fell down, just dropped in the restaurant. I called the ambulance and I rode with him to the hospital. His friend Dr. Daniel Perkins said, 'Don't worry. He's stable, but I want to keep him for a few days.' Joe, you saw him after we had lunch on Friday. He had spunk, remember?"

"I sure do."

"So then on Saturday they put Dad on the list for a scan on Monday, but Perkins said Dad needed to be monitored. His aneurysm could rupture, but worst case it was treatable by open-chest surgery. Then Monday morning my father was dead. His heart stopped. Why?"

"What did Dr. Perkins say?"

"He said he was sorry. This happens."

Dave dropped his head into his hands and said, "Oh, God."

Joe put his hand on his friend's arm.

"I'm so sorry, Dave."

A long moment passed before Dave could speak again.

"Thanks, Joe, but I have to tell you, I'm furious. Dad was strong. He lifted cases of wine. He could work all day.

"And here's the thing, Joe. Dad wasn't the first of Perkins's patients to die suddenly. From what I could find out just from reading obituaries, he was the third of Perkins's patients to die suddenly this *year*."

"The deaths were all suspicious?"

"Yes. Mild heart attack in one case, and two were complications from aneurysms, like Dad."

Joe nodded, thought about Ray. He'd been seventy-two, a *vigorous* seventy-two, but still, an age where heart attacks and strokes were not uncommon.

Dave gently shook Joe's arm, bringing him back to the moment.

"Will you help me, Joe? He never got that MRI, and maybe that scan would have given Perkins a clue. But he didn't get it. I don't know if my father's death was due to gross malpractice, or if Perkins gets off on snuffing his patients. But I do know this: my father died inexplicably under Daniel Perkins's care, and that needs to be investigated."

"What about going to the police, Dave?"

"I don't want to stir up the hospital's lawyers. Not until I have something solid to go on. Joe. Will you help me? I can't let him get away with this."

CHAPTER 29

FRIDAY MORNING, CONKLIN and I were hunched over our computers, fleshing out backgrounds of the people on the Barons' guest list from their recent movie premiere party, building a database of their friends and contacts.

As we worked, we texted notes of interest to each other, and there were tidbits aplenty: affairs, snubs, slights, and fist-fights, parts in movies, book and record sales numbers. We found nothing criminal.

We took a break when Tina Hosier, head of Narcotics and Organized Crime, joined us. We showed her our list, and after a long couple of minutes she said, "I know some of these folks, of course. But I don't see any wholesale drug honchos here."

My phone rang. It was Brady.

"I've got something," he said.

I turned toward the rear of the squad room and saw that Brady was down from his office on the fifth floor. He waved to us from his glassed-in cubicle.

I thanked Hosier for the consult. She said, "No problem. Keep the faith."

A minute later my partner and I dropped into the chairs across the desk from Lieutenant Jackson Brady, friend and chief.

He got right into it.

"A Mr. Alan Newton lives right behind the Baron house. His property faces south. He was walking his dogs with his wife a few days ago and took some neighborhood pics to send to his daughter in Amarillo. Then when he looked at his photos, this shot raised his hackles."

Brady opened a manila folder, took out a photo, and passed it over.

Conklin and I looked at the photo of a woman posing with two dachshunds.

"What are we looking at?"

Conklin stabbed the photo. Behind the dogs was a car pulled over to the curb and a man leaning on the frame of his open car door. He was wearing a camo jacket and a knit cap, and he was holding a short tube up to his eye.

I could hardly contain myself. "That's a gun scope."

"A little fuzzy," said Conklin. "And his face is obscured by his hand, but I'm not throwing it back. When was this taken?"

"Two days before the shooting. Time-stamped, too. Eight thirty a.m."

"Oh, my God. He was casing the target," I said.

"Here's another shot," said Brady.

A second photo crossed his desk, this one of the same vehicle, a Ford, heading downhill. In this shot the vehicle's plate number was clearly visible.

I wanted to kiss someone. I know I was beaming.

"Don't get excited yet," said Brady.

"Too late," I said.

"I know, I know. But right now this is proof of nothing. It's just a guy admiring Saint Francis Wood while looking suspicious. Check him out with our computer techs. See if facial recognition likes him. Report back."

"Yes, sir."

CHAPTER 30

OUR COMPUTER TECH, Mike Stempien, was on loan from the FBI.

He had a free moment and an upbeat attitude.

"I'm looking forward to this," he said.

"Good," I said, "because I'm not wearing my lucky socks."

Mike ran the subject's snapshot through facial recognition, and I'll be damned, we got a hit. Our subject had a name, Leonard Malcolm Barkley, and Conklin and I ran with it.

Back at our desks, after some intense pecking on my keyboard with my partner sitting beside me, Barkley's background emerged.

He was forty, a former Navy SEAL with a distinguished military record. So it was no surprise that Barkley was highly skilled in a dozen weapons as well as hand-to-hand combat. He'd been captured in Kabul, and even though injured, he'd fought his way out of his cage and found his way back to his unit at night.

He was awarded a Purple Heart, honorably discharged, and sent home, where he married Miranda White, also a former Navy SEAL. They bought a house in Silver Terrace, a down-market neighborhood near Bayview.

That was four years ago.

Since then, according to his sheet, Barkley had been on a kind of mad tear and had racked up several arrests: two for brandishing a weapon, several for drunk and disorderly, and the cherries on top, two DUIs. Each time he'd gone to court, he'd told the judges that he was sorry as all hell. Abject repentance, promises it would never happen again, plus good looks and a bad limp from the broken hip and thigh he'd sustained while fighting for our country worked in his favor.

He was fined, given warnings, and released.

"But wait," Richie said, "there's more."

I scrolled down and brought up the next page of Barkley's sheet, dated only three months ago. He'd been arrested and charged for firing a handgun through a window of a bar.

That mention of shooting through a window stopped me cold.

Richie reached across me and keyed the down arrow, pulling up Barkley's statement to the arresting officer.

He'd told the officer that he had been drinking at the bar, called Willy's Saloon, on Third Street. He happened to look out the front window and saw a known junkie trying to jimmy open the door to his vehicle. Barkley threw a shot through the plate glass but didn't hit the guy.

Still, firing at another person, not in self-defense, was illegal. Leonard M. Barkley was arrested, pleaded guilty at his arraignment—not to firing on a person, but to shooting out the blinking beer sign in the window.

He brought a witness to court, the same person who'd called the police. But now this witness altered his story, telling Judge Crosby that he'd been mistaken, that in fact Barkley had only been shooting out the beer sign. Barkley told the judge how sorry he was. That the sign's blinking lights made him think that Willy's was taking on enemy fire.

"I have a touch of PTSD, Your Honor. It comes and goes." Barkley was found guilty of the destruction of private property, and his gun was confiscated. He was given a stern lecture, fined a thousand bucks, and given forty hours of community service at a local food bank. He also had to replace the window and beer sign, all of which he did.

His car was relegated to a detail of the shootout, and the junkie was forgotten. But I was interested in that Ford, same model, same color, same tag number, as the one we'd seen in the photo of Barkley with a rifle scope to his eye, staring down San Anselmo Avenue toward the Barons' back windows.

Barkley was acting like a man with PTSD, all right. He was drinking, fighting, carrying a gun, and firing it, all of which confirmed my opinion that he was armed and dangerous. If he was our guy, he had enough brainpower and a steady enough hand to fire a rifle from three hundred yards through a window and hit his targets. Two shots. Two fatalities.

Barkley's last known address was Thornton Avenue near the intersection at Apollo Street in Silver Terrace. I pulled up a map of that area with a street view. Rich and I homed in on the brown stucco house on this residential block.

"Let's pay a call," I said to my partner.

We high-fived, and I called Reg Covington, our SWAT commander. I filled him in and gave him Barkley's address.

"We'll be there in forty minutes," he said.

Conklin and I jogged down the fire stairs, and when we reached the curb at the front of the Hall of Justice, we signed out a car.

CHAPTER 31

CONKLIN AND I watched from our unmarked car at the crest of a hill where two roads met in a Y-shaped intersection; Apollo to the left, Thornton straight ahead.

The house where Leonard Barkley lived with his wife was one of dozens of small, plain stucco-and-wood-slat houses on both sides of Thornton Avenue.

We saw movement in the Barkley house as the occupants walked past their ground-floor windows. Mercifully, there were no pedestrians. No one was out mowing the lawn, washing the car, or engaging in other activities that would put bystanders in the way of gunfire.

Covington and his team were in an armored vehicle on Thornton. Others of the SWAT team had set up a perimeter ringing the house, extending the line down the hill.

We didn't want to enter the house—yet.

A man like Barkley would have access to firearms as well as improvised explosives, booby traps, God only knew what else. We'd put a spike strip in front of his vehicle. If he tried to make a run for it, he'd blow his tires and we'd have him.

I had Barkley's home and cell numbers. I checked in with Joe, who told me he was still with Dave Channing. He told me that he'd spoken with Julie's nanny, Gloria Rose, who was now in charge of our darling and our home.

I asked myself, as I always did when my gun was in my hand, why I thought I had the right to take chances like this when I had a child. But I didn't take time to search for an answer. A very dangerous man, likely a killer with an agenda, was inside his house only thirty yards away.

I looked at Richie. He said, "I prayed. We're covered." I grinned at the man I loved like a brother and trusted with my life, just as he trusted me with his.

We gripped hands for a second or two, then I spoke to Covington over our channel. I waited until his BearCat pulled up next to our car and in front of Barkley's house. Then I called the subject on his landline.

I let the phone ring until a man's voice spoke on the outgoing recording. Same thing happened when I called Barkley's cell.

I did as requested and left a message.

"Mr. Barkley, this is Sergeant Lindsay Boxer, SFPD. I need to speak with you. Please come out your front door with your hands up. Do it now or we're coming in."

No one picked up the phone, but there was a response, the sound of breaking glass coming from a dormer on the second floor. A gun barrel poked through the opening and shots cracked the air. Covington's team let loose with a fusillade of gunfire followed by a flashbang grenade.

The explosion rang out up and down the street, and finally there was a tense silence.

Time to go in.

CHAPTER 32

THERE'D BEEN NO sign of life from that small stucco home in the middle of the block since the gunshots had been fired from the second floor.

No doubt the flashbang grenade had laid out the occupants, and they were still in shock and misery. I squeezed the bullhorn's pistol grip and blasted my voice toward the Barkleys' house and whoever might be conscious inside.

"This is the police. Come out through the front door with your hands in the air."

I announced again, and then Covington's voice was in my earpiece.

"We're going in."

A half dozen men in tactical gear boiled out of the BearCat and swarmed the narrow front yard. Other armored cars screamed down the hill, and the tac team took positions around the house. Two men and our SWAT commander charged up to the front door.

I heard Covington through my earbud, "On five."

Five seconds passed, then the men with the battering ram bashed in the door. Once SWAT cleared the ground floor, my partner and I went in.

The house was boxy.

A staircase in the center hall rose to the second floor. The kitchen was to the left. There were dishes in the sink and breakfast remains on the table. Refrigerator door was hanging open. A TV room to the right was tuned to the History Channel, showing a World War II documentary. In the center of the house a large Rottweiler mix lay groaning in front of a closed door.

Nothing moved. No one cried out. But our arrival had been a surprise, and someone had fled to the second floor in order to take shots at us. With gun drawn, I took the stairs up and looked into the right-hand bedroom. There was a double bed, piles of clothes on the chair and floor. On the dresser was a framed picture of a bearded man wearing a navy uniform with a SEAL trident. That had to be Barkley.

A Caucasian woman was lying on a blood-spattered carpet in front of the window seat with a .380 handgun beside her hand.

The woman was wearing a large T-shirt with an auto repair shop logo. Her long brown hair fell around her shoulders like a shawl, obscuring the tattoos on her neck. I guessed her age as somewhere between thirty and forty, but in any case, she'd had it rough. Now she was breathing hard, and blood ran from a wound in her upper arm.

I kicked the gun aside, spoke into my shoulder mike, and requested an ambulance. I stooped down and said to the injured woman, "I'm Sergeant Boxer, SFPD. I've called for medical help. What's your name?"

She didn't say. She closed her eyes. Could she hear me? Flashbangs could make a person deaf and sick for a while.

I leaned down close to her ear and said my name again, adding, "You fired on police officers. Do you understand? That's a serious crime."

She gave me a glancing look, gasped for breath, and said, "You are going to feel so stupid."

She groaned, rolled onto her side, and threw up, just missing my shoes.

I got her a wet towel and a glass of water from the bathroom and helped her sit up and use the towel on her tearing eyes. I told her to sip from the glass, but she slugged the water down. With my hand on her back, just us girls, I said, "Help me find Barkley. I only need to establish his whereabouts at the time of a shooting, ask him a few questions. That's all."

She hacked out a short, dismissive laugh I translated as *Forget about it.*

Commandos filled the room where I stood over the injured woman. We cuffed her wrists in front of her belly as she yowled in pain. I didn't enjoy this, but it had to be done. I asked her again, "What's your name?"

"Snow White."

Barkley's wife's name was Miranda White Barkley. Maybe we were getting somewhere after all.

Out on the street, sirens wailed toward Thornton from Venus Street, getting louder, cutting out suddenly in front of the house. Car doors slammed.

I said and meant it, "Miranda. We're running out of time to help your husband. Can you hear me? I want to bring him in safely, but our chief is organizing a manhunt. Barkley can't hide. Every cop will be combing the city looking for him."

Footsteps pounded up the stairs, then Brady appeared in the doorway.

"Got us a Mincey warrant," he said, slapping the folded document against his hand. "Conklin and I are going to grab up laptops, phones, whatever. Did she tell you anything?"

More footsteps sounded on the stairs. Conklin appeared in the doorway with news.

"The dog was lying in front of the door to the basement. There's a tunnel down there. If Barkley was here, he's gone down the rabbit hole."

CHAPTER 33

I LEFT CONKLIN at the scene and followed the paramedics taking Miranda White Barkley on her stretcher down to Thornton Avenue.

By then, because of the SWAT team ruckus, the street was teeming with curiosity seekers and law enforcement officers of every type and stripe. Car horns blatted as frustrated drivers tried to move stalled traffic with the heels of their palms.

I walked up to one obnoxious jerk, who had buzzed down his window and was blowing his horn, yelling at the ambulance, "Move your ass, goddamnit."

I put my badge up to his face and said, *"Cut it out."*

The ambulance hadn't left the street. I jogged along Thornton and caught up with EMT Andy Murphy as he and another paramedic wheeled Miranda's gurney up to the back of the bus.

"Andy, I need to ride with my prisoner."

I held up the handcuff key. He nodded okay, and we

swapped out my handcuffs for Flex-Cuffs and secured Miranda's wrists to the gurney's rails.

Murphy gave me a hand up, said "Brace yourself," and pulled the doors closed. I used the shoulder harness to buckle up, and sitting on the narrow bench, my knees up against the gurney, I also grabbed an overhead strap. The sirens whooped and the ambulance shot up Thornton. I leaned down close to the injured woman's ear.

"Miranda."

"Randi."

"Randi. For everyone's sake, I need to find your husband before he makes another mistake."

"Go away."

She tried to turn away from me, but I persisted.

"If I talk to him first…*look at me*, Randi. I'm trying to stop this from ending in a funeral."

The bus took a hard right on Bayshore Boulevard and Randi yelped. Then she opened her eyes and looked into mine. "Leave him alone. Okay? He didn't do anything except run. He has PTSD."

I squeezed her good arm and gave it a little shake. "That may be true, but that's only one part of what's happening here."

She watched as I took out my phone, then shouted, "He doesn't *have* his phone. It's on the nightstand. *Charging.*"

Well, damn it, so much for giving him a friendly call. I barely clung to my seat on the bench as the ambulance pitched and yawed. If Barkley had executed the Barons, he might not have told his wife about it. If he had told her, she was legally protected from testifying against him.

That thought led to another.

Randi had said that I was going to feel stupid. Why was that? Was she working undercover? Was Barkley?

I needed more information, and at about that time the bus took a hard turn, and with tires squealing, we pulled into Metro's ambulance bay.

The driver opened the rear doors. I jumped out ahead of the gurney and walked around the corner of the building to the main entrance to the ER. I'd been here so many times for family, for suspects like Randi Barkley, for my own injuries, I knew every corner of the bland beige waiting room by heart. Only the diverse collection of loved ones waiting for news and the magazines ever changed.

I knew the intake nurse as Kathleen. She spoke with a trace of an Irish brogue, asking, "How can I help you, Sergeant?"

I pointed to the doors to the ER. She buzzed me in, and I waved my thanks as I breezed through. I searched the curtained stalls and found Randi and a nurse in one of them.

The nurse had cut the plastic restraint on Randi's bad arm and was cleaning up the wound. She said to her patient, "See how lucky you are? The bullet missed the bone."

I entered the stall, closed the curtain, and said, "Randi, how're you feeling?"

"Awesome. Haven't you heard? This is my lucky day."

I pulled up a chair. "Explain something to me, will you? Because I'm a little mystified. Why'd you fire on police with a handgun?"

She said, "Ever read a book called *Competitive Shooting*?"

"You've lost me."

"I used a target pistol because that's what I had. Before you showed up, I was going to go to the range and practice shooting to compete."

I wanted to shout at her, *Are you crazy? You fired on SWAT. You should be dead.*

I just stared at her. She went on.

"SWAT was outside my field of vision. I only saw you and that cop with you. I wasn't shooting to kill. I shot over your heads. Did you notice?"

The nurse was openmouthed. Randi was looking at me—like I was stupid—saying, "Ever hear of a diversion?"

Now I got it. She'd created cover so that Barkley could get away.

"Helping your husband escape from the police makes you an accessory to whatever he's done. Get me? At present, he's under suspicion of committing murder."

CHAPTER 34

IT WAS AFTER 6 p.m. when Brady pulled up a chair to our desks, tightened his white-blond ponytail to keep his hair out of his eyes, and, gripping a red grease pencil, made notes as we summarized our last ten hours.

Item one: Miranda White Barkley was in a cell waiting for her lawyer. Two: Conklin had traveled with SWAT through the tunnel under Barkley's house, which was a short sprint to the nearest commuter rail station; Barkley had probably boarded the train and could now be anywhere.

"Son of a bitch," Brady said.

We talked about Barkley, clever enough and physically able to dig out an exit. No doubt he'd been well trained by the military. At this point, Brady told us, teams were stationed to watch his house, and Caltrain had pulled surveillance footage from the ticketing area at the Twenty-Second Street station.

"Three," said Brady, nodding to Conklin. "Stempien is going through Barkley's devices now."

"Item next," I said. "Randi told me that she deliberately fired over our heads. She didn't hit anyone, so that could be true. The slugs she fired were blanks."

As Brady made notes, I thought about the two bodies, one sprawled across the desk, the other lying faceup on the carpet. Two perfectly placed kill shots had done that.

Who had done the shootings and why? What on earth would have motivated Barkley to murder the Barons, and how did those killings link up with the homicides of drug dealers in LA and Chicago at precisely the same time?

Brady pushed back his chair, linked his hands behind his neck. "Bottom line," he said, "we don't know where Barkley is, the wife ain't talkin', and there's no known connection between Barkley and the Barons. Got a whole lot of parts on the floor of the shop, but can't make a car."

I repeated a version of what Joe always says to me when I'm overstimulated and a wreck about how much time is flying by.

"It's 'day one,' Brady. Day one and we have Randi White Barkley in custody. That's a start."

Brady added that the picture of Leonard Barkley standing behind his car door on San Anselmo Avenue two days before the killings had been disseminated to every cop on the force—Northern, Central, and Southern Stations, as well as the motorcycle cops and the Sheriff's Department.

Brady said, "I don't have to tell you, unless we nab the son of a bitch, we gotta break the wife."

Randi hadn't cracked while she was in pain and with me questioning her. Conklin was good with everyone, but he was especially good with women. His sincerity always came through.

I said, "Sounds like a job for my partner."

Cappy called over from his desk, "Hey, Richie. Cindy's on the tube."

Brady rearranged things on my desk until he got his hand around the remote. He pointed it at the TV mounted on the wall, where it could be seen throughout the squad room, and boosted the volume.

And there was Cindy Thomas standing in front of the Barkleys' house, miked up, made up, a lower-third screen graphic displaying her name and *San Francisco Chronicle*. Brian Whalen, a TV reporter from the local CBS affiliate said, "Cindy, can you bring us up-to-date on the incident that took place here this morning?"

"Brian, this is what we know. This man"—she held up an enlargement of a photo I had scrutinized dozens of times—"Leonard Barkley, is wanted for questioning in the murders of Paul and Ramona Baron."

"You're saying he's a suspect in those murders?"

"The police department is calling Barkley a person of interest. He may be a witness and have useful information. The incident this afternoon involved the police trying to bring him in, but he got away, and his whereabouts are unknown.

"If anyone knows or sees this man, do not approach him. He's presumed to be armed and dangerous. Call the SFPD hotline immediately."

She gave the number.

Then she added, "Mr. Barkley, if you're listening, the police want you to know that your wife has been injured by gunfire and is in police custody. Please call the number on the screen. The SFPD and your wife need to speak to you."

I was pretty sure that if Barkley was watching from his bunker, he was scoffing and loading his weapon. Brady muted the volume on the TV.

He said, "Before you start looking for leakers, I'm Cindy's police source."

I said, "*You* told her?"

"Thanks, Brady," said Conklin. "We owed her one."

"That's what *she* said. Y'all go home now and brace for a deluge coming over the tip line. Let's hope for a lead that pays off."

CHAPTER 35

I CAN'T LEAVE Dave right now," Joe told Lindsay.

He was sitting in his car in the parking lot, watching a rabbit hop across the patio outside the Channing restaurant.

"Hang on a sec," she said. "I'm parking the car."

He heard her shut the door and set the car alarm. He wanted to be home with her, talk to her, hold Julie-Bug on his lap and rock her to sleep.

"He's a mess, huh?" Lindsay asked.

Joe said, "Well, he thinks Ray's doctor murdered him. I don't know if he's grief stricken or delusional or both. But I do know that he's alone and in a bad place."

Joe heard Mrs. Rose speak to Lindsay over the intercom. "Come on up, Lindsay dear."

"Thanks. I'll be right there."

Lindsay said to Joe, "I never asked. Does Dave have a girlfriend?"

"He pays for the girlfriend experience."

"Aw, jeez. Do whatever you need to do," she said.

Lindsay told him that after she put Julie to bed, she'd ask Mrs. Rose to take over for another couple of hours so she could have dinner with the girls.

"I'll bring her a case of Channing's Private Reserve Cab," Joe said.

"And one for us."

"No problem."

Joe said he'd be home tomorrow, and after exchanging good nights and phone kisses, he returned to Dave's small, two-story stone house, which was identical to the house about twenty yards away—the house where his parents, Ray and Nancy, had lived. Dave had left the lights on, telling Joe, "If Ray's restless spirit is still around, he'll want to see the lights."

Dave's living room was sparsely furnished with two up-holstered armchairs in front of the fireplace, a standing lamp, and a handmade end table made from what looked like antique wine crates. A collection of framed oil paintings, including one luminous view of the vineyard at sunup, hung over the fireplace. Joe had taken a close look. They were signed "Nancy Channing."

An aged-plank dining table dominated the dining area. There were four straight-backed dining chairs, and Joe saw a short stack of folders in front of one of them.

Joe took a seat and opened the folder on top. It con-tained a thin sheaf of clippings from local papers, primarily obituaries. Dave brought Joe a cup of tea and said, "Read this one."

"This one" was a glossy Napa Valley monthly publication called *Great Grapes,* which contained a lot of ads, a smattering of local news, and profiles of artists and business owners. Joe opened the magazine to where a slip of paper bookmarked an essay by a writer named Johann Archer.

Archer had written about the death of his thirty-eight-year-old fiancée, Tansy Mallory, a dance teacher and long-distance runner, who'd been taken to the hospital with heat exhaustion. He'd written that Tansy was in every other way healthy and recovering—when she died.

Archer had poignantly expressed his shock about the unexpected and still unbelievable loss of the woman he had dearly loved. The writer hadn't mentioned the name of the hospital or the doctor, only that he disbelieved the hospital's stated cause of death.

He closed the essay by writing, "Inexplicably, a sunny, generous, and optimistic woman is gone. Somehow my heart still beats and I continue to live. That's inexplicable, too."

Joe finished the article and looked up.

"Dave, you got the idea that your dad was murdered from this article?"

"Tansy Mallory's obituary and two others, not counting Ray's, are in that file. It's more than smoke, Joe. I'm calling it a fact-based fire."

Joe's thoughts veered to his training in behavioral science with the FBI. He couldn't read Dave. Of course he was depressed. But he was also edgy and maybe paranoid. That said, in times of tragedy it was common to strike out, blame someone. Dr. Perkins was a logical scapegoat for Ray's death.

Joe asked, "Have you spoken with Archer or the families of these other people who died suspiciously?"

"No. I don't know how to approach them, so I'm going by what I've read here. Two of the obits mention Dr. Perkins, which confirms my strong belief that that son of a bitch is on a roll. That he killed my dad."

CHAPTER 36

EVEN ON A Wednesday night Susie's Café was packed with millennials gorging on cheap, spicy food, old men hanging out at their neighborhood bar, and office workers from the nearby financial district loosening their ties, kicking off their shoes, and doing the limbo.

As for the Women's Murder Club, we had an easy time letting down our hair in this diverse and rowdy atmosphere, so much so that years ago we'd made Susie's our unofficial clubhouse.

The steel-drum band was playing "Happy," and a group of six was heading out as Claire, Yuki, and I scooted past the kitchen pass-through to the back room, where we could speak without shouting.

Lorraine was wiping down the table in "our" booth and said, "Jerked beef is the special tonight."

We thanked her and slid into the banquettes, Claire and I on one side, Yuki sitting across from us. It took only seconds to choose from the menu, which hadn't appreciably changed in at least ten years.

I said to Lorraine, "Cindy's working overtime."

It wasn't a lie, but it was shy of the truth. Cindy had begged off our dinner date because she was still mad at me for asking her to sit on her story that drug dealers were victims of sniper shootings in several cities. It wasn't just any old scoop. The Barons' deaths had gone wide on national TV, while Cindy's name was not on the front page of the *Chronicle*.

I hadn't been able to give her a fullhearted apology, and Cindy knew how to hold a grudge. I explained that to Yuki and Claire, and Claire said, "You're both stubborn." Yuki's two cents: "You had to ask her to hold it. She's a bulldog, but in a day or so she'll get over it and be on to the next."

Lorraine appeared at our table with pencil and pad in hand. Claire and I ordered beers. Yuki ordered a shrimp salad, and Claire said, "I'm gonna say...I'll have jerked beef on a roll."

I asked for gumbo and a basket of bread.

"That's all?" Lorraine said.

"I might order some key lime pie in a little while."

"It could be gone, Lindsay. If not, I'll nail down a piece for you while I still can."

The frisky waitress headed for the kitchen pass-through window, and after she had gone, Claire asked Yuki, "What's the emergency, sweetheart?"

Yuki was clearly dressed for court, in a blue suit, a V-neck silk blouse, and high-heeled shoes.

"Clayton Warren, that junior wheelman I'm charging

with car theft, possession of drugs with intent to distribute, and acting as accomplice to murder of a *cop*."

We both nodded. We knew. If convicted, Warren, who was eighteen, would get serious time for serious crimes.

"His arraignment was set for today. I'm looking for him, and his attorney comes in, tells me that his client tried to hang himself this morning."

"Whaaaat?" Claire and I said in unison.

"Let me restate that," said Yuki. "He *did* hang himself with a bedsheet hooked over a heating pipe in the bathroom."

Claire was consumed with a sudden coughing fit, excused herself, and said, "My asthma." I gripped her hand under the table as she said to Yuki, "He's dead?"

"Not quite. Another prisoner grabbed his legs and yelled for help. He's in solitary with a neck brace and round-the-clock guards. But think about it. He hasn't been indicted, let alone tried. He could go free. And if he's convicted, he could appeal. There's no death sentence in the charged crimes. So why'd he try to kill himself?"

We tossed Yuki's question back and forth across the table, agreeing finally that in the absence of an answer from the kid, his family's lives must have been threatened as a warning not to flip on the actual killer dealer. Claire thought he was depressed, ashamed, and certain he would be convicted.

I said, "Sounds like he would rather die than go to prison."

Yuki didn't buy it. "There's something we don't know. His attorney doesn't know it, either. The kid's been completely passive since his arrest." Yuki shook her head. "Maybe it doesn't matter *why* he's working against himself, but I'm sure he's got a reason. So where does that leave me? I'm wondering if I can just do a C-minus job when he comes to trial."

I said, "Are you kidding?"

She wasn't. Yuki looked at our stunned expressions and said, "Look. I could get away with it. I've got a reputation, you know. I lose cases when I'm *brilliant* and the defendant is *guilty.*"

Sadly, that was true.

CHAPTER 37

CLAIRE SAID TO Yuki, "How about this instead? Tell Red Dog you want off the case. How can you possibly prosecute a person you don't believe in?"

"Okay, say I go to Parisi," Yuki said, referring to DA Len Parisi, a formidable, red-haired, three-hundred-pound hulk who had a fierce reputation for being tough on crime. "He takes me off the case and reassigns it to one of his killer ADAs who eat knives for breakfast. Clayton refuses to defend himself and gets life in prison with no possibility of parole. As soon as he can, he commits suicide."

I said, "It's not your problem, Yuki. You can't direct his life."

Plates were cleared and coffee arrived along with my wedge of heavenly key lime pie. Lorraine bent to my ear and said, "I've got connections." I gave her a thumbs-up, and when I turned back to Yuki, she was scowling.

She said, "Lorraine, a pitcher of margaritas, please. Anyone joining me?" She got no takers.

"Only one glass," she said to Lorraine, who returned with the pitcher in no time.

Yuki is not a drunk, but once or twice a year she succumbs to tequila's siren call. This was the night. Claire was coughing some, but she reached across the table and took Yuki's handbag, dug out her car keys, and handed them to me.

"Fine," Yuki said. "Be that way."

I called Brady and told him that Yuki was going to need a ride home in about an hour. Claire and I clinked our beer mugs to Yuki's salt-rimmed glass, and we toasted her for having a good heart.

Lorraine came by and said to Yuki, "One of our customers is playing your song."

We could hear it now. Jeff Rudolph, a talented amateur with a guitar, was singing about the sun baking, pop-tops and flip-flops. Yuki was cleared for launch and blasted off when Lorraine passed her the mike and walked with her into the front room.

Claire and I joined the parade.

Rudolph had already sung the first stanzas, and his face brightened when Yuki began to sing along with him, her clear soprano voice lifting the refrain.

"'Wastin' away again in Margaritaville…'"

Jeff stamped the floor. "Salt, salt, salt, salt."

Diners were singing and clapping now.

"'But I know…'"

And as everyone instinctively stopped singing, Yuki belted out the last line: "'It's my own damn fault.'"

Someone shouted, "Encore," and there was clapping and more calling out, *Encore. Encore.*

Claire said loudly, "She's done. Really."

Lorraine took back the mike and when we were snug in our booth, she asked, "Coffee, Yuki? Just made it fresh."

Yuki said, "Ha. No, thanks," and drained her glass.

That evening I almost forgot that Claire was facing the challenge of her life, that the Barons' bodies were cold, that Randi hadn't talked, and that Leonard Barkley was still, as they say, in the wind. All of this would wake me up at around three in the morning, but right now it felt so good to be joking around with my buds.

I said, "Lorraine. Coffee all around and pie. Whatever kind you've got left."

"Cherry," she said, wrinkling her nose. "From Monday."

"Sold," I said. "Bring it on."

CHAPTER 38

YUKI WAS LYING on the bed, eyes closed against the light coming from the old-fashioned ceiling fixture.

Brady took off her shoes, rubbed her toes.

"Ohhhhhh," Yuki said. "That's too good."

"Can you sit up?"

"Maybe. I think so," she said. But she didn't actually move. Brady said, "I'm going to try to get your jacket off, Yuki-san. If you can't help, okay, but don't fight me."

Yuki laughed.

Pretty soon Brady was laughing, too. This woman's appealing laughter could send a statue into giggles. He got her jacket off, and her blouse while he was at it, rolled her over, and unzipped her skirt.

She said, "I'm loving this, Brady. You must've done this before."

"You are a silly woman, you know that, don't you?"

"I had a tellible...terrible day."

"I want to hear about it," he said. He unhooked her bra,

brought her a WALK FOR A CURE T-shirt, and asked, "Can you handle it from here?"

"Where you going?"

"I'm going to hit the rain box. Be right back."

When Yuki opened her eyes again, Brady was in bed with her, his hair was damp, and the light was out. She rolled toward him and he put his arms around her. His big arms. Loved them.

"I'm right here, darlin'. Tell me what happened."

"You know what? I'll tell you tomorrow. I don't want to think about it now."

She put her arms around Brady's neck, and he hoisted her so that they were in their best position, her left leg hooked over his hip, their arms around each other, resting her head under his chin. This was as close as two people could get.

He said softly, "So you're saying you want me to take advantage of you."

"I think. I know you want to."

He kissed her. She moaned and squirmed and told him she loved him. He said, "I love me, too."

She laughed.

He said, "I love you so much it scares me."

"I'm harmless."

They rocked together slowly in the big bed. He flipped her so that she was on top, put his hands on her hips, and moved her until they caught fire. Then they held each other until sleep tugged at them, and Yuki slid off her dear husband onto the rumpled heap of bedding.

They nuzzled and kissed and grinned at each other, then

fell asleep holding hands. When Yuki woke up, she separated herself from Brady's embrace, bunched her pillow, and turned her back to him.

While asleep, he wrapped his arms around her and held her against him. Yuki was coming down from the booze, but she was still high on Brady. They needed more times like this. A song was going through her mind.

She sang the last line in a whisper. "'Baby, baby. Baby, you're the best.'"

CHAPTER 39

THE TWO OLD friends sat in front of the fireplace, each with a glass of an excellent house Cabernet.

Dave said, "I'm grateful, Joe. If you hadn't agreed to help me, I really don't know what the hell I would have done."

Joe leaned toward Dave and said, "Let's talk."

"What have we *been* doing?"

Joe just looked at him. Like a therapist would do.

Dave got it. He said, "Okay. Just don't tell me you think that I'm crazy."

He pushed himself closer to the fireplace, extracted a poker from a tool caddy, and stirred the smoldering coals.

Joe thought, *More avoidance.*

Dave had asked for his help, but he wasn't ready to get into the hard stuff. Over dinner he had talked about a woman he'd met online, said he hadn't told her about his injuries. He talked about how even though Ray had been moody, they'd watched sports together on TV; now he watched by himself, or with Jeff the Chef if the game was on early enough.

While Dave threw logs on the fire, Joe sat silently, balancing his good feelings for Dave against his unwanted suspicions.

Dave returned to the table and said, "You were saying?"

Joe said, "I was saying, it's time to really talk about all of it, Dave. You. Ray. Dr. Perkins, and me. I want to talk to you about my limitations."

"You? I wish I had your limitations," Dave said. "Sorry, that didn't come out right."

Joe said, "It's fine. I know what you meant."

He sipped his wine and watched his friend's face cloud over with sadness.

Dave said, "Damn Perkins to hell for what he did…"

Was blaming Perkins a reaction to grief? Or was Dave right?

Joe said, "I don't have a badge, Dave. I'm a freelance consultant. I'll try to talk to Perkins, but if he refuses, I can't force him to talk. That said, I should be able to poke around enough to see if there's reason to bring in law enforcement."

"I can pay you to be my consultant."

"Shut up, Dave. On second thought, pay me a dollar. Then we're official."

Dave thanked him, dug a single out of his shirt pocket, and slid it over to Joe. Joe made a note on the back of his checkbook, "Hired as consultant to D. Channing," then added the date and his signature. He passed the ad hoc document over to Dave, and Dave signed it, too.

Then he put his hands over his eyes and cried.

Joe tried to comfort him, but he was worried. Although he had accepted without question that Dave loved his father, he couldn't ignore the nagging feeling that had come up almost a week ago when he had gone with Dave to the hospital to see Ray.

Ray had treated Dave like a kid or like an employee, sending him to the cafeteria, ordering him around.

"You told me that you were very close," Joe said to Ray, carefully steering his friend back to the present. "So what happens to you now?"

"I don't know. I suppose I'll sell the place. Move to LA or New York. I've been here for so long, mainly to help out my parents. Mom was a buffer between me and Ray."

"More about that," Joe said.

"Well, he was bitter at how things turned out. How I turned out. He made unnecessary cracks. Like, 'Why don't you *run* to the store, Dave?' If he was drinking, he'd tell me that this was God's punishment for getting Rebecca killed."

"Oh, Christ, Dave."

"I've forgiven him. I understand his disappointment. I felt the same way about what I did, a line of thought that deadends on that damned highway. But, as you know, my dad took care of me, gave me a job…responsibilities. And before I do another thing with my life, I have to get to the truth about why Ray died. I have to square things. If Dr. Perkins is killing people, he has to be stopped. He has to pay."

Joe said, "I want to see Ray's medical records, the name of the medical examiner, and Ray's death certificate."

"I've scanned all of that to my laptop. I'll get it."

While Dave went for his laptop, Joe used the bathroom. As he ran the water in the sink, he opened the medicine cabinet. Dave had shelves of medications: antidepressants, drugs for pain and sleep. Joe pointed his phone at all of the little bottles and snapped photos. He had an unwelcome suspicion and he had to allow it.

Like himself, Dave was closing in on fifty. Had he tired of being Ray's disappointing, damaged child? Had he come up with a plan to get away from his father—for good?

CHAPTER 40

THERE WAS AN empty corner office at the end of the fourth-floor corridor that had once belonged to a crooked cop who didn't need it anymore or ever again.

I told Brady my plan to turn that office into a war room for the Baron case, and he said, "Be my guest." Then I told him I was going to form a task force with the primaries on the sniper shootings in other cities.

Brady said, "You're about to learn what it means to herd cats."

"Is that a yes?"

"It's a *hell* yes," he said.

He took the elevator up to Jacobi's former office on five and didn't look back. A half hour later Rich and I had taped up photos of the deceased on the war room walls, our computers had been moved to our new office, and we each had a mug and a thermos full of coffee.

We arranged for a conference call with Detective Richards from Chicago, Detective Noble in LA, Chi and

McNeil from out on the street, and Conklin and myself on whatever lines we could grab at that hour, all of us telephonically together at noon.

Richards's victim was the small smoke shop owner, Albert Roccio. Richards had been miserly with whatever he had gleaned about the shooting, telling us that so far he hadn't made any progress. Noble had taken the lead in the case of Fred Peavey, killed by a single shot outside his son's school. He was coming late to his case and had sounded eager to be part of our team.

McNeil and Chi were the lead investigators on Jennings's assassination at the Duboce Avenue Taco King.

Jennings, the first to die, had been shot from a distance through his windshield. His rear window had been marked with the word *Rehearsal*, written with a finger in the dust on his rear window. However, Jennings had been shot slightly later than 8:30, like the other victims. It was unclear whether Jennings was part of the same collection of executed drug dealers.

Conklin and I were under the most pressure. Paul and Ramona Baron, unlike the other victims, were well known and had a fan base of rich and influential citizens. Those friends were talking to the press and clogging the mayor's phone lines with demands for an arrest of the killer or killers, pronto.

I thought Brady was right that egos would be involved in this task force, but I also believed that to varying degrees the "cats" wanted to be herded if it would result in closing their cases.

Rich and I had an immediate and specific goal.

At one o'clock we'd be meeting with Miranda White Barkley and her attorney, who would be pushing to get his client released and had a fair chance of getting his way. We had no evidence that Randi had participated in the murders.

Still holding her as a material witness, we would have to release her at 2:00. I hoped that by the time the conference call ended, we'd have the leverage we needed to get Randi to talk.

I wasn't just hopeful, I was damned-well determined.

CHAPTER 41

TED SWANSON'S FORMER office had been cleaned, but no flowery air freshener could eradicate the stink of that dirty cop who'd cost the lives of eighteen people.

He was at Chino for life, but that was old stinking news.

I closed the door to our new war room, with its large gray desk and two phone consoles, and my partner and I booted up our laptops.

I clicked on a news link and read the chyron running along the lower edge of my screen: *SFPD has no leads in the deaths of Ramona and Paul Baron.*

Great. Tell me something I don't know.

A box with an arrow appeared in the upper right with the title "The Mysterious Deaths of Paul and Ramona Baron."

"Richie. Come here."

I double-clicked on the arrow and was immediately alarmed to see a slide show of images of the Barons' office after they'd been murdered. There were close-ups of the bullet holes in the casement windows, Ramona's desk chair, the bloodstained carpet, and the taped outline of Paul's body across the surface of the partners desk.

The voice-over reporter was saying, "Acting chief of police Jackson Brady tells Real Crime News that he can't comment while the Baron case is under investigation."

I stabbed the Mute button with my finger and said to Conklin, "Did you see that? Someone leaked the crime scene photos, for God's sake."

"Taking a wild guess here. A CSI was bribed."

"Huh," I said. "Nice little severance package for someone."

I had Clapper's mobile on speed dial. I left him a message, and then I stewed about this wide-open case and kicked it around with Conklin.

I said, "Graphic photos of blood and bullet holes, and the shooter's defense attorney tells a judge that the jury pool has been poisoned. If it ever comes to a judge and jury."

"You're not looking at the bright side."

"You're a riot, Richie."

All we had was a suspect who'd been photographed holding a gun sight and was currently as free as fog. According to Randi White Barkley, her husband had PTSD. He'd run from the police out of fear. My theory was a little different. Barkley had run because he'd killed two prominent citizens and we were onto him. The odds were ten to nothing that he was preparing to kill again.

Still. We had his car, his wife, his laptop, his fingerprints, and his dog. Cops were on his doorstep. Maybe if Randi asked him to come in, he would do it.

I had a question for Richie, the eternal optimist.

"Check me on this. The Barons' murders actually link up with the shootings at the same time in other cities, right?"

"So it seems. Roccio, yes. Peavey, yes. Eight thirty a.m."

"So in your view, selling drugs—major league or minor—is at the root of the murders?"

"Well, do you believe in coincidences?" he asked me.

"Let me get back to you on that."

Detective Richards of Chicago PD had shown a distinct disinclination to share information about his victim, Albert Roccio, but he'd agreed to take our call at noon. I said to Conklin, "Here we go."

I tapped Richards's contact on my phone.

A woman answered, saying, "Detective Wilkens. May I help you?"

"I'm Sergeant Boxer. Detective Richards is expecting my call," I said.

"He just ran out, but he'll be back in a few."

I left my number as Brenda poked her head into the room. "I've got Inspector McNeil for you."

Cappy's husky voice filtered through the car radio mike and whatever he was eating.

"Boxer, you ready for a big pile of nothing much?"

"Bring it."

He laughed, said, "Ready, set, go."

And then he reported in.

CHAPTER 42

I PICTURED CAPPY swiping his bald head with his forearm, replacing his ball cap, setting it just right.

He spoke into the mike, saying, "Okay, so here's what we know from working the Taco King.

"Jennings was a regular. His movements were known. If someone wanted to take him out, they could find him. So he was prob'ly a target, not a random 'rehearsal,' and that goes to motive.

"We spoke with Woody Moynihan. 'Member him? First baseman, .300 batting average until he took a hundred-mile-per-hour fastball to his head."

I said, "Does Moynihan have an idea who shot Jennings?"

My cell phone buzzed, Brenda texting, *Detective Noble is on line three.*

I asked Cappy to hang on, punched the button on the console, said hello to the LAPD homicide detective who was primary on the LA shooting.

Conklin punched line three on his own console and at the

same time activated speakerphone. "Cappy," he said. "Talk to me. Boxer has another call."

"Fine, tell her Jennings was peddling pills to friends. Moynihan says actually he was a customer, but it coulda been a wide circle. Friends of friends. Conklin. You still there?"

"I'm all yours," said Conklin.

"Okay. I talk to myself, but not on the phone. So Moynihan has no idea who woulda capped Jennings, but there's a variety of reasons someone might have gone crazy and offed his dealer. It happens, you know. Narcotics might have a line on it."

I was listening to Cappy and at the same time thinking how Narcotics was a shell of its former self. There were jobs that had to be filled, and this was a great example of why.

Noble said, "Hello?"

I turned my attention back to Noble, saying, "Right here."

He said, "We've doubled up our manpower on this school shooting."

"Excellent. What have you got so far?"

Noble said, "The parents at Little Geniuses, where Peavey was popped, are going, uh, ballistic. We've been bringing them in, giving them a chance to air their complaints and fears of their kids being shot, and hoping maybe someone would finger a suspect."

"How's that going?"

Chi's voice came over the speaker, bringing Conklin up-to-date on the stakeout at Barkley's house.

I tried listening to Chi, but Noble was excited and drew me in.

"Fred Peavey was a dentist," said Noble, "and some of the other parents were posing as patients of his. I've confirmed he was writing scrips for painkillers. I spoke to ten people myself. Nobody wanted him dead. They liked him. We checked them out, and honest to God, except for some with an opioid addiction, they all live in Mister Rogers' neighborhood."

Another drug connection, I thought. This one, pharmaceuticals.

Chi was telling Conklin that he'd briefed Brady on the Barkley house stakeout: cars around the block and a team in the house next door with a clear view of all entrances.

"No sign of Barkley," Chi said. "The dog was impounded pending release to its owner. Maybe you can use that with the wife."

Cappy's voice crackled over the line again.

"I checked out Barkley and his lady. Both of them served in Afghanistan, Boxer. They're both expert shooters. Hey. We're blocking traffic. I'll call you or you call me. Ten-four."

A new text from Brenda. *Detective Richards on two.*

I punched the button and said, "This is Boxer, Detective Richards. You're conferenced in with our team."

Richards got right to it.

"We have no suspects in Roccio's murder, but to your theory of the case, we looked for a drug connection."

I said, "My partner is here. Richards, meet Conklin."

Richards said "How ya doin'?" to Conklin, then told us that a half kilo of heroin had been secreted in Roccio's car.

"He was dealing big and small."

According to Richards, Roccio sold the H on the phone,

and the customers came into the store, bought a magazine, and took the H with them. Same with X and marijuana. Kids coming into his smoke shop would bring a magazine to the cash register and give Roccio a pair of twenties, and Roccio would stick a joint into the centerfold."

Conklin said, "That could've been the easiest sting in the world."

Richards said, "I got a meeting. Nice chatting with you."

Conklin said, "Wait. Hang on, Richards. Any suspects? Any other victims?"

"In a word, no and no. Roccio wasn't the only drug slinger in Chicago, okay? We've got gangs. Organized variety."

"I hear you."

"Later," said Richards.

The line went dead. All of them did. So much for herding cats. I stared at Rich and he stared at me, the unspoken question lying like a dead fish in the space between us.

What now?

"Hello? Hello?"

Shit. It was Noble.

I apologized, asked him to go on.

"It's okay. I was going to say we ran their names. Look in your inbox. I sent you a rundown on Peavey's friends and associates, a mixed bag of moms and dads, white and blue collar, some military types and a couple of patrol cops."

There was a knock on the door as Noble was saying, "Alibis for 8:30 a.m. on the day of the shooting are tight, and no motives we can see. Peavey hasn't ever been sued or arrested. He gets four and a half stars for his dental work.

So maybe our shooting isn't related to the others. But we'll keep going until we hit a wall."

Maybe Jennings and Peavey *were* random. What about the Barons and Roccio?

Random or planned to the second, what was the point of any of these killings and where was this going?

How was it going to end?

CHAPTER 43

I LOOKED UP to see Mike Stempien, our FBI computer tech, coming through the door.

He looked as excited as if he'd found a can of gold coins under his sink. He definitely had something to tell us. Conklin stood up, and Stempien took his chair at the desk and opened a laptop.

"This," he said, "belongs to the Barkleys."

I said, "Mike. I want to hear everything, but we've got a meeting upstairs with Mrs. Barkley and her attorney."

"This'll take one minute. You're going to want to see this before your meeting."

Conklin and I were standing at the edges of the desk.

Stempien said, "This was on the kitchen counter. I pulled up the last sites the Barkleys visited and found—ta-da."

He turned the laptop so we could see it better.

What appeared to be a video game from the Pac-Man era filled the screen. There was a drawing of a carnival wheel of fortune in the center, and a chat box off to the right. Mike said what I was thinking. "I haven't seen a game like this since the '90s. But then I got the feeling there was more to it than it seemed."

"How so?"

"This site doesn't have an internet address. If you want to play, you've got to know your way around anonymous browsing and posting. Meaning, there's a browser called Tor, which stands for *the Onion Routing*. It's got different layers. One layer knows only what the next layer is. You can't see the whole picture. The address isn't something like Google.com or CNN.com. It's like ABQ3d.

"A jumble of letters gets you to a point. Your connection's not so quick because you're bouncing all over the world, and that means you're not going to have the speed to load a site with fancy graphics. Then it's like you need to be in the secret circle to know what site to go to. So if this is just an archaic video game, why the mystery?"

"So a mystery wrapped in an enigma," Conklin said.

I said, "That wheel is a gambling device, right? Are bets being made for prizes?"

I reached down and moved the curser over the wheel, and it started to rotate and make a faint clicking sound. When the wheel stopped, a number flashed at the top of the page.

"So look, Mike. I just got points?"

"Points. Status. A better chance than a different player? My initial feeling was that this site is in disguise for something illegal. Drugs. Or some kind of trafficking. But I was able to make out some of the encrypted chat. The name of the website is the same as the game on it: Moving Targets. And then I got a different feeling."

"What? What kind of feeling?"

"Don't hold me to it, because...well, because. I'm still just turning things over, but I think Moving Targets is a website for hitters. It seems that many of them, from the slang they use, are military or police. The kills they were chatting about could have been your drug dealers. Lots of excitement about the precision of the attacks, about the 'scores.' At least that's the vibe on the site."

I was almost panting with anxiety and anticipation. Had Stempien found the key to the shootings in the Barkleys' computer?

"Can you tell which of the Barkleys was playing?"

"From the activity on their laptop, they both played. But was it just a game? Or was it reflected in real life?"

"Can you figure it out?" I asked.

He was quiet for a moment, thinking about it.

"We'll see," he finally said. "No guarantees."

CHAPTER 44

CONKLIN HELD THE elevator door for me, then reached over and pressed the button for the seventh floor.

I stared up at the row of floor numbers as I collected my scattered thoughts. A couple of minutes from now we would be talking to Randi White Barkley and her attorney, Lynn Selby. We had a hint of leverage, knowledge that someone in the Barkley household played a suspicious video game. It wasn't much and it was late in coming. Still.

I played it out inside my head, our ADA addressing the judge, saying, *Your Honor, we're charging Miranda White Barkley with shooting two rounds over law enforcement's heads and possibly playing a violent video game.*

Yeah, right.

The doors slid open, and we walked out onto the worn gray tiles and crossed to Bubbleen Waters, desk sergeant and local karaoke singer of note. We exchanged greetings, and Sergeant Waters presented the log. I signed us in, and we followed a guard along a long corridor ringing with inmate voices and the clanging of doors and the echoing sounds of our footsteps.

We stopped at the gate to the small, barred room with a table and four chairs in the center, and the guard let us in.

Randi didn't look up. She wore the standard orange jumpsuit and cuffs and had braided her hair into one long plait hanging down her back. She'd gotten help, no doubt, as her wounded arm was bound in a bulky and conspicuous bandage.

Randi's attorney, Lynn Selby, was a public defender with a future. She was blond, with pale-pink lipstick and a light-gray suit, but I knew her, and although she looked like a pussycat, she had a bulldog's bite.

There were stiff greetings all around, and after we'd taken our seats, Selby said sweetly, "Assuming there are no new charges against Mrs. Barkley, your forty-eight hours expires in an hour."

"How're you feeling, Randi?" I asked.

"Peachy," she said.

I smiled at the sarcasm.

Selby said, "Please address your questions to me, and quickly please. I want to get my client out of here."

Randi White had done two tours in Afghanistan. She'd been trained to withstand interrogation, to give up nothing but her name, rank, and serial number. And along with her military programming, she also had a guard dog of a lawyer to protect her from us.

I said to Selby, "Lynn. Randi knocked out her bedroom window and threw two rounds at our marked car. She knew we were police. That's reckless endangerment to start with.

She has admitted to providing cover so that her husband, Leonard Barkley, could escape. He's a suspect in a double homicide. That makes Randi an accessory."

"Come on, Lindsay. Accessory to helping her husband run away? He's a psychological mess due to his time in our armed services. She fired blanks. Over your heads. On purpose. You know that. Furthermore, Randi White Barkley is the only person who was injured in this assault on her home and on her person. That's a lawsuit against the city waiting for me to dictate it to my transcriber."

"Take it down a notch, will you, Lynn? I haven't asked her a question yet."

"Go ahead, Sergeant."

As we'd planned, I said, "Rich, why don't you take it from here?"

CHAPTER 45

MY EASYGOING, GOOD-DOIN' partner got comfortable in the metal chair, linked his long fingers together, and placed his hands on the table.

He kindly addressed the woman in standard jail orange.

"Randi, you feeling okay to talk for a few minutes?"

"I guess."

"This won't take long. You were in the ER when you asked my partner if she'd ever read *Competitive Shooting*. You need a how-to book on shooting?"

"I can always get better. I was heading off to a range when you and your fellow gangsters pulled up. You go to a range, too, don't you?"

Conklin smiled and changed the subject.

"There was a video game on your open computer when we ruined your day. Something called Moving Targets."

Randi scoffed. "You ruined more than one, I'd say. Anyway. Moving Targets. Len and I both play."

"So, what's the appeal of target shooting? I looked you up. You're proficient with just about any kind of weapon."

"Target shooting is fun and it keeps me sharp—"

Selby interjected, "That's enough, Randi. Are we done, Inspector?"

Randi overrode her lawyer. She said to us, "You know—or maybe you don't. Some people like to *shoot* and some people like to *kill*. I like to shoot—at targets."

I said, "Can you explain what you mean about people who like to kill? Are you talking about psychopaths?"

"Maybe. I've seen some military people who get addicted to shooting humans. In particular, bad humans. Enemies. You get permission and a weapon, and for some people it's the greatest high. That's how they talk about it."

Conklin said, "I've never seen that. I mean, sure, I've seen people without conscience, but tell me more about this thrill or high."

I knew he was hoping Randi would implicate Leonard. Would we get that lucky? Selby put her hand on Randi's to get her to stop, but her client wanted to talk.

"Here's something I'll never forget. Me and three others from my platoon were in a parking lot outside the base camp, same parking lot we're in every day. Do you know the term *Blue on Green*?"

I shook my head no.

Randi said, "Green is the friendly host-country forces, the ones that we were mentoring in Afghanistan. We're the Blue. So we're getting into our jeep, like we do every day, and a shot is fired, and Major Buck Stanley is hit in the face and goes down.

"And there's a truckload of Greens fifty yards away coming back from the range. I run to Stanley. I'm guessing one of the Greens became radicalized or was turned by the insurgents, and he looked for an opportunity to shoot an American. He might have palmed some rounds at the range....

"And in that same moment one of our officers comes out into the lot and starts shooting the Greens we were *training*. We knew them. Worked with them every day. Oh, my God, the screams, the blood spraying, men climbing out of the truck, running. Our guy was firing and firing and walking over to the fallen and shooting each one in the head.

"We should have had an investigation. Done the right thing."

Randi shook her head, then looked at me and Conklin.

She said, "I looked at this officer's face. He felt good. Maybe great. Was he a psycho? Maybe. Or he'd become addicted to killing. I still don't know. And no, it wasn't Len. The officer who killed, I don't know, twenty-five Greens was a US Navy lieutenant name of Tom DeLuca. Don't bother looking for him. He didn't come back."

No one spoke for a long moment, taking in Randi's words and the shock on her face.

And then Conklin said, "We're looking for a killer, Randi. An expert sniper or sharpshooter, maybe military, maybe not. I'm thinking I might get a bead on the killer, even identify the shooter, if I join Moving Targets."

"I can't help you with that," said Randi. "I'm ready to go now. Okay?"

"Sure," Conklin said. "I'll get your dog home to you by the end of the day. What's his name?"

"Barkley."

"His name is Barkley Barkley?"

Randi said, "Yeah, and he barks. But stop. It only hurts when I laugh."

Conklin grinned. "Sure, Randi. I'll see you later."

CHAPTER 46

I FOUND CLAIRE in the autopsy suite, still wearing her scrubs.

"Claire?"

She looked up, surprised to see me, and said, "Oh, my God."

She pulled a sheet over the dead man, patted his hand, then called out to her assistant, "Bunny, can you put Mr. Ryan away? Thanks."

Those closest to Claire had made a care plan, each of us with an assigned role. Edmund would be meeting us at the hospital. Cindy and Yuki would be going to see Claire at the end of the day. I would be driving her to Johnson Hughes Cancer Treatment Center and staying with her until she was tucked into her bed at one of the best facilities in the country.

She said, "I'm sorry, Lindsay. I forgot you were coming. Paging Dr. Freud."

"We still have time. How are you feeling?"

"Never better."

"Right," I said, playing along. "So get dressed."

Twenty minutes passed like a snail race, and finally Claire was sitting beside me, buckled into the passenger seat of my car. When I'd parked this morning, I'd found an empty spot on Harriet Street, convenient to the ME's office and the Hall.

I switched on the ignition and noticed Claire had kicked off her shoes and folded up her legs, and was hugging her knees to her chest.

"I need to talk," she said.

I turned off the engine and faced her.

"Here I am, Butterfly."

"You never heard me say this before, but I'm scared. Really, truly freaked out of my mind."

"Who wouldn't be? You've got surgery in the morning. Talk to me."

Claire threw a long sigh and leaned back against the headrest. "I spent some time online looking up imminent death."

"Number one," I said. "Don't think that way."

"You know, I see more dead people in a day than most people see in their entire lives. Not even close. You'd think I'd be fairly blasé by now. I'm thinking I know too much."

"You're not looking at imminent death, Claire. Come on. You're going to a *great* surgeon. World class. He's going to take that tumor out with a piece of lung about this big—"

"Two tumors this big."

"Two? You said…you said one."

Claire said, "What happened is, over the years the pictures showed a spot. A little spot. Left lung, right here.

Couple weeks ago, had the biopsy. Then yesterday they asked me to come in for a PET scan. And whaddaya know? They saw another little spot. If it's spread…if it's spread, I could be looking at a year, more or less."

I felt hollow and cold. Claire was telling me this for the first time, and she was mad and scared. As for me, I wasn't ready to accept it. I said, "I don't believe that—"

"No, no, let me talk. I'm a doctor and you're not."

"I don't have to take your word for it."

"So when people hear that they have a death sentence, they either tell themselves, 'I have only this much time, so I'm going to make the most of it.' They take a trip around the world or learn to ski black-diamond runs."

"Or they accept that sell-by date and just give up," Lindsay continued. "Like, 'Why am I doing anything? It's over.'"

Claire, who'd been staring out the windshield at nothing, not looking at my stricken face, turned to me.

"See, neither of those two options apply to me, Lindsay. I can't quit my job and run off to see the world. I have a husband who is twelve years older than me, and this is killing him. He's literally getting angina. I have a little girl at home. She needs her mother."

I pressed my lips together. I wanted to yell, *You're talking* crazy. *You're looking at a worst case that may not exist.* But I had to let her talk.

"So this is why I'm freaking out. They're going to cut me open, and I know where and how. They're going to take out something I should have worried about instead of kissing off, and something else, to be determined. Lindsay, you know I'm conscientious. Right?"

"Absolutely. Totally."

"But doctors are notorious for feeling invincible. I mean me. Death is a colleague."

I was shaking my head, *No, no, no,* and wondering why I hadn't been more vigilant. Why hadn't I kicked her ass? Because I didn't know shit about non-small-cell lung cancer.

Claire was saying, "And then Dr. Terk is going to stamp my forehead with my expiration date, and I'm going to see it in the mirror every morning. And I swear, I don't know what I'm going to do."

Tears were running from her eyes, spilling onto her shirt.

"Claire. Claire, *listen* to me. You're *afraid.* I get that. But you don't know what the doctors are going to find until they analyze what they take out."

She nodded. But I wasn't getting anywhere.

"And after the surgery," I said, "you recuperate. You do what your doctor tells you, and if he says radiation or chemo, you do that. And if he says it's okay to work, you decide if you're going to do that. You take care of your family and let them take care of you, and you take some time for yourself. But along with all of that, you fight like hell, Claire. You use all of your contacts and build a team. Check into the latest treatments and alternative treatments. You've got to put on your brass knuckles and load your gun and fight like hell. And that's how you *win.*"

My best friend reached out to touch me, but I had to pull away and cry into my shirtsleeve. I grabbed tissues out of the glove box, and when I could speak again, I said, "Hear me?"

"I haven't had a cigarette in twenty years. How could my

body betray me like this? How could I ignore the symptoms? I'm not ready for this, Lindsay. I'm not ready to die."

"Did you hear me?"

She nodded. Tears were running down both our faces.

Claire coughed long and hard and painfully.

Then she said, "Yeah. I hear you. Fight like hell."

"I'm glad we got that straight."

I hugged her over the console and the gear shift. We rocked within the confines of that front seat, and I told her that I loved her, and she said, "I love you, too."

I started up the Explorer and heard Claire say, "Lindsay? Look at me."

Posing like a boxer, she showed me her fists. "I hear you."

CHAPTER 47

I DROVE BACK to the Hall on autopilot, using a soft touch on the gas, watching the lights and signs, but my mind was on Claire.

When I'd left her private room, she'd been covered in a light cotton blanket, wearing headphones, listening to the San Francisco Symphony, featuring Edmund Washburn on percussion. From the serene look on her face, it appeared that she was in a high-quality, low-stress zone. I suspected there might be some sedative in her IV bag.

I said to her long-devoted husband, "Edmund, you'll call me when Claire is out of surgery?"

"You're number one, Lindsay. First call goes to you."

I leaned down, kissed Claire's cheek, said, "I'll see you tomorrow."

"Tell the girls," she whispered, but didn't open her eyes.

Edmund got to his feet and hugged me tightly. There was nothing to say that hadn't already been said, all of it cheer-leading with stark fear lying just beneath our words. I kissed

Edmund's cheek, too, and after he released me, he squeezed my hand, hard.

I told him that I'd speak with him soon and fled before emotion took me over.

The stoplight at Seventh Street was red. When it turned, I parked at the next empty spot on Bryant and fast-walked to the Hall, where I badged security and took the elevator to four. Instead of turning left to the Homicide squad room, I turned right and headed back to the corner-office war room.

I hit the light switch, got my computer bag out of the desk drawer, and was stuffing the charger into the outside pocket when there was a knock.

"Boxer. Got a sec?"

It was Brady.

I said, "Sure. What's happening?"

"Do you remember Bud Moskowitz?"

"He was with SWAT. He retired. Wait, Brady. You don't think Moskowitz had anything to do with the shootings?"

"No." He laughed. "Bud saw that news clip this morning with the crime scene photos. He has an idea."

"Great. Give me his phone number."

"He's in my office. I'll send him back."

CHAPTER 48

I WAS STRAIGHTENING up the desk, organizing my notes, when Moskowitz said, "Hey. Boxer."

"Hey, Bud. Come in, come in."

I stretched out my hand. We shook and I offered him a chair. Harold Moskowitz, known as Bud, was more than twenty years older than me. I hadn't known him well, but I had a good feeling about him.

"So, you have a tip for us, Bud? Because we could use one." Moskowitz looked fit, as well as focused and competent.

"You mind if I take a look at those photos?"

"Go ahead."

He walked over to the wall and looked at the crime scene photos taken of the victims from different angles. He spent time with each one, slowly, methodically examining them, taking a couple off the wall to hold under the light, asking me about the victims and the caliber of the rounds.

I told him what little I knew, that the shells were of different types, that the casings hadn't been found, that Forensics hadn't gotten any hits in the database because of the bullets' impact with bone or plaster or brick.

I asked Moskowitz, "What do you see?"

"All the shots were taken from a good distance. Very professional work."

"We all agree."

"Boxer, I don't know if this is worth anything, but when I read in the paper about all these shootings taking place at the same time, it reminded me of this website I used to belong to."

"Moving Targets, by chance?"

"Well," he said, slapping the desk, "you stole my tip. I'll be going now."

I laughed and told him to stay. "No, really. Our computer tech also came up with Moving Targets, but we're still in the weeds. Tell me what you know."

"My wife is waiting for me downstairs, so let me give you the short version. I used to belong to the site. I played the game as a *game*. For target practice. But at some point I started to think that some of the guys on the board were highly trained experts, very competitive, and that they were crazy. They talked in the chats about killing like it's the greatest high in the world.

"But I didn't know. Were they talking shit? Or were they for real? The site held virtual events. Competitions. And there were team events; points were awarded for the best shots and for teams shooting multiple targets. The more difficult, the higher the points and the bragging rights. It looked like it was pretend, cartoon murder. But after a while I wasn't entirely sure.

"So then the newspaper stories and something I saw on the internet. A picture of two bullet holes through a second-story window, two shots that took out two people—it set off alarm bells."

"This is really getting to me, Bud. I'm thinking along the same lines. I'd like to get into this site. Can you give me a password or something? I can pretend to be you."

"I opted out ten years ago and my codes have expired. Understand, Boxer, I never matched up guys boasting about kill shots with actual deaths. There were groups within the group. I didn't belong to any subgroup. I wasn't working under cover, and I wasn't a serious player."

My mind had been dull with pain just minutes before. Now it crackled like a downed electric wire.

"Let me make sure I understand. You're saying that Moving Targets appeared like a sports forum. People who were known only by screen names, shooting off their mouths, playing virtual ball. But instead of making bets on lineups and game outcomes, they're bragging about killing people? Why did you keep this to yourself?"

"Boxer. First of all, there were no names or pictures of real bodies, just chatter and cartoon drawings with x's over the eyes. Bang. You're dead. And a sound effect.

"Also, I told Tracchio about it."

Tracchio had been police chief before Jacobi. Many years had passed, and Tracchio was long retired.

Moskowitz went on.

"Tracchio gave me a direct order. He said if I didn't have real names, bodies, facts, to get the hell off Moving Targets. I did what he said. I was with SWAT. I had plenty of shooting in real life. I quit the site and never went back."

It was more than I'd known ten minutes before, but I still had nothing actionable. Not yet. I thanked Bud and invited him to be part of our team.

"Thanks, no, I'm going to the Bahamas tomorrow with Bev. Our nephew is getting married. So look, I left my contact information with Brenda."

I wished him a good flight, and after he was gone, I headed down the corridor to debrief Brady. A half hour later, keys in hand, I left the building focused on facts.

Drug dealers had been killed. Mostly nickel-bag nobodies, except for the Barons, celebrities who'd bought massive inventory but hadn't yet launched their drug business. Shooting them through the windows had been much harder than killing the others on the street. Were those executions extra points for a video sniper?

Brady had agreed with me that it appeared to be a military operation, and Stempien, too, had said that he thought Moving Targets was heavy on military.

Had the drug dealer hits been organized by the members of Moving Targets? Was Leonard Barkley one of those hitters?

The answers were just out of reach.

The lights were out. And I couldn't see a thing.

CHAPTER 49

I WAS STARTLED awake by a shout or a shot or a dream—but I couldn't remember a bit of it.

My heart was hammering and my eyes were wide open. A hint of sunrise was backlighting the gray sky as I reached across Martha to better see the clock.

Its luminescent hands pointed to half past five.

That's when it hit me.

Claire was in the hospital and would be having surgery in a few hours. *Going under the knife.* Was she awake, too? I stared at the ceiling, finally clapping a pillow over my face, and when I woke up again, Martha was licking my ear and the sun was rising over the windowsill.

I tousled Martha's coat and put my feet on the floor.

It was still too early to call Edmund, but I had things to do. I fed Martha, made coffee, and caught up on TV news while unloading the dishwasher. I peeked in on Julie, then showered, dressed, and checked my text messages while I took sweet Martha for a quick walk. Joe had written to let me know he was going to stay longer with Dave.

Julie-Bug was still sleeping when we returned from our rounds, and I made up a wake-up song on the spot. My voice was a little rusty but not bad for an impromptu performance.

"Bumblebees, bumblebees.
Time to wake up the banana trees.
Bzzzzz, bzzz, bzzzz."

Julie's eyelids flew open, and she laughed at my singing, then told me that I was wrong.

"Bees *don't* wake up banana trees."

I challenged her on that point, saying, "Well then, who wakes them, smarty?"

"Bees wake the flowers, Mommy."

"Okay. But rhyming counts."

She giggled, I kissed her head, and she gave in.

"We both win, Mommy. I'm hungry."

I made oatmeal, and using a magic trick I'd swiped from the back of a cereal box when I was a kid, I pierced the banana skin with a needle near the stem. Using the needle as a little knife, I sliced the fruit crosswise every quarter of an inch from stem to stern, leaving the skin whole. The pinpricks were almost invisible, and I didn't give anything away.

I watched Julie peel the banana, and her look of disbelief and amazement as perfect banana slices fell onto her cereal.

"Mommy. Look at this!"

"Bumblebees did that," I said, very pleased with myself.

"Noooooo. Really?"

The doorbell rang at eight on the nose, and Mrs. Rose came into the kitchen and, clapping her hands, said, "Children wait for school buses. But school buses don't wait for children."

Julie ran to the doorway and I was right behind her. I gave her the pink-and-silver backpack and received kisses and hugs in return. And once the door was closed, the worry I'd been stifling crashed in on me.

I called Edmund, got a wrong number, tried again.

"Hang on, Lindsay. I'm outside the hospital looking for a quiet spot. Can you hear me?"

"I can. How's Claire? What's happening?"

There was a pause; maybe it lasted only a few seconds, but all of my attention was focused on that connection.

"She's changing the scope of the surgery, Linds."

"What? Why?"

"She was brainstorming with the surgical team. That's all she wrote. She's not in her room right now."

I said, "I don't think I'm getting this."

"The docs have been watching this little spot in her lung for years. I'll bet she didn't tell you that."

"No. She only just told me."

"So she's saying, 'Spot, spot, it's just a spot,' and even Dr. Terk thought so. She skipped her X-ray last year, and now it's two spots, 100 percent cancer. Terk planned to take out the spot, but now that it's two and visible, he's gotta get it all."

"Edmund. It didn't metastasize?"

"Nobody said that. As far as I know, Dr. Claire had a change of heart about what kind of surgery, something she read or thought up or wanted to bounce off the surgeons. She sent me a text saying, *I got this. Love you,* then shut off her phone. I can't reach her or her doctor. Nurse said she's in radiology, then on to the operating theater. I'll call you, Lindsay. As soon as I know what's going on."

I said, "I'll call you when I get to work." That wasn't a question.

"Makes more sense for me to call you. I promise I will."

"Okay," I said. "I hear you, Edmund. I'll wait for your call."

CHAPTER 50

I SNATCHED THE car keys from the coatrack in the foyer and was halfway out the door when my phone rang.

I grabbed it. "Edmund?"

"It's Brady."

"Brady. I just spoke with Edmund Washburn."

"How's Claire?"

I condensed what Edmund had told me, and Brady made appropriate sounds and comments but asked no questions. I pictured him standing in Jacobi's old office, impatiently staring out the window at the morning rush on Bryant, and I got it. Something was on his mind, and once I stopped talking, he was going to tell me.

I took a breath.

He said, "Are you on the way?"

"What's wrong?"

"There were three fatal shootings," he said. "Two in Houston and another in San Antonio. The MO looks the same as the others. The victims are known drug dealers. All were shot at the same time, at eight thirty a.m., local time."

"So you're saying the shootings are connected to the Baron murders?"

"Could be. Or it's a hell of a coincidence."

"What can you tell me?"

"At eight thirty a shot was heard on Warm Springs Road in the residential Westbury neighborhood in Houston. Cops responded to the 911 call. Couple of minutes later Anonymous phoned the tip line, giving the address of one of the dead men and the location of the gun."

"He didn't want to get involved."

"Right," said Brady. "Tip was accurate. Houston PD recovered the weapon a half mile away from the victim, Vincent Morris, black male, fifty-three, unarmed. Shot through the temple while driving. Naturally, lost control of his late-model Mercedes and crashed into an empty van parked at the curb at McKnight Street and Dunlap Street. Morris was killed with one shot."

"You're saying the victim was shot dead while driving and from a half mile away? Is that even *possible*?"

Brady sighed. "Several bystanders saw the Mercedes plow into the parked van, but there were no witnesses to the shooting itself."

I asked, "Is the gun registered?"

"Number is filed off. It's at their lab. That's all I know.

"What about the other two victims?"

"Where're you at, Boxer? People are piling up outside my office. Conklin has everything—photos, coordinates, contacts. See him soon's you get here. You two should reach out to Houston. I'll call San Antonio. See if we get some new puzzle pieces."

He hung up.

My thoughts were bouncing like a handball inside my skull. My best friend was consulting in her own life-threatening disease, and possibly convincing the surgical team to improvise on the fly.

And now there was a new direction in the sniper case. Three dead people in Texas, and at least one of them had been shot through a car window. I had to wonder if that long-shot marksman was our lone suspect, Leonard Barkley.

If not, was the shooter a member of the same Moving Targets club? Or worse, had psycho copycats seized on a fresh new idea: real-life target practice on random subjects?

I had many questions and one answer: anything was possible.

Minutes after speaking with Brady, I was driving toward the Hall of Justice, cautioning myself to keep my scrambled mind on the road.

CHAPTER 51

BRENDA FOLLOWED ME into the war room, handed me a pile of messages, set up a coffee machine, and, pointing to a plastic-wrapped platter, told me, "I made those cookies from scratch. Peanut butter and chocolate chip."

"Awww. Thanks, Brenda."

"Anytime, Lindsay."

Cappy was taping up the new crime scene photos, and Conklin was on the phone, saying, "Got it. Thanks."

He turned to me and said, "Lindsay, open your laptop. You've got mail."

The email from Conklin had the pictures and names of yesterday's shooting victims with appended details: age, marital status, occupation, police record, known associates. All had died where they'd been shot. ID on all had been recovered, as well as drugs on two of them.

"Cindy hooked me up with the Houston PD," Conklin told me, speaking of his beloved roommate, my pissed-off girlfriend Cindy Thomas. "She's been on this since 6 a.m.

You know, Linds, she sleeps with the police scanner next to the bed," he said. "Brings it to work, which is where she is now. Don't get between my girl and her Pulitzer."

I laughed and sighed at the same time.

Conklin went on. "She says all three victims are known dealers. Victim number one was shot by a single bullet from a long distance."

"According to Brady's contact, the shot was fired from a half mile away."

"Wow. Wow. Wow," said Conklin. "A half mile away? That's gotta be some kind of record."

Conklin got up, walked to the wall, and scrutinized the enlarged photo of the crash: Morris's Mercedes having come to rest halfway through the rear compartment of the panel van.

He moved a couple of feet to the next photo.

"Victim number two is still unidentified, also shot in his car," Conklin said. "The light had just changed, and the driver was heading south on San Pedro Avenue when he caught a few rounds to the left arm, chest, and head. Same time as the one in Houston, eight-thirty a.m."

I got up and took a good long look, trying to work out what had happened from this photo. One of the vehicles had the dead man in the driver's seat. The other was the recipient of a rear-end collision that had turned the intersection into a four-way gridlock. The photo credit in the corner was from a Channel 7 Eye in the Sky chopper.

"Reminds me of the so-called rehearsal murder at Taco King. That could have been personal," I said.

"Maybe this one, too," said Cappy. He was taping up the

last photo, victim number three, who'd been taken down in Houston. The photo showed a body spread-eagle on the sidewalk in front of a coffee shop.

Cappy said, "This killing happened across town from the man who ran his car into the parked van. No way it was done by the same hitter. The victim has been ID'd as Linda Blatt."

"She was a cafeteria worker during the day, delivered dope after hours," Conklin added. "Had a few dozen packets of crack in her bra."

My phone tootled. A text from Brady.

Boxer, Houston's Det. Sgt. Carl Kennedy waiting 4 yr call.

I tapped in the number, broke through the gatekeepers with my authoritative mad-dog-cop-in-a-big-hurry voice.

A man answered.

"Hello, Sergeant Kennedy?"

"Yes. Oh. Sergeant Boxer, good to finally make contact with you. I was with LVPD ten years back. Charlie Clapper and I were in Homicide together. We're old friends."

We exchanged mutual admiration for the esteemed head of our crime lab, and then I had to get to it.

"Kennedy, I've been on the case for a week now. I know a lot about the San Francisco victims, Paul and Ramona Baron in particular. But we're not getting traction on their shooter, who looks to be a sniper with incredible skill. Our suspect has gone into hiding. We have a lead of sorts."

I told Kennedy about Moving Targets, that our suspect, Leonard Barkley, was a member. And I told him that our FBI tech had found the site in a hidden pocket on Tor Browser.

"Getting access to Moving Targets has proven impossible so far, but we're still working on it. As it turns out, a former cop on our force once had access and played target games. But it appeared to him that the website might hold competitions for kills in real life."

"Is that right? Here's some news for you, Boxer," Kennedy told me. "A small business called Moving Targets has a brick-and-mortar hole-in-the-wall in the strip mall on North Shepherd Drive in Houston."

"You're joking."

"It's next door to an auto parts store. I've passed it a hundred times. Always has a 'No Walk-Ins' sign on the locked door. I peeked in through the glass once and saw a dark room with a half dozen folks on computers. I checked tax records to see the name of the company because it looked so sketchy. The name is Moving Targets, but what is it? The company description said 'Computer repair. By appointment only,' and they didn't list a number.

"My caseload heated up," Kennedy continued, "and I lost interest in this small-time little computer store. Now I'll do more research. Maybe I'll pay Moving Targets a visit."

"That would be great, Kennedy."

We signed off, and I summed up the whole story for Cappy, Chi, and Conklin. Brenda brought in a fresh pot of coffee, and I got a text from Edmund.

For the first time since my lovely second honeymoon less than two weeks ago, I felt good.

CHAPTER 52

SEVERAL TWO-STORY, brick-and-glass medical buildings stood within a mile of Saint John's Hospital in Napa.

Joe was inside one of those buildings, sitting in a small chair in an L-shaped waiting room shared by a pediatrician and Dr. Daniel Perkins, cardiac surgeon, the man Dave Channing believed had murdered his father.

The pediatric side of the room was awash in primary colors. There was a bulletin board centered on the largest wall, pinned with dozens of children's crayon drawings, a circus rug on the floor, a pile of blocks, and two little boys playing with toy cars, revving them up: "Vrooooom, vroooom."

Joe waited in the cardio side of the room. There was no decor to speak of, just a rack of magazines and pharmaceutical company brochures and some NO SMOKING signs on the off-white walls.

Between the two waiting areas was a shared nurse's station behind sliding glass windows.

Joe flipped through a month-old *Newsweek* without reading it. He felt like some kind of fraud, a sometime G-man, now a private eye without a license, helping out a friend he hardly knew in a twisted endeavor he no longer believed in.

He'd done the spadework, read the medical examiners' reports, met with family members who'd lost a loved one in the previous year to an unexpected heart attack while at Saint John's in the care of Dr. Daniel Perkins.

With the exception of Archer, the writer whose now-deceased thirtysomething fiancée had been a long-distance runner, none of the family members had hinted that Dr. Perkins was to blame for the death of their loved one. And so Joe had stirred up grieving people with nothing to support a suspicious cause of death.

And why had he done this? Because Dave Channing had become more restless and paranoid as the visit had gone on, and Joe had promised that he would do his best to clear it up: either validate or debunk his concerns.

Before leaving the Channing Winery this morning, he'd gotten Dave to agree that whether he accepted Joe's conclusions or not, Joe was going home that night.

Now he was wondering if he was wronging his friend by setting an arbitrary deadline. Good investigators didn't do that.

Joe and Lindsay had spoken on the phone an hour ago as she drove to work. Her voice had been strained as she told him about Claire and how helpless she felt. He pictured Lindsay's face, taut with fear and exhaustion.

He had done his best to comfort her, but Lindsay had been too agitated to hear more than "I'll be home tonight."

"God. That would be great," she said. "Promise me."

"I promise to try like crazy."

Joe tossed the magazine on the chair beside him and hoped that soon he could resolve the complicated feelings of disloyalty and suspicion by determining one of two possible truths, that either Dave was losing his mental grip—or that Dr. Perkins had caused Ray Channing's death.

CHAPTER 53

A FIFTYISH NURSE with graying cinnamon-colored hair, wearing green scrubs, paused in the entrance to the waiting room.

"Mr. Molinari, if you'll come with me, the doctor will be with you shortly."

Joe followed her down a hall to a small office and took the offered seat across from the desk. Perkins's office was a plain brown study with a tidy desk opposite a couple of bookcases. There was a plastic model of a heart that could be broken down into valves, ventricles, and arteries on the desk. Between the bookcases was an oil painting of vineyards at sunset. Joe recognized the style. Nancy Channing had painted that.

"I'm Carolee Atkins," said the nurse. "We spoke on the phone yesterday."

Joe said, "I remember. Thanks for fitting me in."

"Would you like me to weigh you and take your blood pressure just for the hell of it?"

Joe grinned and said, "No, thanks. I'm up-to-date. Six one, 178, 127 over 70."

Atkins smiled and said, "Very good, Mr. Molinari. How's Dave doing?"

Joe made the universal hand motion for so-so and added, "He doesn't understand why his father went from alive and well to suddenly dead."

Atkins said, "That happens with thoracic aortic aneurysms, but that's my unofficial opinion. Ray has been a patient and friend of Dr. Perkins's for over five years. I guess I can tell you that the doctor is heartbroken. He considers Dave a friend, too. Hold on. I'll see how much longer he'll be."

Joe said, "Wait. Explain 'heartbroken.'"

The nurse hesitated, then stepped back into the office.

"Obviously, Dr. Perkins cared about Ray Channing very much, and he cares about Dave, too. Dave is taking his grief out on Dr. Perkins, which is so unfair and maybe a little bit unbelievable."

"Really?"

"See for yourself. I don't know exactly what *salt of the earth* means, but I'm pretty sure Dr. Perkins fits the definition. I'll make sure he knows you're here."

Five minutes later Dr. Perkins entered the room. He was a white-haired man in his sixties, about twenty pounds overweight, wearing metal-framed glasses and a bright-red tie under his lab coat.

He smiled as he introduced himself and shook Joe's hand. Then he said, "You look familiar. Do I know you?"

Joe said, "You might have seen me on the news years

ago. I was with Homeland Security during the Bush administration."

"Maybe that was it," said Dr. Perkins. He went around his desk, sat down, felt his coat pocket for his glasses, then touched them on the bridge of his nose.

"These things are so light, you can't even feel them." He smiled, then said, "You're Dave Channing's friend. I've gotten his letter giving me permission to discuss Ray's condition up to and including his death."

"I'm trying to help Dave reconcile how his father seemed so healthy before he died."

"I understand. I know you and Dave are very close. Ray showed me pictures of you two in your football uniforms. He talked about you like you were a second son."

"Ray came to all of our games. We always knew where he was sitting in the stands from his yelling and cheering."

"Back to the future—if you don't mind my asking, in what capacity are you here today?"

"Friend of the family. That's all."

"Okay, Joe. I have a patient in fifteen minutes, so how can I help you?"

CHAPTER 54

JOE FIXED DR. PERKINS with a hard *Don't dare lie to me* stare and said, "Dave feels that something untoward happened to Ray."

"He's made that pretty clear," the doctor said. "He barged into the waiting room last week and accused me of murdering Ray. Murder. Me. In front of a roomful of people."

The doctor shook his head. "Maybe I should be asking you how you can help *me*. I don't want to have him arrested. Kid got dealt a beautiful hand, then it all got taken away, and he blames himself for that. Then his mother dies. Now his father. I feel terrible for him. But if he can't get a grip on himself, he has to get help."

"I have a couple of questions myself, Dr. Perkins. Dave gave me a look at Ray's medical charts, and the ME's report says that Ray died of complications from his thoracic aortic aneurysm. Is that your opinion?"

"No doubt about it."

Perkins lined up his pens, straightened the plastic heart and the papers on his desk. He had a slight tremor in his hand.

He went on, "Ray refused to believe that he wasn't in perfect health. He was seventy-two with the arteries of a man ten years older. I would tell him, time for a prostate test. Colorectal. Calcium score. CMIT. He wouldn't take statins. He stopped taking his blood pressure meds. When he came to the ER, he told admissions that he felt tired and a little weak. He said he'd been working hard, not sleeping. Mr. Molinari, those are symptoms of about fifty things. You know what I call it? He had an invincibility complex."

Perkins stared over Joe's head at the painting.

When he spoke again, his anger had cooled. He said, "Saint John's isn't Cedars-Sinai. It's a country hospital, and we did our best, you understand? Ray's blood pressure was high. Cholesterol was high. But he was stable. As I understand it, you saw Ray the day after he was admitted."

"Yes, I did," Joe said. "He looked good to me, sounded good, too, but I'm no expert."

"I am an expert. I saw him on Saturday. I told him that after he got his MRI on Monday, if everything looked okay, we'd release him. I put in some provisos. That he was going to have to see me more often, do what his doctor ordered, blah, blah.

"Monday comes, he turns down the MRI. He said, 'I don't need it, Doc. I'm fine.' I stopped by on Monday late afternoon to see his chart, make sure it was okay to release him the next day. He wasn't hale. But again, he was stable. I prescribed a mild sleep aid.

"I was shocked when I got the call on Tuesday that he had died."

Nurse Atkins leaned into the doorway.

"Doctor, your ten o'clock is here."

Perkins patted his jacket pocket, touched his glasses perched on his nose, and looked at his watch.

"Time got away from me." To Atkins he said, "Just be a minute."

When she had gone, he said, "No, it wasn't the .5 milligrams of valium that killed him. It was his heart. Complications from his aneurysm. I feel terrible that we lost Ray. I miss him. But Dave is being very unfair to me. I save lives, Mr. Molinari. I don't take them."

"Dr. Perkins. Thanks for your time. I'll have a stress test when I get home."

"Smart. Take care of yourself."

CHAPTER 55

THE FORMER ROOMMATES shared a late lunch at the plank table in Dave's great room with its soaring ceiling and 180-degree view of the vineyard.

"Talk to me," Dave said. "What did that son of a bitch have to say for himself?"

Joe said, "Dave, you remember that I came up through the Behavioral Analysis Unit of the FBI."

"Yes, yes, I've seen the TV show. You were some kind of profiler."

Joe sailed past Dave's snarky humor and said, "I'm good at reading psychological cues."

"I also watched *The Mentalist.*"

"I missed that one, Dave. So shut up for a minute, will you?"

Dave threw a sigh, drank wine, said, "Go ahead. Please."

"Here's what I gleaned from my meeting with Daniel Perkins. He's a little distracted. He's got a slight tremor in one hand, and that's neurological or stress. He's busy. And he's highly pissed off at you for calling him a murderer in front of his patients, which, by the way, could get you sued."

"I'm up for it. Tell him to go ahead and sue me. My countersuit will be quite a revelation to him."

Joe gave Dave a warning look and went on. "He's quite regretful about Ray, but he also fought his corner."

"Arrogant asshole." Dave emptied his glass.

"You know what he said to me, Dave? Words to the effect of, 'I wish I'd been harder on Ray. But I know it wouldn't have done any good. You can't make people do what they don't want to do. I tried. I'd tell him to take his blood pressure meds, and he'd tell me to fuck off.'"

Dave said, "So he won you over completely. Not a doubt in your mind."

"He told me your father wouldn't take his meds, and that was the truth, Dave. I've toured Ray's medicine cabinet, and there are prescription drugs, blood pressure meds and statins, unopened, with expiration dates from last year and the year before."

Dave pushed his chair back from the table, got more bread and brie from the kitchen, and returned with it to the table. When Dave was facing Joe, he said, "Let me ask you this."

"Shoot."

"Are being a bad patient and becoming a murder victim mutually exclusive?"

Joe said, "You're asking, if it's true that he didn't take his meds, can it also be true that his doctor killed him?"

"Exactly. He could have gotten fed up with side effects

and didn't take his meds. And still, his doctor could have killed him along with a few others in the same one-year period."

"Say you're right, Dave. What was his motive? Because unless you tell me that Perkins is going to inherit the winery, I can't think of one."

"What about compulsion? What about psychosis? What about a God complex?"

Joe said, "Possible. What about Occam's razor?"

"There were no razors involved, as far as I know."

"Occam's razor is—"

"I know what it is. I went to a good school, you know. Occam's razor. Don't multiply motives unnecessarily. The simplest explanation is usually right."

"Yep."

"So in your estimation, it's easier to believe that Ray and another three of Perkins's patients died from heart disease rather than were murdered by their doctor."

"Dave, Ray's chart for the day before he died is marked 'Patient refused MRI.' The ME's report says cause of death was complications from a thoracic aortic aneurysm. The other three patients you identified also died of heart ailments. I'm just one man and I don't have a badge, so I'm going on leads and these documents."

"You have a lot of charm, Joe. Always did."

"Thanks. I remember when you had charm yourself."

The two men grinned at each other, and then Joe said, "I'm going home tonight, Dave. I'm still only going to be a text and an hour-and-a-half drive away. If you need me, call me. If you have any evidence that Ray was murdered, I strongly suggest you call the police and let them do a complete investigation."

"Thanks for all you've done, Joe. I know I sound like an ingrate or maybe a crank, but I know I'm right. And I also really appreciate your help."

"I know. We're good."

CHAPTER 56

I WAS ELATED to see Joe's car parked outside our apartment building.

When I opened our front door and shouted, "I'm home," Joe appeared in the foyer and hugged me, rocked me, kissed me, danced me, and hugged me some more. It was as if we'd been separated for months, not days.

The small entranceway filled up, Julie tugging at me and hugging Joe's legs, Martha yipping, and Mrs. Rose off to the side, beaming, saying, "This is like something out of a movie."

I laughed. Joe thanked her for standing in for him over the last few days.

"Gloria, you're the absolute best," he said, then told her he'd brought her a souvenir from the Channing Winery.

He said to me, "Be right back," and carried Gloria's case of wine across the hall for her. I unbuckled my gun, locked it in the antique gun cabinet Dave Channing had given us as a wedding gift. Then, swinging Julie up into my arms, I asked her if she'd like to go with me to take Martha for a quick walk.

"We already did it, Mommy. Look what Daddy brought me!"

I marveled at her stuffed cow, yet to be named, and when Joe returned from across the hall, he opened our case of wine, uncorked the Channing Winery Private Reserve Cab. I poured juice for Julie, and Joe and I kept our glasses handy as we made dinner.

While Joe prodded the winery-made pizza in the oven, I brought him up-to-date.

"Claire is out of surgery, asleep in her private room. I wasn't allowed to see her. Believe it or not, I'm not in her immediate family."

He grinned. "How do they know that?"

"They had a list. Edmund told me that she's resting comfortably, considering they took out half of her lung."

"Half? A half of her lung?"

"Edmund told me that Claire argued for the most aggressive treatment—and that's what she got. Sounds like she decided to take her best shot."

Julie came back to the room with Martha, demanding to know what we'd just been talking about. Joe distracted her.

"You know, if you have a cow, that makes you a cowgirl."

"Really?"

"And even cowgirls eat dinner."

Joe's reheated Channing Winery pizza was delicious, and so was the arugula salad with shaved Parmesan and fresh Napa fruit. The Channing vino was also mighty good.

As soon as was reasonable, Julie-Bug plus her new cow

were tucked into her bed, the dishwasher rumbled, and, after changing into sweatpants and T-shirts, Joe and I stretched out together on the long leather sofa.

Of course we both fell asleep.

I heard his phone and tried to slip it out from his pant pocket. Woke him up, of course. I said, "This is the second call, Joe."

He looked at the screen, saying, "It's from Perkins's office." He pressed the Talk button, but the caller had hung up.

He played the message on speakerphone. It wasn't Dr. Perkins. It was a woman's voice.

"Mr. Molinari. I couldn't tell you today for fear of being overheard. One day I saw Dave Channing hurl a potted plant at Ray. One of those heavy terra-cotta urns. And he threw some punches, too. Thought you should know."

The call ended abruptly.

Joe clicked off and said to me, "That was Nurse Atkins, Dr. Perkins's nurse. She says that Dave got physical with Ray."

"Hit him?"

"Yeah. And threw things at him. My brain is closed for the night," he said. "How about it, Blondie? Bed?"

"You don't have to ask me twice."

CHAPTER 57

JOE HAD ANNOUNCED that his mind was closed for the night, but that was an aspiration more than a fact.

The late call from Dr. Perkins's nurse had rattled him, and hearing that Dave had gotten physical with Ray aroused Joe's worst fears.

I held on to Joe, my arm across his chest, my leg over his thighs, and I listened as he ticked off the first three items on an investigator's checklist when considering a murder suspect.

"Dave had the means," Joe said. "He has sleep meds in his medicine cabinet. Could he have crushed an overdose of sleeping pills, loaded up a glass of juice, and handed it to his father? Yes. 'Here, Dad. Drink this.'

"He definitely had opportunity. He visited Ray in the hospital several times, and Ray had a private room. You're going to ask me about motive, Blondie, and that's the tough one. So what could be his motive to kill his only living relative?"

Joe rolled onto his side and put his arms around me.

"Exactly," I said. "Ray was Dave's everything. His life is going to be a lot poorer without the love and support of his father. Without Ray, who is there for him? His by-the-hour hot dates? The seasonal workers? His virtual friends online? Sounds lonely."

Joe said, "Well, I can imagine it a different way. Ray ran everything. Dave worked for Ray. He took orders, and I saw that, Lindsay. 'Run to the cafeteria for me, son. Hand me my tablet. Give us some privacy, Dave.'"

"You're saying Dave resented that."

"I'm saying that reporting to his father at his age could have been more than annoying, it could have been a motive for murder. Ray owned the business, and Dave ate there, lived there, worked there. Dave's income and way of life depended on his father, and his father was sick. He was demanding and sick. Maybe he's looking at the lives of other fortysomething men, who have careers, homes, wives, kids, even grandchildren. Maybe if his father was dead, he could leave the small-town restrictions of Napa Valley with a sizable nest-egg inheritance. Move. Reinvent himself. Make sense?"

I saw Joe's point and said so.

"But did he murder his father, Lindsay? Or did Dr. Perkins do it? And I have to ask the same three questions of Perkins. Did he have the *means*? Yes. He's a doctor. Did he have the *opportunity*? Yes. Same reason. So what's a possible *motive*? Why would he kill his own patient?"

I said, "Isn't it most likely and utterly probable that no one killed Ray but Ray? Perkins told you, Ray neglected his own health."

Joe rolled over onto his back and sighed. "I really would love to know for certain that Ray died of natural causes."

"Me, too. I like Dave. And answer me this. If Dave killed his father, why would he have you looking into it? If he did it, you'd have to turn him in."

Joe thought about it for a long minute. Then said, "How about guilt? If he killed Ray, he could have so much guilt we can't even imagine it. He might want to be sure he's covered his tracks by involving me. Or he might have an unconscious motivation."

"Meaning?"

"Dave might want to get caught."

CHAPTER 58

JOE FELL ASLEEP fast and slept silently and still, his mind and body resting after a long run of worry and wakefulness.

I couldn't sleep for thinking about Joe's theory, that Dave had killed his father out of resentment and then felt so much regret, shame, and guilt that he wanted to be punished.

Eventually, I slept—a light, dream-tossed state in which I envisioned shooters lining up shots at moving targets. I saw Paul and Ramona in their office, making morning small talk. And then the sound of broken glass, Paul sprawling across his desk, blood sheeting over the edge, soaking into the carpet. Ramona standing, another shot. My eyes opened and I pictured the cabochon ruby pendant on a gold chain hanging an inch above the bullet hole through her chest.

I must have fallen back asleep, because when my eyes opened again, I was thinking about Claire. Had she been drugged into a dreamless sleep? Was she in pain, staring at the ceiling, thinking about her precious young daughter? Had her doctor given her good news or bad? I needed to know.

It wasn't yet six when I slipped out of bed without waking my husband. I padded softly into the main room and then peeked in on our sleeping, curly-haired cowgirl. I watched her for a little while, wondering what kind of woman she would grow up to be.

Martha mouthed my hand. I assured her that I was on it, and quickly dressed in jeans and sweatshirt to take my good dog for a walk. I remembered something told to me by a stranger on a train. She was holding her baby, and she jerked on her dog's leash to pull it under the seat.

She saw me looking at her, I guess with judgment in my eyes. She said, "Before you have a baby, your dog is your baby. When you have a baby, your dog is a dog."

I stooped down to look Martha in the eyes.

"You know I still love you, don't you?"

She wagged her tail, whined, and licked my face. I leashed my old friend, and we rode the elevator to street level.

It was still early morning. Other people walked their dogs, crossing the nearly empty street against the light. Martha wanted to play, but I gave her the next-best thing, a sprint to the corner of Lake and Eleventh and back.

All night my mind had flopped like a beached tuna. Claire. Dave Channing. Dead bodies in cold boxes awaiting burial and justice. My job.

We took the elevator up, and once inside our home, Martha cocked her head and whined, *Feed me.*

In the kitchen I filled a bowl for my fluffy old girl, brewed my morning joe, and flicked on the small under-cabinet TV to keep me company. The first morning show was in full swing when a bright-red breaking-news banner streaked across the screen.

What now? What the hell is it now?

CHAPTER **59**

EARLY THAT MORNING Cindy was in her office, checking the East Coast news feeds, when her cell phone rang.

It was Lori Hines an old friend. They'd gone to Michigan together, and Lori had recently moved from Chicago to San Francisco for a high-profile job with KRON4.

"Cin, I've just heard that one of the snipers has issued a memo to the press," she said. "Check your mail."

With Lori on hold, Cindy scanned her mailbox and opened an email headed *For Immediate Release.*

Every word contained in its four paragraphs was a stunner.

She read it out loud to Lori, who said, "Get ready to break news, girlfriend. I'm in a satellite van less than ten minutes from the *Chronicle*'s front door."

Cindy said, "I'll call you right back."

She read the email again.

It shook her as much on the second read and appeared

to be every bit a blockbuster—raw, bloody, and ready to be splashed across TV screens everywhere. If it had been widely disseminated, the clock was ticking and the deadline was *now.*

She printed out the email and phoned Tyler to bring him into the loop, but at 7 a.m. her call went to voice mail.

What to do?

It was risky to go on the record with a story based on a totally blind lead, but it was done often enough. *Unconfirmed at this time. Confidential sources say.* And then there were the breathtaking Deep Throat leaks during Nixon's last days.

Cindy thought over her options: take a moon shot, or go by a more cautious route. If she broke the news, she owned the scoop. If she waited…

She called Lori. "Give me ten minutes."

Opening a new email file, Cindy wrote to Tyler, saying that a news bomb was about to drop, that she had judged the lead as authentic, and that she had moments to go live with the story before the competition broke it.

Cindy roughed out the story, and it was ready for edit in nothing flat. She gave it a headline, attached the unverified email, and, marking the package *Urgent,* fired it off to the publisher and editor in chief's inbox.

Then she stuffed a copy of the email into her coat pocket, darted into a closing elevator, and rode it down to the street.

Lori was waiting for her on Mission, already set up for the interview.

The two friends and colleagues talked over the upside-downside ramifications while standing in the shadow of the *Chronicle*'s clock tower and agreed—the risk was worth taking. The business they were in, it was either go big or go home.

They took their seats in the tall director's chairs facing the camera, their backs to the Chronicle Building, an umbrella shading their faces, the morning breeze messing with their hair.

The sound man tested the level. The cameraman counted off five seconds to go with his fingers, and then tape rolled. Lori introduced Cindy as the star reporter and head of the crime desk at the *San Francisco Chronicle*.

She said, "You have big news this morning, Cindy. A *bombshell* email that you've just posted on your crime blog, from someone claiming to have inside knowledge about the recent sniper attacks that have terrified people in five cities."

"That's exactly right, Lori. I received an email just minutes ago giving reasons for the sniper attacks and warning of future executions," Cindy said. "I find the email credible. But viewers must understand that, like the Zodiac Killer's letters to the *Chronicle* decades ago, the email is unsigned.

"I've weighed both sides of the argument carefully and have decided that it's better to release this email than keep it quiet."

"Cindy, is there a time stamp on that?"

"It landed in my inbox early this morning. The heading was 'For Immediate Release.'"

"Can you read it for our viewers now?"

Cindy raised the sheet of paper from her lap and began to read the highlights.

"Quoting now: 'This is a warning to all drug slingers, the pushers who sell grass, coke, meth, and Molly, the sickos who sell oxy, heroin, fentanyl, unprescribed pharmaceuticals, and designer drugs, or name your poison. Deaths from overdoses have risen to seventy thousand Americans per year, nearly half of those from opioids like fentanyl. It's not okay. It's not stopping. It's getting worse.

'A coalition of citizens across the country has had enough of ineffectual ad campaigns and political slogans. We've launched a new war on drugs. A real war. Nine scum dealers are dead so far and we're just getting started. We have a list. If you're part of the problem and value your life, stop selling drugs now, whatever it costs you. Destroy your product and get straight.

'Or spin the wheel. You'll never know when your number comes up.'"

Lori said, "Cindy, correct me if I'm wrong, but until right now we have not known the motive for the shootings that have taken place here and in Chicago, LA, and, as of yesterday, Houston and San Antonio. Is that right?"

Cindy said, "There have been theories that there was a drug connection, but to my knowledge, this email is the first public communication from someone asserting a connection with the shooter or shooters and that their mission is to rub out drugs.

"We have to take it seriously."

CHAPTER 60

CINDY WOVE THROUGH the maze of cubicles in the messy, crowded newsroom.

Artie Martini, sportswriter, called out over a partition, "Great interview, Cindy. I sent you the clip."

"That was fast, Martini. Thanks."

Cindy glanced through the glass wall of her office while fishing her keys out of her coat pocket. She had cleared her phone lines before the interview, and twenty minutes later, barely seven forty-five, all twelve buttons were in a blinking frenzy. She hoped that a cop friend, of which she had many, had called to confirm what she'd just told the entire freaking world.

And there was something else. The anonymous writer had said that *nine* victims were down.

She counted *eight*. If the writer was telling the truth, one victim had not yet been accounted for, or had not been connected to the others.

Either way, victim number nine was news.

Cindy retrieved her phone from her coat pocket, dropped into her chair, and turned on the Whistler TRX-1 scanner on the windowsill.

She started her beat check, again listened to the police radio, checked the wire services and network feeds on her laptop. Satisfied that there hadn't been a big earthquake or a fire on the West Coast, that no terrorists were holding an airliner hostage, she checked incoming email.

Her interview with Lori Hines had been widely covered.

There were bulletins on Google and Yahoo!, and a request from the *New York Times* for more information, and she saw that other journalists who'd gotten their own copies of the war-on-drugs email had released it far and wide—but not first.

To her great relief, nothing in her mailbox claimed that the email was a hoax.

Cindy pulled the office phone toward her and began punching buttons.

The voice of Brittney Hall, Henry Tyler's assistant, came over the speaker: "Cindy, Henry wants to see you at eight."

Why? Slap on the back, or had her impromptu interview with Lori Hines put her in trouble of the job-threatening kind?

The next caller was Lindsay: "Cindy, I just spoke with Claire. She's out of the ICU. Room 1409, doped up, but receiving visitors for a couple of hours a day. She sounded okay. Considering. Hey. I saw your interview. You were terrific."

Another dozen messages followed—more compliments

on her interview, an art department query, an editor asking for a call back, but nothing that shook her world.

She called Johnson Hughes Cancer Treatment Center and was relayed from operator to nurses' station to Claire's room, until she spoke with a nurse's aide who told her that Claire was with her doctor and took Cindy's number.

Cindy went back to work and was googling *Warning to drug dealers* when her phone rang. The number on the caller ID was from a local exchange, but she didn't recognize it. She picked up, hoping it was Claire.

"Cindy Thomas?"

The caller was male, and Cindy got a sudden chill when she realized that he'd disguised his voice with a digital voice changer.

"Speaking."

"You read my email. I saw your interview, and you've earned a reward. We just put down another dirtbag in Chicago. A perfect hole in one. Have a good day."

"Wait. Wait just a minute."

The line was dead.

She tapped Call Back, but the unidentified caller didn't pick up. Shit. She looked up the phone number and there was no listing. Of course the caller was using a burner phone.

Cindy scribbled notes, a verbatim account of what the caller had said. The ninth victim had been shot in Chicago. She sent the memo to Tyler, even as she checked the Chicago PD blotter. There was nothing there about a sniper shooting. It was early yet. For the moment, she had what the caller had implied; her reward was an exclusive.

She left a message for Lori to call her and simultaneously opened the *Chicago Trib* website. There was nothing there about a new sniper shooting. Nothing, nada, zip. If her anonymous caller had told her the truth, a Chicago drug dealer was dead, and the *Chronicle* still owned the story.

The digital clock in the lower right corner of her computer screen blinked 7:57. Pulling a mirror out of her pencil drawer, Cindy fluffed up her hair, slicked on some lip gloss. Then, clutching her phone and her tablet, she took off for Henry Tyler's office.

Tyler's PA, Brittney, betrayed not the smallest emotion as she waved Cindy into the office of the publisher and editor in chief.

Tyler was there. And so was Jeb McGowan.

CHAPTER 61

I TIPPED BACK my chair so that I could better see the TV hanging above my desk in the squad room.

News anchor Jason Kroner was reporting from the studio of ABC7 Chicago.

"According to a police source, this morning an unidentified man was found shot dead on the pavement on the Chicago Riverwalk at approximately 7:00 a.m. An hour later a person of interest in the shooting was apprehended on the Michigan Avenue Bridge, standing at a distance from his SUV, the engine left running and a .308 Remington rifle in the front seat.

"There's a sight line from several places on the bridge to the pavement where the victim was discovered. The shooter may have fired from a vehicle."

I sighed as the reporter gave a rip-and-wrap of the other sniper killings, all unsolved cases, starting with ours. And then there was a cutaway from Kroner to a thirty-second clip of Cindy reading the war-on-drugs manifesto.

Cindy could be annoying for sure, but she was really admirable—smart, professional, and I have to say it, adorable. Richie was beaming and we shared a grin. And then the camera was back on Kroner, who closed, saying that the station would update the story as news became available.

I said, "Could be a break. The guy said, 'Stop selling drugs....Or spin the wheel.' Who says that? You say, 'Take your chances.' Or, 'Roll the dice.'"

"It's a reference to Moving Targets, all right."

"Jesus. And the guy Chicago PD has in custody. I wonder if he was looking through a gun sight."

"You feeling lucky?"

"If this is Christmas, the suspect has a beard and his name is Leonard Barkley."

We stopped for coffee in the break room, then took the short walk down the hall, past the interrogation rooms, the elevator bank, and the virtually empty Robbery Division detail, and unlocked the door to our war room.

I sat down at the phone, punched in a number I'd put on speed dial. When a phone rang inside Chicago PD, I asked for Detective Richards.

He picked up, saying, "Boxer, are you haunting me?"

"I guess I am. Have you spoken to the unnamed gunman?"

"I processed him. His name is Jacob Stoll. He's a former marine lieutenant, did a couple of tours in the 'Stan. His prints match what we got off of AFIS. He's currently employed part-time as a school bus driver. The gun is registered to him and it wasn't recently fired. We're holding Stoll as a person of interest, but if he shot the guy found dead in the park, he didn't use the rifle in his car."

"No?"

"The gun hasn't been recently fired. We'll hold him as long as we can. It's possible he shot the victim with a different firearm, maybe tossed it off the bridge."

Conklin said, "Maybe he's revisiting the scene to watch what the cops do."

"Possible," said Richards. "After we get him in the box, we'll hear what he has to say."

I said, "Richards, the so-called video game, Moving Targets. The person who tipped off the press used the phrase 'spin the wheel.'"

"Yep, I got your email and saw your screen shot of the site. I'll try to work it in when my partner and I talk to Stoll. Would you be interested in watching our interview, live streamed from our house to yours?"

"Hell no."

"Excuse me?"

"Just kidding, Richards. That would be great. What do I have to do?"

"Stand by for a password. One more thing, Boxer."

"What's that?"

"You owe me."

CHAPTER 62

CONKLIN AND I sat side by side at the old desk in the war room, staring into a computer screen that was, in effect, a window into an interrogation room at the Chicago PD Violent Crimes Division.

We got our first look at Detective Sergeant Stanley Richards. He was fortyish, of average height and weight, a restless, hands-in-his-pockets, coin-jingling man with a five-o'clock shadow at ten in the morning.

He took his hands out of his chinos and dropped into a seat at the table approximately twenty-one hundred miles away from our desk in the war room. Sitting beside him was his partner, Detective Suzanne Waltz. She was wearing a man-tailored white shirt, a navy-blue blazer a lot like mine, and a hint of a smile, an expression I would have loved to wear myself. She looked calm, relaxed, and unreadable.

The suspect, Jacob Stoll, sat opposite from the detectives and had sprawled across both chairs on his side and folded his arms over the table. His body language was saying that he owned the table, the room, the story he was about to tell.

My hope that Stoll was Leonard Barkley by another name evaporated. Unlike Barkley, who was a Fidel Castro look-alike, Stoll had a fleshy face. He looked to be six foot two to Barkley's five foot nine, and he had a wide, toothy grin, perhaps prompting Detective Waltz's *Mona Lisa* smile.

He said to her, "You're a really good-looking woman, Detective, you know that?"

Waltz said nicely to Stoll, "Jacob? Okay if I call you Jacob? Mind taking a look at this?"

She held up her phone so that Stoll could see a photo. Richards had forwarded it to us, and I recognized the shot of the recently deceased man. According to the police report and the dead man's bloodstained shirt, he had taken a bullet through his heart. According to Richards, he'd also had a boatload of heroin in his backpack.

Stoll said, "May I?" Without waiting for an answer, he took the phone from Waltz and gave the screen a good long look. Then he handed it back.

"I don't recognize him, at least not from that angle. I can't swear he wasn't one of the three thousand enlisted men I trained or served with. But this I know: when you check my rifle, you'll see it hasn't been fired. You checked my hands for GSR, so you know I haven't fired a weapon. Anything else?"

"Yeah," said Richards. "Where were you at six thirty this morning?"

"Is that when that guy in the park bought it?"

"Where were you, Lieutenant Stoll?"

"I was at the South Blue Island Avenue bus depot having

coffee and joking around with three other drivers and my supervisor, Jesse Kruse. We cleaned the buses, and I started my route at seven. Picked up thirty-six little kids and took them all to school. Drove nowhere near the Riverwalk. I got more eyewitnesses to my whereabouts than you got time in a week to interview.

"And now I have a question for *you*," said Stoll. "Are we done? If not, I'm through talking without a lawyer. If so, I'll take my gun and go about my business."

Richards said, "Remember when I read you your rights?"

"I remember. But this is ridiculous. You didn't arrest me. I thought you just wanted me to tell you what I saw from the *bridge*."

The confident body language was gone. Stoll was getting exercised. It wasn't going to do him any good. My partner and I looked at each other, brought our eyes back to the screen as Richards said, "Stoll. You're a person of interest in a homicide. We're holding you in custody until we check out your alibi, and if you've been honest with us, we're gonna clear you. Understand? We have to do that, if it takes a week, or longer."

Richards continued, "Furthermore, now that you said you want a lawyer, we have to stop talking to you."

"Fuck that. I waive my rights."

"Good thinking," Richards said almost kindly. He pushed a pad of paper and a pen across the table.

"After you sign the waiver, we're gonna need names of all the people who can vouch for your whereabouts during the hours before we brought you in."

CHAPTER 63

SITTING BESIDE ME, Conklin exhaled loudly and ran his hands through his hair.

He said, "Is Stoll innocent, arrogant, or dumb and dumber? It's hard to know."

Stoll signed the waiver. Richards signed it. Waltz signed it, too, and sat with Stoll as Richards took the waiver out of the room. He returned a minute later, took his seat, asked Richards if he wanted anything—soft drink, coffee?

Stoll shook his head no.

Richards said to Stoll, "Explain the rifle."

"I was going out to DeKalb County to shoot at tin cans. It's my brother's land, and I have permission."

"So I don't get what you were doing on the bridge."

"I was taking in the view. It was looking to be a gorgeous day. Man, when I'm wrong, I'm really wrong."

Detective Waltz asked Stoll for his brother's name, contact information, location of the property. She also took the number of Stoll's supervisor. Then she left the room to run down Stoll's alibis.

Richards said, "Stoll, have you ever heard of a website called Moving Targets?"

"No. Oh. It's a video game, right? A buddy of mine used to play. Compete, you know. I didn't find it very challenging. Not for someone trained like me."

"Is there more to it than a game? In your opinion, could Moving Targets be a front for targeted hits on drug dealers?"

"What? Where'd you get that? That's nuts. If we're talking about the same thing, it's like a kids' game. Anyone saying otherwise is just full of crap."

Richards drilled down, asking the same questions in different ways, taking his time, playing up to Stoll's military expertise, asking Stoll's opinion, looking for Stoll to contradict himself.

But Stoll was consistent.

Richards returned to the subject of Moving Targets, saying, "That website has come up during our investigation. I'd like to talk to your buddy. Ask him about how the game works."

"I'd like to talk to him, too. Name is Sid Bernadine. He's dead. Stroked out two or three years ago. I miss the hell out of Sid."

Stoll looked empty. Like he'd given up everything he had to give. Richards had done a good job. I don't know anyone who could have gotten more or better out of Stoll—not me, or Conklin, or Brady or Jacobi.

Waltz returned to the room with another cop.

Stoll said, "So what's this now?"

Richards said, "I told you, Stoll. We're gonna make you comfortable here while we check your alibis and your gun. You get a phone call. You want to do this nice? Or should we go ahead and cuff you?"

Richards put his hands in his pant pockets, and that opened his jacket. I caught a flash of yellow, the handle of his Taser gun.

"I'll take that phone call now."

The room emptied and our screen went black.

CHAPTER 64

HENRY TYLER HAD been breaking news at the *Chronicle* since before Willie Brown was mayor.

Cindy liked him, respected him, and was anxious to get his thoughts on the anonymous email and its writer who called out the "new war on drugs."

When Cindy entered Tyler's office and saw McGowan, she had a visceral reaction. Why was the nervy *Chronicle* cub in Tyler's office?

What kind of meeting included the two of them? She flashed on him prowling around, his leaking her news to the competition, showing signs of marking her territory for future acquisition.

She said "Hey" to McGowan, "Morning, Henry" to her boss, and took a seat next to McGowan on the edge of the leather sofa. She hoped that Tyler wasn't going to give her hell for airing an unconfirmed story with McGowan in the room.

Tyler said, "Cindy, I just saw your interview. Well done.

I've got to ask if you've got confirmation that your tipster has an actual connection to the shooters."

"Not yet, but then again, he called me, Henry, a few minutes ago. He disguised his voice and used a throwaway phone, but he let me know that there'd been a shooting in Chicago. Same kind as the others. One kill shot from a distance. I sent you a memo."

"Sorry, I missed it."

"I posted the article on my blog. We broke it first."

Tyler said, "A solid verification and in that order? Victim of a shooting. Call from your source, and that shooting is confirmed?"

She nodded yes, and Tyler said, "Okay. Very good. Two scoops in one hour. Nice work, Cindy. You're on a great streak."

He smiled at her from behind his desk, then said, "I called you both in because the SFPD still has nothing on the Jennings murder, and likewise, the Baron case is getting cold. Also, Houston and San Antonio have nothing on their victims. I want you two to work together. See if you can't get something on what appears to be a cabal of military-grade killers.

"McGowan, report to Cindy on this and make yourself useful."

"Yes, sir," McGowan said.

"Cindy, you still have my mobile number?"

"Tattooed on the palm of my hand."

Tyler smiled.

"Go get 'em," he said.

CHAPTER 65

MCGOWAN HELD THE door for Cindy, and as they made their way around the newsroom together, Cindy couldn't help but notice that McGowan was high on enthusiasm.

"Wow, Cindy. Look. I'm going to help you in every way I can. I'm your guy."

"You asked Henry to give you this assignment, right?"

"Wait, Cindy. He said that we should work together, didn't he? In my mind, we're on track to land the story of the year."

He gave her an undeniably winning smile, which Cindy did not return. She thought, *We, huh?* but said, "Okay, then."

Once inside her office, she closed her door and called Richie.

"This is an official on-the-record call," she told the man she loved. "Got anything on the dead man shot on the Riverwalk in Chicago at the crack of dawn? Anything at all?"

He said, "We're working with Chicago PD. I can only tell you this as my friend and lover. Confidentially, Cindy. Okay?"

"Damn it. I mean, okay."

"Chicago police have a suspect in custody. As soon as I've got something I can talk about, I'll call you first."

Cindy said, "Gee, Richie. I can never thank you enough."

He laughed, said, "Be good."

She clicked off, swiveled her chair so she was looking out over Mission Street rather than through her office wall at McGowan's cube only twenty feet away. The killer or killers had committed the Chicago murder less than four hours ago.

The story was so hot it was sizzling.

The combined killings amounted to a killing spree that was unprecedented in style and geographic range. It had started here in San Francisco. Her beat.

And now the fear and fascination with this peripatetic shooting gallery had galvanized the country.

Who would be next?

Cable news, even the president, had weighed in on this spate of assassinations. "We're a nation of laws," the White House spokesman had said. "We deplore vigilantism. Innocent people will be killed, and they are *all* innocent—until proven guilty by a court of law."

Cindy agreed in principle, and she still had a job to do.

She had to unlock this story.

She went to her doorway and called out to McGowan, who stood up and came over to her.

"Jeb, work on this morning's Chicago victim. Who, what,

when, where, and if you uncover a shiny new why, that would be great. Then, separately, build a timeline starting with Jennings. Next, the Barons. Roccio. Peavey. The three Texas victims. Today's guy, too. Profile of each. We'll update this timeline, keep running it as a sidebar—"

McGowan held up his phone.

"Chicago victim's name is Patrick Mason."

"Good. Follow up and I'll reach out to Houston. See if the killers there had the same MO."

McGowan smiled and did a pretty good imitation of Henry Tyler, saying, "Go get 'em."

CHAPTER 66

CINDY WAS IN a fury when she sat back down at her desk.

Jeb mocking Henry. That snotty kid.

She opened the email from her anonymous source who'd tipped her to the war on drugs and given her today's scoop. Drug dealer shot dead in Chicago.

Cindy had the feeling that this was another Zodiac or Son of Sam, other serial killers who'd buddied up to the press. This time it was serial killers, plural. But who were they, and why and how were the shooters and their intended victims chosen? She wanted to read the email again, this time looking for dropped bread crumbs or any lead that she had missed.

He had written, "If you're part of the problem and value your life, stop selling drugs now whatever it costs you. Destroy your product and get straight.

"Or spin the wheel. You'll never know when your number comes up."

Spin the wheel was an odd phrase. Was it his manner of speech? Was it something meaningful? She'd like to know.

That's when it hit her.

Her source had written to her. And he had called her.

Her return call to the burner phone had failed, but *she hadn't written back to him.*

She had to do that, and if she made a good enough pitch, maybe he'd write back. Maybe she could sell him on her being his press conduit to the world. She was known. The *Chronicle* had reach. Tyler was a friend and mentor. It was a good idea.

But before she fired off her return email, she wanted to think about it some more.

Cindy opened her blog and her mail, checked every feed in the US and abroad, noting how much coverage the sniper killings had drawn.

She also detected something else that surprised her. The public was cheering on the vigilantes. When she opened the comments section on her blog, that same unexpected element was present. Readers were thinking that the shooters who were picking off drug dealers were the good guys.

She left her office deep in thought, headed toward the coffee station. McGowan was outside his cubicle, standing with his back to her. He was chatting with a pretty, young intern.

He was talking about *her.*

"Cindy does a good yeoman's job," McGowan said. "She has ten years in grade here, so she knows what she's doing, but she has no style. She's not a writer's writer, if you know what I mean."

"A hack, you're saying?" said the intern.

McGowan laughed. "Right word. Exactly."

Cindy had to decide quickly.

Show McGowan that she'd overheard him? Or hold it back for a better, more pivotal time? She walked around him to the coffee station, poured herself a paper cup of hazelnut bold, feeling the back of her neck getting hot.

She heard McGowan calling out to her over the din of the newsroom. He was saying, "Cindy. *Cindy,* I want you to meet Robin Boyd. She just started working here as an intern. Her father works for—"

"Nice to meet you, Robin. McGowan. Get to work. I want those profiles, every one of them, before noon. Show me what kind of writer you are. Try not to let down the team."

CHAPTER 67

CLAIRE'S ROOM WAS lined with flowers of all heights and colors, grouped on the windowsills, in a row along the chair rail across from her bed, and there were bunches of get-well cards woven into the slats of the window blinds.

I was so glad to see her. When she smiled and stretched out her hand, I went to her, gave her a long, gentle hug.

"Be careful of my lifelines," she said of the tubes running hither and thither from IV bags, into and out of her thin cotton hospital gown.

"Bossy even now," I said, moving a big chair up to her bed. "How are you feeling?"

"Like I've been run over by a team of horses. Those Budweiser ones. Clyde-somethings."

I laughed with her, picturing that.

"Well, they didn't trample your sense of humor."

"No, thank God. I need it, but I'll tell you a little secret."

"What's that?"

She signaled me to come close. I moved in so my ear was almost against her mouth.

"You can ask me anything," she said. "I'm so doped up, I'll spill all my beans."

I paused to wonder if she had any secrets that I hadn't already discovered over the last dozen years.

"How about this? Tell me what the doctors told you."

"Thassit?" she drawled. "That's like you got one of those genie lamps with the three wishes and you wished for a sausage on the end of your nose."

I couldn't help cracking up at the image from that ancient parable or fable or whatever it was. But I refused to be side-tracked. And so I persisted.

"What did Dr. Terk say?"

"Oh, you know. Looks like they got it all, but they're not committing, not yet."

"When are they letting you out of here?"

"What day is it?"

"Tuesday?"

"What year?"

"When, Claire? When can you go home?"

"When the docs are sure my lung isn't leaking."

"Do you hurt?"

"Not now. Man, I never realized how boring you are, grrfren'."

I laughed out loud. I knew it was the drugs talking, but still, I was so glad to be in her face, annoying her to death.

"And work? Did they say when you can come back to work?"

"Why? Did someone die?"

I laughed again. "The usual number. Lots. And no more pushing me around. Doctor said you have to go for a walk, so we'll go together to the end of the hall."

"He did not. You're lyin'."

I buzzed the nurse, and when she arrived a moment later, she detached a few lines and helped Claire from her bed. I got a laugh out of her flashing her big butt down the hallway, and she laughed, too, wheezing some, telling me she'd get me for this. I put my arm around my best friend's waist and told her to shut the fuck up.

She said, "Did you catch that sniper or snipers yet?"

"Working on it."

And then she started to sing. Yeah. As I had one arm around her waist and was holding the IV pole with the other.

"Hup two, three, four. What the hell we marching for? Sound off."

I stared at her.

"Lindsay. You say 'sound off.'"

"Sound off."

"Thassit. Sound off, one, two. Three, four," she sang.

I shook my head and helped her make a two-point turn.

"What? What are you thinkin', Lindsay?"

"I'm thinking I want what you're having."

She laughed and laughed some more, wobbling enough on her slippered feet to scare me. The nurse and I used considerable strength to hold Claire up and walk her back to her room, and it took three of us to get her into bed.

I promised her I'd come back the next day, and not long after that I hugged her good-bye.

CHAPTER 68

I CHECKED MY phone as I walked through the exit doors out to my car.

Richie had called a couple of times. I climbed into the driver's seat and called him back, and he picked up on the first ring.

I wasn't expecting him to say, "Bad news."

"What is it? Please don't make me beg."

"Kennedy. That detective in Houston. He was shot a couple of blocks from the Moving Targets storefront he was checking out. He took one slug to the back of his head. This can't be a coincidence."

I was stunned. I liked Kennedy. He was perceptive. Curious. Outgoing. Proactive. I'd felt as if I knew him.

I didn't speak, and so Rich said my name a couple of times.

"I'm here."

"I know, I know how you feel," he said. "It's sick. They're going after cops now?"

"How could they have known he was a cop? Did he tell them? Or did they just make him when he walked into the shop? And then what? They followed him out, tailed him for a few blocks, and shot him?"

"Houston PD is on it. They crashed Moving Targets and the space was empty. No computers. No nerds. No fingerprints. No cameras. Back door open to the loading dock. No one was home but the dust bunnies and a sign hanging inside the door."

"Sign saying what?" I asked him.

"'Gone Fishing.'"

"That's a sly way of saying 'Gone hunting.'"

"Right you are."

I told Rich I was on the way back to the Hall, but in fact I wasn't ready to drive.

After we hung up, I sat in my car looking out at the hospital parking lot, and I thought of Carl Kennedy. He'd been upbeat, quick with an idea, and now he was dead. He and Clapper had been tight, having worked together in homicide, LVPD. I didn't want Charlie to hear about Kennedy on TV or the internet.

I tapped Clapper's office number into my phone and waited for his assistant to locate him. When he got on the line, he said, "Boxer, you heard about Kennedy? He told me he was working with you."

"I just heard. Charlie, I'm very sorry."

He said, "Thanks," but his voice was all wrong.

He sounded removed.

"Charlie?"

"Lindsay, got a minute? I'll take this to my office."

I turned off the police radio, pressed my phone to my ear, and waited for Clapper. And then he was back on the line.

"Boxer, what do you know about what happened?"

I gave Clapper background on Moving Targets and said that Kennedy knew of an in-real-life location that was possibly Moving Targets' HQ.

I said, "Kennedy was going to check them out. Then he was shot a few blocks from their store. Houston PD found the store had been cleaned out."

"I hadn't heard that part, Boxer. I'm starting to form a theory."

"Tell me."

"What if Kennedy knew these Moving Targets people? I should tell you, he was known to cross the line."

"Like how?"

"Skim cash. Pocket drugs. Stash a gun. My just-formed theory is based on his character, Boxer, not on evidence. Maybe he told Moving Targets he wanted to make them an offer. They pay him off. He keeps the cops in the dark."

"And so they shot him."

"Evidence will tell, Boxer. Regards to Richie."

And then he hung up the phone.

CHAPTER 69

CINDY DRAFTED AN email to the mystery man who had given her the tip of a lifetime: the motive for nine killings and counting, a manifesto on a "new war on drugs," followed by a lead to a new shooting in Chicago.

The man wanted exposure. He had proven that he had inside knowledge. He wanted to get the word out that he and/or others were eliminating drug dealers, one piece of crap at a time.

He'd obscured his identity, but he wasn't being coy.

His message to drug dealers was twofold: Do you want to live? Or do you want to "spin the wheel"?

The final draft of her email to him was short and simple. "I am sympathetic to your cause and have an idea for spreading your message. Please write or call me again so we can discuss."

In fact, she abhorred frontier justice, but if she could be this man's conduit to the worldwide press, he might give her the key to the whole shooting match. She would love to draw the killers out of their hidey-holes and into the hands of the SFPD.

But she was impatient. She felt a breeze. It was the passage of time. The clock on her computer screen read a couple of minutes after noon. Where was the mystery man right now? Was he at his computer, reading the news, basking in the growing public praise for what he was calling the "new war on drugs"?

Cindy sent her two-sentence email. Got the *Message sent* notification. And now she was on the hook, waiting for his reply.

She turned her mind to other things. She spoke with Claire, who told her she'd never been so bored in her life. They laughed when Cindy added, "Better bored than dead."

She texted Richie to say, *Can you tell me ANYTHING?*

Ah. No.

Screw you, buster, she responded, forcing herself to add, *Kidding!* She got up, made a wide counterclockwise circle around the newsroom so that she could avoid not only McGowan but Tyler as well. The lunch wagon was in the outer corridor near the elevator. She bought an egg salad sandwich and a bag of pretzels, then took the long way back to her desk.

She checked her email, hoping that the man of the spinning wheel had replied in the ten minutes since she'd invited him to be her confidential informant.

Nope. He hadn't. And he hadn't called, either.

So she opened her crime blog, skimmed the new comments on her original post, and found a thread she was least expecting. It was about the love of killing, the high of shooting, of slicing arteries, of stabbing and hacking off body parts, of taking trophies.

Oh, my God. What door to hell had she opened?

CHAPTER 70

CINDY SKIMMED THE new comments on her blog, gobbled them down, then went back to the top of the page and read them again. The posts were about the love of violence and, to her mind, had been written by psychopaths.

Like this one: "Daily life is gray. When you're a soldier, you're trained to kill, given direct orders from your CO, and compensated with the guilt-free experience that's the greatest high in the world. Then you come home, and everything is gray again. If you're like me, gray is not good enough."

The post had been signed with a screen name, and the writer hadn't confessed to a specific killing. Interestingly, he'd gotten dozens of likes.

Other writers had expressed similar thoughts, sending her anecdotes about blood lust that only war could satisfy. Some veterans of foreign wars had detailed the taking of trophies—ears and hands and fingers—spelling out in loving specificity the pleasure of taking body parts, as well as taking photos of piles of the dead. The language used to describe these atrocities was too graphic for the *Chronicle* to print.

More to the point, the posts were about killings in war.

Nowhere in this avalanche of gory imagery was there a connection to the snipers and the victims in American cities. Cindy kept reading, and finally, at the bottom of the fourth screen, she found a post with a completely different feel, a declaration.

Her vision narrowed. She knew who he was. She read fast, then again more slowly:

There are killers who torture, who revel in taking life, sometimes in rage, sometimes for pleasure. This is not my style. When I kill a drug dealer, I am in control. My fellow travelers and I know our targets long before we fire a gun. They are guilty of ruining lives and of taking them by the tens of thousands as a byproduct of their sales jobs.

I'm proud of the recent work we've done. We've saved countless lives while only taking a few. I feel no pleasure in the shootings. I feel proud of the results. I'm doing good work. And I stand by it.

The post was signed *Kill Shot,* and Cindy knew from the cadence and structure of his post that this was the man who'd declared the "new war on drugs."

She grabbed the phone to call Tyler but stopped because McGowan had appeared in her doorway. She put down the receiver.

"What is it, Jeb? What do you need?"

CHAPTER 71

CINDY STARED UP at the creep Tyler had forced her to take under her wing, wishing that she could make him disappear just by looking at him.

"See how you feel about this," said McGowan. "I roughed out the profile of the first victim."

Cindy knew a lot about Roger Jennings, the ballplayer who'd been killed at the Taco King. She and Jeb had seen the car, the pregnant wife who'd been spared, and the hole punched in the windshield by a bullet before it killed the Giants catcher. Thanks to Richie's friend Kendall, she had a photo of the word *Rehearsal* written in the dust of the Porsche's rear window.

It had been verified that the veteran ballplayer had sold recreational drugs to his teammates. That wasn't even news. She'd assigned Jeb to writing victim profiles, so now he was saying he'd done it.

It was put-up-or-shut-up time for McGowan.

"Let's see it," Cindy said.

McGowan placed a sheet of paper on her desk and stood watching her.

"It's a first draft," he said, "but I want your early read on the tone."

"Be quiet and let me read," she said.

Jennings's name was at the top of the sheet.

The text read:

There's more than one kind of head shot.

Some head shots are close-up photos that can get you a part. Another can drop you to the mat in the eighth round. Others you catch and throw back to the pitcher. Those are known as high, hard ones.

Roger Jennings was versed in high, hard ones. He knew they were coming because he would call them. He didn't do it often—it wasn't his style—just when he needed to ruffle a hitter.

As a batter himself, he was quick to react. He could duck or fall flat to the ground. He was seldom tagged as the target of pitches, let alone those thrown at his head.

But the head shot that killed him wasn't a baseball. It was a bullet, and he never saw it coming.

Cindy looked up at Jeb, who'd been nervously watching her read.

He said, "And then his bio, thirty-eight years old, survived by his wife, Maria, twenty-nine, blah, blah, blah—"

"It's good, Jeb. It's very good. Poetic. Evocative. Compelling. And yes, I like the tone."

"Really? Thanks, Cindy."

"You're welcome. Keep going. Make sure you mention that witnesses report that Jennings was selling drugs. Maybe that's the kicker at the end of the piece. Maybe it's a refrain or a summary. Try it a few ways."

"Can do."

"Good. We're looking for eight more profiles and counting."

"Right," Jeb said. "I'll have those for you before we close for the day."

"Go get 'em," said Cindy.

And when he was gone, she dialed Tyler's extension.

He picked up his phone.

"It's Cindy," she said. "Hold a spot on the front page for this: 'Anonymous Shooter Confesses.' Sending you a draft in five."

CHAPTER 72

JOE WAS WORKING in his home office, outlining a security analysis proposal for the TSA.

It was pleasant work. He'd written the book on the Transportation Security Administration when he was in Homeland Security, and figuring out the new TSA specs gave him a chance to use comfortable tools that were right at hand.

Julie had left her stuffed cow, Mrs. Mooey Milkington, on his desk to keep him company. Martha was snoozing next to his feet. Bill Evans's soothing "Peace Piece" was coming through his earbuds, and in about an hour Joe was going to break for the meat loaf sandwich that was chilling in the fridge.

It was while Joe was in this fine-tuned contemplative mood that his phone rang, breaking it all into shards.

Joe glanced at his caller ID, which read, *NAPA COUNTY JAIL*.

He let the phone ring a few more times as he decided

whether or not to pick up, but by the third ring he really had no choice.

"Molinari."

"Joe. Thank God you're there."

"Dave. Please don't tell me you're in lockup and that this is your one phone call."

"You want me to start lying to you now?" Dave said. It was a joke but not a good one.

"What happened? Give me the condensed version so you don't use up your quarter."

"Okay. This morning, after I drank my breakfast, I went to Perkins's office and called him out. His nasty nurse—"

"Atkins?"

"Yeah. Her. She barred the door. So I made a general announcement in the waiting room that Perkins had killed my father, and I was shown the door. I saw Perkins's Beemer in the parking lot, so I rolled past it and keyed the side of his car. Next thing, cops came, lifted me out of my chair, and carried me into the squad car."

"What are the charges, Dave?"

"It was vandalism with a side order of defamation."

"How bad was the scratch?"

"Headlight to taillight. I don't need a lawyer to tell me it was more than four hundred dollars in damages. I could go to jail for, like, three years."

A muffled sound coming over the phone was Dave crying, and Joe had to strain to hear the guard tell him, "Say good-bye. Time's up." Dave argued with the guard, said that he was talking to his lawyer and that he needed to get bailed out.

"Thirty seconds," said the guard. "Make it count."

Joe said, "Dave, what's the bond?"

"It's 10K. Look, Joe, I know I have a goddamn lot of nerve, but can you come back and pay the bail? I can repay you as soon as we get to my place. Also, I have a few more documents you're going to want to read. And, Joe, I gotta be honest. It kills me that you don't believe me about Perkins."

Joe thought about all of the sleeping pills Dave had saved up in his medicine cabinet. If he didn't want to spend the rest of his life blaming himself for Dave's suicide, he had to see him, try to get him into therapy. At the very least, throw out all the pills he could get his hands on.

"Your bed is all made up," Dave was saying. "And I have a couple of New York steaks and a bottle of Private Reserve Cab that Ray had been aging for ten years."

Joe said he had to make arrangements, but he'd try to be at the bail bondsman by 4:00 p.m.

"Thanks, Joe."

"Take it easy," he said, but the call had been disconnected and there was a dial tone in his ear.

Over the next couple of hours Joe spoke to Lindsay, made an arrangement with Mrs. Rose, squared away his notes, and wrote a couple of emails. He went to the bank, and then he was on the road, heading north to Napa Valley.

As he picked up speed, Joe was starting to look forward to what would come next. He wanted to see the new documents Dave had mentioned, and more than that, he wanted to have an honest conversation with Dave.

There was a question he'd never asked him, and he wanted to watch Dave's face when he finally did.

CHAPTER 73

DAVE WAS USING a disreputable wheelchair that had been ridden hard in the Napa County Jail for a couple of decades.

Dave's own chair had been lost and there was no finding it.

He said, "Don't worry, Joe. I have a spare at home."

A guard helped Joe transfer Dave from the chair into his passenger seat, and Joe got behind the wheel. He checked to see that Dave was buckled in, then drove away from the jail and took the first right turn onto the highway. Dave thanked Joe effusively for all he'd done and then sagged against the car door.

When they'd cleared the town limits, Joe asked, "Tired?"

"Yeah. Tired and beat. That was fucking brutal. "Real jail. Real bad guys. No joke. I was afraid to sleep."

Joe winced. He said, "You fix the damage, make some promises and keep them, get a good lawyer…"

"Do you know anyone?"

"I'll ask around."

It got quiet again and Joe turned on the car radio, fiddled with the dial until a classical station came in strong. He tried to relax. He was fine with Beethoven and an open road. But it was seven thirty. He was hungry and he needed to think. He wondered, not for the first time, what the hell he was doing here.

Nearly an hour after leaving the jail, Joe pulled onto the dirt road leading up the side of the hill to the winery. A minute or two later he'd parked in front of Dave's cottage and, following his directions, located the key under a stone rabbit and entered the dark house. He located the lights and the spare wheelchair folded up in the hall closet.

Returning to the car, he found Dave sitting with the door open, his legs outside the car and a look of mortification on his face.

"Dave? What's wrong?"

He waved his hands in the general direction of his lap until Joe got it. Dave had peed his pants.

Joe felt heartsick for Dave and positively ashamed of his own selfish feelings.

If he took Dave at his word, his friend had suffered an incalculable loss. His father was dead. He was facing one to three for the childish vandalism, and a good lawyer might or might not keep him out of jail. It was becoming clear to Joe that even if Dave was acquitted, he couldn't run the winery by himself.

This was an awful and desperate situation.

Joe helped Dave into the chair and pushed it to the foot of the ramp. Dave was saying, "I've got to clean up."

"Do you need help?"

"No, no, I can do it. And I need to go online for a couple of minutes. Make sure no one is suicidal. I never go twenty-four hours without checking into my website."

Joe knew he was speaking of his support group for paralytics.

"I'm good to go now, Joe. Just hold the door."

"Sure."

"There should be a bottle of wine around somewhere."

Joe cracked a smile.

"We're fifteen or twenty minutes from a steak on the fire."

"Take your time," Joe said. "I'm fine."

As Dave rolled his chair to his quarters at the back of the house, the thought Joe had had so many times before came back to him. What had happened to Ray? Had he simply died? Had Perkins killed him, as Dave insisted?

Or was Dave behind it all, doing a head fake, playing the victim, and in so doing, covering up his real crime?

CHAPTER 74

JOE SAT AT Dave's big plank dining table and called Lindsay.

"I have to stay overnight," he told her. "Dave's a wreck."

"Call me after lights-out," she said. "I want to hear about Dave, and I have a few things to talk about."

"He's in the shower. Tell me now."

Lindsay filled him in quickly on the Houston cop, Carl Kennedy, who had been part of her task force. Her voice was strained when she told him that Kennedy had been killed, shot from behind, and that Moving Targets might be involved.

"They had an office," she said. "By the time the cops got there, it had been cleaned out to the walls. And of course no one witnessed the shooting."

"So who do you think shot him?" Joe asked.

"Hang on a sec," Lindsay said. "There's more. Clapper just spoke with Houston's forensics lab. Kennedy was armed when he was shot. One bullet had been fired from his gun, and he had a shell casing in his pocket."

"I'm not getting it."

"Here's the thing, Joe. A drug dealer who was killed in Houston yesterday was found with crack hidden in her bra, and when the slug was removed from her neck, it matched—"

"It was a match to Kennedy's gun?"

"Yes."

"So who shot Kennedy? What are you thinking, Linds? I'm not my sharpest tonight."

"I'm speculating here. Say that Kennedy was with Moving Targets. It's a wild thought, but according to Bud Moskowitz, ex-SWAT and former Moving Targets player, cops and military were members of the inner sanctum. Let's also say that for some reason, Moving Targets turned on Kennedy. Did he know too much? Did he threaten them? Had he just found religion when he took out that female drug dealer and was going to turn himself in?

"Joe, I just don't know. Listen. You've never heard me say this before. These vigilantes outnumber us. They're more organized than we are and probably smarter."

Joe listened to Lindsay's breathing. She was exasperated and maybe on the verge of tears.

He said, "Okay. I get it. Now that you've got that off your chest, what's your next move?"

She groaned, but Joe wasn't letting her go without an answer.

"Come on, Blondie. From your gut. Out with it."

"Okay. I have one thought."

"And that is?"

"Paul and Ramona Baron are being buried on Saturday. Rich and I should go to the funeral. See who's there. Take some pictures. And hope a suspect shows up with a long gun."

CHAPTER **75**

THE PRISONERS' WARD at Metropolitan Hospital was grim, but no grimmer than the rest of the place.

Same pale-green paint job, same dust-encrusted windows and gray-speckled linoleum floors. The ward had six beds, two of them in use. The bed closest to the door was occupied by a tattooed man the size of an oak tree, chained hand and foot, howling for something for the pain.

The bed in the farthest corner was filled by Clay Warren, the eighteen-year-old miscreant Yuki would be prosecuting for possession with intent, car theft, and acting as an accomplice in the murder of a cop, though all concerned knew he'd merely been the wheelman. Also, it was widely known but legally suspected that the real perp was a major drug dealer who had ditched the kid and the car and gotten away clean.

Said drug dealer was very likely living in a cute little cliffside hacienda overlooking the ocean, while the patsy had been stabbed in the chest with intent to kill him.

No wonder he wouldn't talk, even for a pass to a lighter

sentence and the possibility of breathing free air in his twenties.

Yuki knocked on the doorframe and, after passing the raging oak tree, headed toward Clay Warren.

"Clay?" Yuki called out. "I brought you something. I hope you like sweets."

The young man turned his head toward her and almost instantly looked away.

She noted the flex ties cuffing his wrists to the handrails. His ankles were under the sheets, but Clay Warren wasn't going anywhere. There were tubes running from his chest, from under the sheets, from the IV above his head, to the monitors behind him.

It was then that Yuki saw an older woman sitting in a chair at the far side of the bed, keeping the patient company. The woman, who was probably Clay's mother, stood up. She was Yuki's size, about forty, wearing drab gray clothing that hung to her ankles. And she was furious.

Yuki said, "Hello, I'm ADA Castellano—"

"I know you. I've seen you in court. How could you do this to my boy? Look at him. *Look* at him."

Clay, just barely conscious, was present enough to say, "Mom. Stop."

"Mrs. Warren?"

The woman didn't answer. She stood facing Yuki, her eyes locked in a hard stare, her fists clenched.

"Mrs. Warren, I want to help Clay. Please understand that I need him to help me with the guy he worked for so I can go to the DA."

"You're lying, ADA Cutthroat. ADA Career Woman. You

don't want to *help* Clay. You want to *win*. How much time do you get for lying to his *mother?*"

Yuki looked down at the floor, not out of shame or to avoid the woman's anger but in an effort to compose herself and explain her position. If Mrs. Warren could get Clay to agree to testify against Antoine Castro, Yuki would be able to get the charges against him lightened significantly.

"Let's go to the cafeteria and talk," Yuki said. "Maybe together we can make a plan."

"You should *leave*. That's what. Leave my son *alone*."

"Please tell me what happened to him."

"Do you need glasses?"

Yuki was actually wearing glasses, through which she watched Clay's mother point a shaking finger at the whole length of Clay's chest and abdomen, bandages wrapped around him. He must have been stabbed multiple times.

"He was shanked in the shower," Mrs. Warren said so loudly she got the attention of the huge man at the front of the ward.

"Is that right?" he said.

Clay's mother ignored him. "You have children, ADA Castellano? Try to imagine it. My son had lost gallons of blood by the time they got him here. His heart even stopped. Grace of God he's alive. He should be out on bail, not in that place with those *animals*."

There was laughter from the oak tree. "You don't mean me, right? Because I didn't do it."

"Mrs. Warren, I have no power over Clay's situation if he doesn't help himself. He was driving a stolen car with a trunk full of dope. A cop was shot dead. The gun was inside the car. If Clay won't testify against the real criminal, I cannot do a thing but try to convict him."

"If he talks, he'll be dead before his birthday."

After strafing Yuki with her condemning eyes, Clay's mother, who had dressed as though she was already in mourning, returned to her pale and motionless son. She sobbed as she leaned over the side rails and caressed her boy's head. Yuki went over and touched her arm. She was roughly shaken off.

Yuki knew damned well she shouldn't be here, shouldn't see Clay without his attorney present, but she felt sick for the kid. His mother didn't really get it. It was highly probable that Clay wasn't talking in order to protect *her.*

If Yuki couldn't turn him around, he was cooked.

Could he hear her?

"Clay. Here's my card again. Feel better soon."

Yuki placed the card and a bag of small chocolate bars on the side table, said "Take care" to Clay's mother, and headed for the doorway.

Mrs. Warren shouted after her, "Pull some strings, damn it. Throw your weight. Be humane. If you don't stand up, you will think of Clay every day he is in prison, and then, when they kill him, you will think of him *forever.* Welcome to hell, ADA Castellano."

Yuki called for a taxi, and one was waiting by the time she got to the street.

"Hall of Justice," she said to the driver.

She stared out the window as she headed back to work. Parisi would have to listen to her. This wasn't justice. This was closing a case by charging the wrong man.

241

CHAPTER 76

I WATCHED YUKI blow through the swinging gates to the squad room in a great big hurry.

She waved at Brenda without stopping and landed at my desk, saying, "Lindsay, you've got to come with me."

"Where are we going?"

She pointed to the far end of the room, took me by the wrist, and led me to Brady's office. He was working, head down, but he looked up when she spoke his name from the doorway.

"I can't go downstairs," she told him. "Can we use your office for a couple of minutes?"

His look said, *Why?*

"We need some privacy."

"Okay. Sure thing. Have fun, darlin'."

He headed to the front of the bullpen and appropriated my desk. Yuki dropped into Brady's well-worn swivel chair. I closed the door and pulled up a seat. We settled in, but I didn't think we were going to have any fun.

I was highly agitated. My brain was sparking from three sugared cups of black coffee and my newfound obsession with the so-called "new war on drugs." I pictured the photos on the casualty wall of the war room, starting with Paul's body splayed across the desk, Ramona's dead and staring eyes, and the ruby cabochon hanging just above the bullet hole through her chest. From there I ticked off the victims in LA, Chicago, San Antonio, and Houston. At that point I stopped ticking off and dwelled on Detective Carl Kennedy, a murdered cop, leaving even more questions about Moving Targets.

As is completely normal for detectives, I was obsessing, or as I call it, searching what I knew for a missed clue, an anomaly, or a pattern, beyond the one obvious correlation. The victims had all sold drugs.

Had Kennedy been killed because he threatened Moving Targets? Or had he been marked as a target because he, too, sold drugs? I didn't know and neither did Houston PD. But we knew the shooters were active in multiple cities and states, either a constellation of groups or one group making their kill, then changing location and killing again.

Cops in five major cities had no idea where the snipers would strike next. But we agreed. There would be a next.

Yuki was also agitated, and it had nothing to do with high-octane caffeine or snipers.

She said, "I've just been to the hospital prisoners' ward. You know the kid I'm prosecuting—"

"Clay Warren."

"Right. He got shivved in the shower last night. Someone

upstairs loves him, because it's a miracle he survived. So I went to see if I could, you know, talk him into giving up the actual drug dealer and cop shooter. He's bandaged from here to here," she said, demonstrating from below the waist to collarbone.

"But, noooooo. His mother kicked my butt around the room, told me to do something. That he's going to get killed. Lit my fuse but good, Lindsay. And she was right."

I nodded and said, "Go on."

"So I charged into Red Dog's office," she told me. "He was meeting with a couple of suits," Yuki said. "I didn't recognize them, and I didn't care. I just let Red Dog have it at the top of my voice. Picture me screaming, 'We can't prosecute a man who is not guilty. Clay Warren was a kid wheelman, and now he's in the hospital with a dozen holes in his guts and a compromised kidney. Now I'm supposed to send him to prison for things he couldn't have done? Come on, Len. Have a heart. We're doing this?'"

I clapped my hands over my cheeks and leaned in.

"What did he say?"

"He stood up, all six foot three of him, and he barked, '*Grow up, Castellano. We have a dead cop.* This so-called kid wheelman either shot him or witnessed the shooting, for Christ's sake. You've been here too long for this candy-assed crap. A good prosecutor can prosecute anyone.'"

Yuki put her elbows on Brady's desk and lowered her head into her hands. Her next words were muffled by her palms and a blackout curtain of blunt-cut hair. She shook her head, then lifted her face to look at me.

"I was standing my ground, but he was coming toward me.

I started backing up. This was his parting shot, Lindsay: 'I don't appreciate you barging in here. We're done.'"

"Yow," I said.

"I'm mortified," she said. "I almost said, 'I don't give a flip what you appreciate.' Am I trying to get fired?"

"Are you?"

"When I quit before, I was sad all the time. Len begged me to come back."

"I remember."

"I emailed him an apology, but I didn't grovel."

"Good. On both counts. What now?"

"I'm going to avoid Red Dog for a couple of days if I can. I've got to tell Zac that I saw his client and what happened, and he has to get a continuance for the latest possible date."

I said, "Could be when cops come to take Clay back to jail, his mother will change her mind. Get him to give up the crime boss in exchange for witness protection."

She said, "Yeah, I saw *GoodFellas* a few times, too."

I smiled, and my phone buzzed. I glanced at the screen.

"It's your dearly beloved," I said. "I gotta take it."

Just as I hung up with Lieutenant Brady, Yuki's phone rang. She handed it to me. "It's Conklin."

I looked over my shoulder and saw Conklin through the glass wall. He signaled to me and at the same time spoke into my ear, "Need you, Lindsay. We have to make a plan."

"I'm coming," I said. I walked Yuki to the elevator, hugged her good-bye, and rejoined Conklin. "We've got to get organized for the funeral tomorrow," he said. "And please do not fight me on this. In the interest of domestic harmony, I'm bringing Cindy."

CHAPTER 77

CONKLIN AND I were attending the Barons' funeral because there was a chance that their killer might show up.

It happens. Sometimes a killer will return to the scene of the crime to gloat or bathe in the memories. Funerals are the after party, not only to exult in and rerun the bloody memories but also to enjoy the grief of the bereaved.

We were in the town of Bolinas, population sixteen hundred, on the edge of the Pacific. If the Barons' killer paid a call, he would see that it was a beautiful day for a funeral. Soft sunlight warmed the clean lines of the old Presbyterian church. The cemetery was across the road, an acre of sloping clipped grass, marked with old tombstones and ringed with a stone wall. There was also an imposing wrought-iron gate.

Dozens of people would be in attendance, but the hundreds of fans, press members, tourists, and curiosity seekers were not welcome.

Warren Jacobi, former chief of police and my close friend, had volunteered to be a consultant, my undercover escort for the day. Partnering with him was like old times, and as clueless as we were about whodunit, the whole team was revved up. We were hoping that Leonard Barkley or Jacob Stoll or a previously unknown suspicious character might crash the funeral.

I wore a skirt and a boxy black jacket to hide the holster at the small of my back. Jacobi and Conklin were both armed, and Cindy wore a somber gray dress, playing her part as Conklin's civilian date.

We all blended in and took our seats in pews at the front and the rear of the church. The church was lovely inside and out, and the funeral service was touching and hopeful, given the circumstances. Reverend Grandgeorge was elderly and sweet; he talked about the Barons being at home in heaven and said that he knew we hoped they were comfortable and at peace.

I had a different take on that.

I thought that if there was a heaven and they were in it, they would be enraged that their lives had been cut short and that their children would be raised by other people.

The organ played. People prayed. And when the service ended, we all left by the double-wide front doors.

Outside the church, in parked cars camouflaged by a fringe of woodland around the parking area, our colleagues Chi and McNeil, Lemke and Samuels, were armed with guns and cameras, ready to pursue a fleeing suspect.

Jacobi offered me his arm and I took it, tottering a bit on my high heels as we crossed the dirt road between two lines of yellow tape, backed by local police who were charged with keeping the press in check. Which wouldn't be easy.

Photographers jostled for good angles as reporters shouted questions about the police investigation. Paul Baron's parents were long dead, but we accompanied Ramona's family—her parents, Jill and Charles Greeley; her sister, Bea; and the two small children, DeeDee and Christopher—through the cemetery gates. We mingled with mourners, walked a few hundred yards across the acre of grass, coming at last to the white tent over the two open graves.

The mourners gathered. Remembrances of Ramona as a child were offered, as well as shared laughs, hugs, and tears. The children clung to their grandmother.

I looked around surreptitiously and noticed a beefy man in a canvas jacket, red-faced with clenched fists, standing off to the side. I nudged Jacobi. Conklin was already looking at the big man as he stepped toward the tent.

When he was standing near the open graves, the man in canvas said loudly, "What a load of crap."

He then coughed up a wad of phlegm and spat on Paul Baron's coffin.

CHAPTER 78

THE FORTY PEOPLE standing under the tent gasped as one.

Even *I* was shocked, but my reflexes snapped me out of it. At the same time someone shouted, "You asshole," and two men moved toward the one who'd spat on Paul's coffin. They each took an arm and pulled the man in canvas away from the gathering—but he stuck out a leg and snagged the tent pole, and the pole bent.

The tent wobbled and slowly, hypnotically collapsed.

Screaming broke out and anger rose up. Men began milling in a loose circle. Jackets came off and were flung to the ground. Provocative curses flew, and the circle of men broke into two groups. It looked to me as though it was Paul's friends and family against those of Ramona.

There were many obstacles on the hill of the cemetery lawn: trees, headstones, stunned women and children. The local cops were three hundred yards away out on the street. I couldn't gauge how bad this would get. Guns could come out. Knives. We, the undercover team, would have to prevent violence, and yet if we drew our guns, we could set it off.

I looked for my teammates and made eye contact with Conklin.

My badge hung from a chain around my neck, inside my jacket. I pulled it free and held it up.

"SFPD. Everyone freeze."

The red-faced man was six feet tall and heavily muscled, and he acted like I wasn't there. He waved his arms and yelled to the opposing group, "Don't you see the *hypocrisy* of *burying* them together? It's his fault. Paul *corrupted* her. She would never be in that box if not for him. He might as well have shot her himself."

He was shouted down, called names, and that made him even wilder. He was on the move, dodging, weaving, swinging his head around, shouting accusations. And since the collapse of the tent, the media had jumped the tape. They outnumbered the local cops and were now climbing over the walls.

Still yelling "It's Paul's fault," the red-faced man ranged in and around the broken group of mourners.

Charles Greeley was fit, in his late fifties. He'd been watching, but he couldn't stand still any longer. I watched as he broke away from his wife, a slim woman who looked like her daughter's death had broken her. Greeley reached the red-faced man and shoved him hard, sending him staggering back and away from the fermenting crowd, hissing, "Anderson. You bastard. Control yourself. This is my daughter's *funeral*."

Greeley pushed Anderson a couple more times, his hands flat against Anderson's chest, Anderson saying, "Get your hands off me, Mr. Greeley. I don't want to hurt you," as the older man backed him into the stone wall.

I saw potential for tragedy. I shouted, *"Freeze. Everyone freeze!"* but no one was listening.

I was closing in on Anderson when he *really* snapped.

"I'm sorry, *Mr. Greeley.*"

A shovel had been leaning against the wall, and now it was in Anderson's hand. He drew back his right arm and swung the shovel, connecting with Greeley's shoulder. Greeley cried out and spun into a tombstone, where he crumpled and dropped.

Jacobi helped the dead woman's father to his feet. Once he was standing, Greeley tried to pull free of Jacobi's grasp, cursing, "You son of a bitch, Anderson. How fucking dare you?"

I drew my nine and went for Anderson, shouting, "Hands behind your back."

He started to do it, but as I pulled my cuffs from my jacket pocket, Anderson turned and, seeing an opportunity, punched me square in the face.

I hadn't seen it coming. I stumbled back, my ankle twisting in my stupid high-heel shoes. I lost my balance and sat down hard on the ground.

Someone reached a hand down to help me up, but as soon as I was standing on my wobbling feet, Anderson swung at me again.

This time I ducked, and then I decked him.

CHAPTER 79

REPORTERS SCRAMBLED ACROSS the sloping field of the cemetery, joined by bystanders, and together they outnumbered the local gendarmes ten to one.

Reverend Grandgeorge held up his hands and asked for the commotion to stop in the name of God, but he had no chance against those who believed deeply that Paul Baron was filth and the others, friends of the Greeleys, who reasonably saw the funeral as sacrosanct.

Barefoot and bleeding, I retrieved my gun from the grass and ordered Anderson to stay facedown on the ground. Conklin intervened. As I rubbed my jaw and tried to clear away the fog behind my eyes, Conklin arrested Anderson for assault on a police officer and read him his rights.

Jacobi helped Anderson to his feet and marched him to the car across the road. The noisy crowd followed.

Conklin said loudly, "Who else wants to go to jail?"

I got into the passenger seat of the unmarked car, and Jacobi took the wheel. He backed out of the churchyard and pointed us southeast toward San Francisco, about an hour away. But he had a hard time keeping his eyes on the road.

"Are your knuckles broken?" he asked. "Let me run you by the emergency room."

"Jacobi. I'm fine. Really."

I knew without looking that I had a fat lip, a swollen eye, a scraped cheek, and a pulsing ache in my right ankle. I didn't think I had broken bones, but I was pissed.

I held my bloody right fist in my lap and picked up the mike with my left hand. I reported to dispatch that we were on our way back to the Hall. The dispatcher's voice came over the radio along with a big pile of static, and she confirmed.

I dialed down the noise, rotated my bad ankle, and looked out the car window, ignoring the kicking and cage rattling from the back seat. Anderson was freaking out, but he was cuffed. The doors were locked, and no one had been shot or maimed.

An hour later we were back at the Hall.

I washed up and iced my face, and after Anderson was booked, he was brought to Interview 2 in an orange jumpsuit. He didn't ask for anything, not a cold drink or a phone call or even a lawyer. Good. Jacobi and I were experienced working together, and we gave Anderson a thorough three-hour interrogation with tape rolling.

Since Anderson punched me, I was throbbing all over. Maybe I just wanted it all to be done with, but I believed Anderson's story. He had no independent knowledge of the Barons' drug involvement, but he'd seen the news. His story was short and bitter. He had loved Ramona when they were in high school. And he hated Paul. He put his head down on the table and cried.

"Lock me up," he said. "I deserve it. There's no other place I want to be."

By then we knew that Anderson didn't own a gun, had never been in the military, had no priors or outstanding warrants. He didn't even have a computer, owing to the iffy wireless service in the area. He wasn't one of the Moving Targets shooters, but we were keeping him in lockup while Greeley got a lawyer and pressed charges.

As a guard took Anderson to holding, he said to me, "I'm sorry about...hitting you. I'm sorry for what I did."

"Tell it to the judge," said Jacobi.

Back at my desk, I slumped down in my chair and said to Conklin, "It's still Saturday, right?"

My partner grinned at me. "Want to go out to dinner with me and Cindy?"

"Thanks, but no. I have a date."

CHAPTER 80

MY DAUGHTER SCREAMED and ran into her room when she saw me.

Martha made quite a racket, too, took a stance outside Julie's door until my little girl let her in. And poor Gloria Rose stood by, wringing her hands.

"What happened? Lindsay, what happened?"

I put my gun away and peered into the hallway mirror. I looked worse than I'd thought. My swollen lower lip was split, and one of my front teeth was chipped. Dark-blue circles had come up around my eyes, and I was starting to worry about my knuckles. I couldn't straighten my hand.

I said to Mrs. Rose, "I had to break up a brawl. I'm fine. If you keep looking at me like that, I'm going to start to feel sorry for myself."

"I'll get some ice. Be right back."

"Gloria, I'm going to look like a beauty queen again by this time next week."

She was supposed to laugh, but our good family friend and nanny nodded and said, "Sit down, Lindsay. Pull your hair away from your face, so I can see if you need stitches."

"Make that ice pack for the road," I said.

"That's why God made sandwich bags."

I sat down like she'd told me, and I let her clean my face with alcohol, hardly screaming at all, but enough that Julie crept out to see what the ruckus was all about.

"What happened, Mommy?"

"It's a long story, honey. But the bad guy's in jail."

"Ohhhhhh. And he'll never get out?"

"No, I wouldn't say that. He flipped out. Hurt some people. It's a long story. I'll tell you later. Do you want to go to the park?"

"And bring home noodles for dinner?"

"I'll have to ask Daddy what he wants, but I'm sure we can find a couple of noodles for you."

"A couple?"

Mrs. Rose led me to the sink, unwrapped and washed my knuckles. While I told her what a good person she was, she poured alcohol over my right hand, telling me that I needed to take a nap.

"Don't take offense, but you look like you crawled out of a dumpster. This was a nice suit, but you'd never know it."

She showed me the rip under the armhole, the grass stains on the elbows, the bloody lapels.

"This is what I get for wearing heels. Let me up, Gloria. Martha? You want to go to the park?"

Did she *ever*. I told her and Julie to give me a minute and repeated to my darling daughter's nanny, "I have to get into jeans, okay? And spend some time with Jules. I need it. She needs it, too."

"You've got a point," she said. "Go change. Put on some lace-up boots. You're limping."

A bit later, while we still had late-afternoon sunlight, I hugged Gloria Rose good-bye. I leashed my good old border collie and helped Julie on with a jacket, and we took a leisurely three-block walk to Mountain Lake Park.

It would have been a great idea but for the phone. Brady called. After I briefed him, Conklin called to make sure I was okay.

The park was busy. New rules were now posted about keeping dogs on leashes and not feeding the ducks. Not a problem for Martha in her old age. She was more of a flock herder than a duck fetcher. I found a seat on a bench where I could see everything. Julie and Martha lay down in the grass, and Julie told Martha a story involving bad men and her big, strong mother.

I couldn't help but laugh, and then Chi called, a methodical man with a list of witnesses, two of them who said I'd thrown the first punch.

"How many say I didn't?"

"More."

Chi went down the list of mourners, giving their opinions on who had reason to shoot Paul and Ramona Baron.

"Here's the net-net," Chi told me. "Anderson is popular. He played football. He can fix anything. And he has friends. They thought Paul Baron was a dirtbag, that Ramona was the real deal, and they felt sorry for Anderson, who had loved her for twenty years. None of them had any thoughts about the snipers, nothing. 'Moving Targets? What's that? Never heard of it.' But they trusted we would crack the case. And nobody is filing charges against you."

I sighed into the phone, told Chi I'd see him on Monday, and I'd just hung up when my phone rang.

"Joe! What's your ETA?"

"Not tonight, sweetheart. If I could leave Napa right now, I would."

"But…why not? Dave?"

"Yeah. Long story."

He said he'd call me after the child was asleep. Julie climbed up on the bench and asked if I was talking to Daddy.

I handed her the phone.

"Daddy. Chinese noodles for dinner, okay?"

There was a moment of silence. Then the question "Why?" was repeated several times before she said, "Okay. Bye," and handed me the phone. Joe had hung up.

"Sorry, Julie, but his friend Dave is in a bad way and only Daddy can help him."

Julie threw her arms around me, and Martha dropped her head onto my knees.

"It's okay, Mommy," Julie said. "I just love being with my two best girls."

I laughed at that direct quote from her father. I hugged her and ruffled my doggy's head, and after a while we walked home, stopping off at the Chinese noodle joint, of course. Bought takeout tan tan noodles for two.

We were home and halfway through our noodles when my phone buzzed.

I looked at the screen. It was Brady. Damn.

I grabbed the phone and prepared myself to tell him I'd be fine after a day in bed, but he spared me the trouble. Jacobi had briefed him through the right hook to my face and let him know that the perp was booked.

But that wasn't why he was calling.

"There's been another shooting, Boxer."

"No. Where?"

"LA. One shot to the head. The dead man was a retired cop."

"No, Brady, no. What the hell is this? Was he dealing?"

"I've got more news, Boxer. Stempien ran the pictures Lemke took at the funeral. He got a hit on Barkley."

"I'm speechless."

"I sent you the photo. He shaved, but it's Barkley with a rock-solid alibi for the shooting today. He couldn't have been in Bolinas and the City of Angels at the same time."

I looked at the picture of an average-size white man, clean shaven, wearing a black sports coat, white shirt, and a tie. Had I seen him and not recognized him?

"Lemke will circulate the photo," he said. "You take the day off." I laughed. It was about 6:30 p.m.

"See you in the morning," said Lieutenant Brady.

CHAPTER **81**

JOE HAD BEEN sleeping in Dave's spare bedroom on the second floor when he was jarred awake by the squeal of hydraulic brakes and the sound of shouting.

He peered out the window and saw Dave directing a crew in overalls, carrying furniture and boxes from Ray and Nancy Channing's house next door and loading up a large truck.

This disturbed Joe, as it would any investigator. Was there something in that house that could be evidence against Dave? If so, there was nothing he could do to stop him. In fact, the whole situation stank of secrecy, misdirection, and Dave's uncharacteristic anxiety and paranoia.

Joe showered, dressed, packed, and took his bag downstairs. He left the house by the front door and watched the move of furnishings, garment bags, plastic tubs, and whatnots into the truck. Dave waved and called out, "This is all going to auction," he said.

260

"Can I give you a hand?"

"We're good," Dave said.

Joe shouted back, "I'll make breakfast."

Comfortable in any kitchen, Joe found the coffee, set up the pot, took eggs out of the fridge, and whipped them in a bowl. There was a loaf of bread in a basket, and he sliced it.

He lined a pan with bacon, then went outside and gave Dave a five-minute warning.

A few minutes later Dave came into the house with items on his lap: a paint box, a pair of men's boots, and a rifle.

"Wow, it feels good to send all that stuff to auction," he said. "Anything that doesn't sell goes to Goodwill. I got cash for Mom's paintings and Dad's clock collection."

"I put cheese and onions in the eggs," Joe said.

"Take a look."

Dave took an envelope from his shirt pocket, opened it, and showed a check to Joe. "I can pay you back and meet the payroll, too. Okay?"

"Sure. That's great."

Dave placed the boots on the floor, the paint box and the gun on the chair in front of the fireplace, before pulling his chair up to the table. It wasn't long before he began rolling it back and forth. He appeared to Joe to be preoccupied and anxious.

"You need something?" Joe asked.

"I *need* to see Dr. Daniel Perkins in *handcuffs.*"

Dave backed up, made a sharp turn to the fridge, got his hands on a carton of juice—and it slipped from his fingers onto the floor.

Joe grabbed a dish towel, but the juice outran him. He turned his head so he could look up at Dave.

He said, "You're the same guy who could throw the pigskin in a perfect spiral from the fifty-yard line to the end zone."

"Yeah, well. That was a lifetime ago."

While Joe mopped up, Dave went to the sideboard and pulled out dishes and coffee mugs and set the table. Joe watched him do it. His hands were shaking. Why?

Joe finished frying the bacon and cooking the eggs, and when the toast popped, he buttered four slices, set it all up on a pair of blue china plates, and brought breakfast to the table. Dave brought over the coffeepot, and as Joe would have predicted—it slipped from Dave's hand, dropping from three inches above the tabletop.

Joe steadied the sloshing pot.

He said, "Dave, what the fuck is going on?"

"You mean besides watching a truck drive off with my parents' stuff that I've grown up with my whole life? Besides my upcoming trial? Besides that I've lost my father, my best friend? And you, Joe, you look at me like you'd like me to get the electric chair."

Joe sat down across from Dave and moved all of the plates out of the way. Dave was rolling the chair again, to and fro, to and fro, staring down at the table.

"Look at me," Joe said.

Dave stared at the table.

Joe said it again, but this time not as a demand. Dave had every right to his feelings. And Joe had every right to his.

"Dave, I'm not the law. I work for you. You're acting like a man with a bad conscience. I have to know the whole truth in order to help you. Did you have *anything* to do with Ray's death?"

Joe braced himself for Dave to flip the table, knock the coffeepot to the floor, and then open his veins with a bread knife.

"No," he said. "I didn't do a damned thing to Ray but love him. Let me ask you, Joe. I've met your father. He's a good guy. Could be a bit of a jerk. He had a lot on his hands, all you kids, afraid the money would run out. He said a few rough things to you in front of the coach. In front of me. Did you ever think of killing him?"

"No."

"No. Under what circumstances would you have done it? If he was hurting someone? If he was a criminal? Not even then, right?"

"Right."

"Even if he was sick and told you to put him down, you wouldn't do it."

The pause lengthened, and then Dave spoke again.

"I swear to you on the memories of my mother, my father, and the love of my life, Rebecca, that I had nothing to do with Dad's death. Someone did, but it wasn't me."

Throughout this speech Dave had fixed a direct and un-wavering look into Joe's eyes.

Joe said it with feeling. "I'm sorry, Dave."

"Apology accepted. And don't you dare ask me if I killed Ray ever again."

Joe got up, walked around the wheelchair, and put his

arms around Dave's chest, hugging him from behind. Dave nodded his head and held Joe's arms. They stayed this way for a long time, until Joe spoke.

"I'm going to cook up some more eggs, and then let's go to work."

CHAPTER 82

DAVE AND JOE moved into the sitting room, where Dave had laid out papers on the coffee table.

"I pulled these from funeral home websites," he said. "I've got five question marks and four suspicious deaths, all of them patients of Doc Perkins."

"Playing devil's advocate for a minute."

"Oh, jeez. I thought we were done with that."

"People die, Dave. Older people with heart conditions die all the time. Perkins is a cardiac surgeon. His patients all have heart disease."

"Correct, Joe. And their deaths aren't investigated because of that. Old person is brought into the hospital with heart issues and dies overnight. End of story. What if Perkins is ending the story a little early?"

"Humor me, Dave. If it wasn't Perkins, who could be the angel of death? Who had the means, the opportunity, and the motive?"

They kicked it around as cars pulled up to the winery.

And they made a list of nurses, aides, orderlies, other doctors, and a couple of laundry workers Dave knew by name.

They quickly, almost arbitrarily, cut the long list of possible killers into a manageable short list: A charge nurse who manned the ICU and cardiac station at night. An EMT who'd brought in 60 percent of the patients who had died. There was Perkins's favorite anesthesiologist, Dr. Quo, who checked in on post-op patients.

But Dave's opinion didn't waver. Perkins still held the number one spot.

"Ray had a roommate when I was there with you. Ted somebody."

"Scislowski. Ted Scislowski. He was scheduled for a triple bypass the day after Dad died."

"You think he has checked out of the hospital?" Joe asked.

"Or did he, you know—*check out*?"

"Was Perkins his doctor?"

"I'm not sure."

Joe got on his phone, called Saint John's, and asked to speak with a patient, Ted Scislowski. The front desk put the call through.

Joe reintroduced himself to the man he'd met casually the other week and said that he'd like to drop by for a visit.

"Wonderful," Scislowski said over the phone. "Ray said a lot of good things about you."

"Can I bring you anything?"

"Nope, but I might have something interesting to tell you."

CHAPTER 83

AN HOUR LATER Joe walked into room 419 in the recovery wing.

"Ted, hi. How are you feeling?"

"Ha. Like my rib cage was wrenched open and my sternum was cracked. Oh, yeah, and my arteries were re-arranged, but I'm still breathing. Watch your cholesterol is my advice to you. Please have a seat, Joe."

Joe said, "I have a little gift for you. I think it's going to have to wait until they let you out of here."

"Hey," said Scislowski, examining the bottle. "Channing Winery Private Reserve Cab. I'm going to save that for a special occasion. Like the first night I'm home. My wife and I are going to drink to poor Ray."

Joe pulled up the offered seat and told Scislowski that he felt terrible that Ray had died, that Ray's son was inconsolable.

He said, "Dr. Daniel Perkins was your surgeon?"

"Sure. One of a couple or so in the operating room. You

know, what I wanted to tell you is that I had an out-of-body experience."

Joe said, "Really. I want to hear all about it."

"Okay, because it was amazing. I'm in the operating room, I guess unconscious. And then I was up above the operating table, my back to the ceiling, and I was watching the operation. You've heard these stories before, haven't you? Patient dies and he hears what the people in the operating room are saying?"

Joe leaned in, said, "Ted, you're saying you died?"

"I'm not just saying it. Dr. Perkins told me. My heart stopped. I was officially dead. Yeah, believe it. I watched the heart-lung bypass machine squeeze my heart. They were listening to classical music, talking over the violins.

"I was in a state of…I don't know what else to call it but wonder. Or grace. I could see and hear everything, including the flat line on the monitor. Then here they come, regular beeps. My heart beating in my chest. A nurse says, 'He's back.' I wake up in the recovery room. What do you think of that?"

"Damned good story, Ted."

"And all true." Scislowski laughed.

Joe laughed with him. It felt great to be in the presence of a man so happy to be alive. He said, "So, Ted, Dr. Perkins brought you back to life?"

"God, I love that man. I'm only sixty-three. I have a lot to live for."

"Ted, Ray was a good friend when I was in school with Dave, and I feel awful that he died. Were you with him when he passed away?"

"I'm sure I was," said Scislowski, "but I was knocked out, so I'd get sleep before my operation. I very dimly remember a nurse calling, 'Mr. Channing. Mr. Channing.' I opened my eyes and called out to Ray, but she had closed the curtain. There was some fussing going on, as if she wasn't supposed to be there, and then the nurse and an orderly, I think, wheeled him out. I said, 'So long, Ray.'"

Joe wanted to ask who else was in the operating room when Ted Scislowski came back to life, and what nurse and what orderly had wheeled Ray Channing's body out of the room, but it felt wrong to do that. As if he were questioning Scislowski's memory.

And then he did it anyway.

Scislowski said, "I heard voices but didn't see any faces when they rolled Ray's gurney out of the room. I do remember the sheet over his face. Now, when I was in the OR, I was just watching Dr. Perkins. Everyone was wearing gowns and masks, but I know Daniel. He's been my doctor for ten years. Joe, why do you ask?"

"Favor to Dave. He's grief stricken."

The two men talked for another few minutes about Ted's upcoming stay at rehab and how long Joe would remain in Napa. They were making small talk about their families when a nurse came into the room with Ted's medication.

Joe made a mental note of the nurse's name, and after she left, Joe put his card on Ted's nightstand and shook his hand good-bye.

He got into the elevator thinking of Scislowski saying, "God, I love that man," and continued thinking about Ted Scislowski's story about his life-and-death-and-life operation.

Dr. Perkins, the nice white-haired doctor with the metal-framed glasses and bright-red tie, had opened Ted Scislowski's chest, cut away the arteries that had led to his heart attack, and effectively, scientifically killed his patient. After that, he'd reconnected the arteries in a medically precise procedure and, using a heart-lung bypass machine in an almighty-God kind of way, palpated his patient's heart and brought him back to life.

Joe had a new thought about Perkins. If he was a killer, he was a very, very smart one.

CHAPTER 84

I'D BEEN PUZZLING all night about Brady's call saying that the man who'd been shot in LA was a retired cop.

I didn't understand this twist in the Moving Targets' MO, and I sure didn't like it. I put my Kevlar vest on under my Windbreaker and kissed Julie and Mrs. Rose good-bye.

I got to the Hall at eight, alarming the security guard in the lobby with my Halloween mask of a face.

I said, "I got a few licks in, too."

The guard said, "I don't doubt it for a second, Sergeant."

I held my face as I laughed, knowing that there was going to be more of this kind of talk as my bruises spread.

Upstairs in the squad room, Conklin said, "You'll be fine. You'll be fine."

The repetition made me think otherwise, but I let it pass. "Who's in with Brady?"

"Detective Noble from LA."

"He flew in? Does Brady want us to join them or take Noble to the war room?"

Conklin said, "War room. I brought churros. Only ate one."

He picked up the phone and tapped the keys. My long view from the front to rear of the squad room included the back of Noble's head and Brady, behind his desk, picking up his landline. He and Conklin had a short exchange about logistics, then they hung up.

"I'll set up the room," said Conklin.

"Allow me," I said.

Conklin said, "I got it," and went to make coffee. I sighed and walked to Brady's office, steeling myself against his comments when he saw my face. I introduced myself to Detective Noble, who winced when he stood up to shake my hand and got a good look at me. Brady didn't even blink.

Noble and I walked through the empty bullpen to the war room, which was now wallpapered with photos of the sniper victims. Conklin played Inspector Mom, offering refreshments, including churros and just-brewed police department mud with a choice of flavored creamers. Then Detective Noble brought us up to speed on yesterday's shooting.

"It's not in the papers yet," he said, "but three people were killed yesterday. One was former LAPD narc Barry Pratch."

Noble showed us pictures. First one, Pratch was in his dress uniform, possibly for his photo ID. The second photo was nearly identical to those of the other sniper victims.

Pratch was spread-eagle, facedown in a street that had been cordoned off and banked by cruisers. He wore civvies: jeans, polo shirt, running shoes. His khaki jacket had reinforced shoulders, patches on the elbows—a hunting jacket or what you'd wear to a shooting range.

I looked up and asked Noble, "Do you know anything about who killed him? Why was he wearing a shooting jacket? Please say you've got witnesses."

Noble said, "If only. No. The whole thing is odd. Pratch had been with LAPD for a decade but got written up a number of times for suspicious shootings on the job. Rumor had it, never officially stated, that he was using oxy, very likely taken off perps. Maybe he was selling, too. Wouldn't surprise me," Noble said.

Clapper had said similar things about Detective Carl Kennedy. The only difference that I could see was that Kennedy had moved from LAPD to Houston and was on the job when he was murdered. Maybe Pratch and Kennedy had been friends.

Noble said, "Pratch was about to get canned, so he took early retirement three years ago. But listen to this. He was *going after the shooters*. And he killed two of them. He was hunting down drug dealers like he was still *on the job*."

"What does this mean to you?" I asked Noble.

"My theory is that Pratch took out two of the snipers and would have kept going. But someone, a third shooter, capped him first. Dead men don't shoot."

Noble went on to tell us about the shooters' bodies.

One of the dead men had been found on the roof of a two-story office building. The other had been standing outside an apartment house. Neither of the snipers had been identified yet. But LA's overworked Forensics Unit had photos, prints, and expended bullets, and would ID the dead men as soon as they could.

"Which could be weeks," Noble said.

We refilled our coffee cups and kicked it around.

Why had a disgraced police officer killed two trained assassins? How had he known them, and how had he known where they would be? Was he one of them? Had he gone straight and decided that shooting drug dealers was dead wrong? Or had he had Moving Targets in his sights from the beginning and joined them? Maybe he'd seen a way to redeem himself by bringing them down.

All good theories, but where was the key to the answer?

Would we ever know?

Noble had said, "Dead men don't shoot."

Correct. And they don't talk, either.

CHAPTER 85

BRADY STIFF-ARMED THE door and burst into the war room, saying, "Barkley was just seen entering the Sleep Well in Portola."

I knew the place. The Sleep Well Motel was pinkish in color with a traditional motel design: a square-U-shaped building enclosing a parking area, which faced San Bruno Avenue.

Brady snapped out his orders. "Take Lemke and Samuels. I can't raise Nardone. Boxer, you're first officer. SWAT's on the way."

I followed Brady down the center aisle with Conklin right behind me. Lemke and Samuels were at their desks. Lemke's jutting lower jaw made him look like an old pit bull. Samuels was round shouldered with glasses and could pass for an accountant. People underestimated him. They were wrong to do so. They were both good cops, inseparable, and now Lemke had a halo because one of his snapshots at the Barons' funeral had turned out to be Barkley.

Conklin conveyed Brady's orders.

Samuels forwarded their phones to Brenda, and the two of them grabbed their jackets. We were all hoping for another crack at Barkley. I wanted him alive and in the box because he was all we had—and he might be a key to the whole Moving Targets operation.

The four of us jogged down the fire stairs to Bryant and signed out a couple of squad cars. Conklin took the wheel of ours and we went to Code 3, switching on our sirens and flashers, Conklin stepping on the gas.

I reported in, requesting a dedicated channel, and signed off. A minute later four-codes streamed over the speaker. Officer needs emergency help. Send ambulance. Requested assistance responding. A second request, send ambulance.

Traffic parted ahead of us, and within ten minutes we were on the main road through Portola, a working-class neighborhood on the edge of the city. We flew past the small businesses—shoe repair shop, bakeries, grocery store, a couple of restaurants—and then I saw the blinking neon sign up ahead.

SLEEP WELL MOTEL. VACANCIES. FREE WI-FI.

By the time we arrived, the motel's parking lot was filled with law enforcement vehicles and cops on foot who were attempting to clear the area of bystanders.

My job as primary responder was to stabilize the scene, secure it for CSI, and determine what had happened for the record and for the lead investigator, who, please God, wouldn't be me. I reached out to Clapper and filled him in. "We need prints right away."

"In a motel room. Wish us luck."

"All the luck in the world."

I looked past the cruisers, ambulances, and guest vehicles, trying to get a fix on what the hell had gone down. Where was Nardone? Brady had said Barkley had been seen. Given time spent relaying orders and driving through noon traffic, it was a fair bet that Barkley was long gone.

I was out of the car before Conklin fully braked. I hobbled on my twisted ankle to the ambulance that was taking on a patient. The paramedic wouldn't let me inside.

"He's got a head injury. Please. Get out of our way."

"What's his name? What's his name?"

"Glenn Healy. Officer Healy."

"Where are you taking him?"

"Zuckerberg San Francisco General."

The rear doors closed, sirens shrieked, and the bus moved onto the main road. Someone called out to me.

"Sergeant Boxer. Over here."

Sergeant Robert Nardone was sitting on the third step of a staircase running from the parking area to the second floor. Cleaning supplies and toiletries were heaped around Nardone's feet as if Mr. Clean and Bed Bath & Beyond had purged their trucks, haphazardly flinging samples across the area.

My eyes were drawn to an overturned housekeeper's cart that had crashed into a vintage Buick some twenty feet from the foot of the stairs. That explained the toiletries.

But I still couldn't picture what had happened here.

Nardone would have to tell me.

I asked him, "Bob, are you all right?"

"We lost him, Boxer. Bastard stole our car and booked."

CHAPTER 86

NARDONE WAS PALE and had a nasty abrasion down the left side of his face, and he was holding his left arm tightly to his chest.

Any minute now paramedics would load him into an ambulance, but I held on to hope that before then I'd get his statement. I'd known Sergeant Robert Nardone for years. He had a sharp eye, worked hard, and was angling for a job in Homicide. Although he'd been injured, he was sitting up, speaking, and seemed to be tracking the scene as it devolved.

I said, "Nardone. Are you okay?"

"Good enough."

"The guy who did this. Was it Barkley?"

"I forgot to ask for his ID."

Sarcasm was a good sign. Nardone had a gift for it.

I brushed little bars of soap, bottles of shampoo, sponges, and a spray bottle off a step and sat down beside him. I now had a wide view of the parking lot.

Tourists, paying guests, and local looky-loos meandered across the two hundred square feet of asphalt, stepping on possible evidence and getting in the way of the cops who were doing their best to clear and cordon off the area. No one was taking witness names or statements. A lot rested on what Nardone had to tell me.

EMTs with lights flashing and sirens whooping filed into the area, and civilian drivers leaned on their horns as they tried to leave.

I told Nardone I was concerned that Barkley had hijacked a police cruiser. An armed criminal driving a patrol car could speed without being stopped, could pull drivers over, and if he could get them to step out of their vehicle, he could rob them, kill them, take their car. That stolen black-and-white made Leonard Barkley more dangerous than before.

Nardone gave me his car's tag number and I called it in, requesting an APB, forthwith. And now I saw another victim. Standing beside the second bus, Lemke and Samuels talked to a patient who was strapped onto a gurney. She was sobbing, and I saw blood running down an arm.

I turned back to Nardone. "Who is she?"

"Housekeeper. Accidental casualty."

He'd dropped the bravado and was fixing me with a hurt look in his eyes.

"He kicked the shit out of us, Boxer, and took everything but our skivvies. Healy got the worst of it. Way worse."

"Okay," I said. "Please start at the beginning."

Nardone sighed and gingerly touched his face with his fingertips.

When he was ready, he said, "Healy was driving. We were looking for a coffee shop when I saw a guy looked like Barkley cross the road, heading to the motel. I was pretty sure it was him, but the picture I have of Barkley, the dude had a beard."

"Yep. He shaved. Go on."

"So we pulled in the lot and saw him take the stairs to the second floor and enter room 208. You can see it at the head of the stairs. We parked over there, where we could watch the room, and I called in a sighting of a suspect wanted for questioning, and we requested backup."

"But he saw you, right?"

"Yeah. He peeks through the curtain, then opens the door, and I see him assessing his next steps. He's going to either bolt for the elevator at the end of the building. Or he's going to vault over the railing. Healy and I get out of the car, draw our weapons, and I yell, 'Stay where you are. Show us your hands.'

"That's when the cleaning woman comes out of room 206 and slow-walks her cart along the second-floor walkway, blocking our view of the suspect. She's wearing earbuds and she's humming. I can't see around her, and she doesn't hear me."

"And then?"

"And then fucking Barkley lunges, grabs her, and shoves her and her cart down the stairs. I'm in front and she bowls me over. Strike! I fall on top of Healy, who hits his head against the railing. Now all three of us are in a pile, right? Disoriented. Out of breath. The suspect, assumed to be Barkley, grabs Healy out of the pile, pushes him against our car, and yells into his face, 'I'm the good guy, you dumb shit.'"

"Aw, jeez."

Nardone swallowed, coughed, and then he continued.

"I'd lost my gun while rolling down the stairs with four or five hundred pounds of people and a cleaning cart on top of me. I hear Barkley gut-punching Healy, who's grunting and trying to get free of him. Then I see that Barkley has bent Healy over the hood and he's patting him down, saying, 'Give me the keys.'

"And then the keys jingle. He's got them."

CHAPTER 87

NARDONE WANTED TO tell the story as much as I wanted to hear it, but he was running out of gas.

There were some small plastic bottles of water among the litter of toiletries. I got one from under the cart and brought it back to Nardone.

He thanked me. Sipped from the bottle.

Then he said, "I tried to shove that poor woman off me. But she's dead weight. Unconscious. By the time I'm out from under her, I find Healy lying in his vomit, bleeding from the side of his head. Our guns are gone. The dude has also stripped off our shoulder mikes. I didn't even feel him do it. But now I'm on my feet, and I see him get into our car and pull out. My phone is in the car."

"And your badge?"

"I have mine, but he ripped Healy's off his shirt pocket. I gotta say this, Sergeant, and not as an excuse. We didn't have a chance. The dude is MMA or something."

"If it's Barkley, he's a Navy SEAL."

"That explains it."

"You did your best, Bob."

Paramedics approached with a gurney. Nardone protested. They insisted. Paramedics won.

Out on the street in this light commercial area, horns blared, hydraulic brakes squealed, uniforms closed a lane and tried to control traffic. If the runaway psycho was Barkley, he had PTSD. Now he had weapons and a badge and a police cruiser. And he thought he was the good guy. The mayhem could set him off.

Conklin came over and said, "I spoke with Cappy."

McNeil and Chi had been assigned to watch the Barkley house, in hopes that Barkley would need clean underwear and maybe a conjugal visit. But according to them, Barkley hadn't shown up and Randi had been followed whenever she left it.

I called Brady, told him we needed to move Barkley's wife, put her in protective custody. He said he'd get a warrant.

I got into our squad car, turned on the radio, checked in with dispatch.

Specialist Hess told me, "Good news, Sergeant. The cruiser was found on San Bruno, near Cliff's Auto Body. Abandoned, engine left running."

"Were there guns inside?"

"No guns. No nothing."

Barkley had given us back the car. Good news. I no longer had to worry about him flipping on the siren and driving at 100 mph to parts unknown.

But that wasn't enough.

Where was Barkley?

Maybe he was across the street, watching us.

CHAPTER 88

BY TWO THAT afternoon I was settling Randi White Barkley into her safe house in Parkside, which in my humble opinion was several grades above the shack she and Barkley called home.

It had two freshly painted, sunny rooms, comfy furniture, an ocean breeze, and a park only a few blocks away. Barkley Barkley, her large Rottweiler mix, climbed onto a white sofa and fell asleep.

He felt at home, but Randi complained while uniforms secured the windows and checked the door locks. She didn't know that we had court orders allowing us to set up hidden cameras, bug the landline, and hack into her laptop.

Randi asked, "Is this actually legal?"

"Yes, and again, Randi, it's for your protection."

"Protection from whom? My husband?"

"Consider this. Say he gets in here to visit you. We tell him to come out with his hands up. He resists arrest. There's shooting. You both die."

Randi shrugged. "We knew that could happen from the beginning. We have a pact with death. Don't you?"

She paused to watch my face. I pictured my young daughter. My getting shot was always a painful possibility.

Randi read my expression and sneered, "Yeah, I thought so."

She went into the kitchen and opened the fridge. From where I stood, I could see that it was empty.

I said, "There's a cruiser outside. Officer Carol Ma Fullerton is your contact. Here's her number."

I used a fridge magnet to attach the note to the door. "She'll get you what you reasonably need," I said. "Meaning, groceries. Keep the shades down and stay off the phone. Fullerton or her alternate can take you and your dog to the park once a day."

"When can I get out of here?"

"Look, Randi. If you prefer, I can put you in jail and hold you as a material witness."

That was true, but only for forty-eight hours. Cops are allowed to lie, and I don't think my nose grew even half an inch.

"I'm gonna need tampons," she said.

"I'll tell Officer Fullerton on my way out. There's a drugstore about a block from here."

Randi joined her dog on the sofa, put her feet on the coffee table, and clicked on the TV.

"You got HBO here?"

"Make yourself comfortable, Randi. Keep your phone charged in case we need to make contact."

"And ice cream," she said. "Double chocolate chip."

Would Leonard Barkley try to find her at their actual

home on Thornton? Had he followed us as we moved her to this swell safe house? What were his plans?

Randi would never tell me.

She was playing with her dog's ears and watching the first season of *The Sopranos* when I let myself out.

CHAPTER 89

CINDY WAS IN her office writing a victim account of a carjacking, while tuning in to her police scanner at the same time.

She was on deadline and deep into her writing when someone knocked. It was Henry Tyler, saying, "Returning your call."

Cindy invited him in and told him she'd have the story for him shortly.

"I only need a teaser on the front page," she said, "then maybe half a page anywhere in the B section."

"I'm leaving tonight at six. On the dot."

"You'll have it before then."

Cindy went back to her draft of the story, checking the quotes against her interview transcripts—when the police scanner went crazy. She dialed it up. Something was happening and it sounded big. This was why she kept her scanner with her at home and work and in between like it was her flesh and blood.

First thing she heard clearly was a call for backup, followed by dispatch saying that backup was on the way. Then there was a string of four-codes: officer needs emergency help, send ambulance, requested assistance responding, and send ambulance again.

Officer needs emergency help was like an electric shock to her spine.

She speed-dialed Rich, pressed the phone to her ear, and listened for him to pick up. No answer.

Cindy looked through her glass wall. McGowan was not at his desk. She sent him a text message saying, *Hold the fort. I'll be back in an hour.*

She wanted to call Rich again but throttled the impulse. If he was at his desk, he'd call her. If he was out, he was busy. A new voice came over the radio, an officer asking dispatch to repeat the location.

The dispatcher answered: "The Sleep Well Motel, 2701 San Bruno Avenue."

Cindy couldn't tell what was happening, but her instincts were on high alert. She felt a big story coming to life in Portola. If she got clear road, she could be at the Sleep Well in fifteen minutes max.

Cindy slipped her phone into her handbag, zipped up her baseball jacket, and slung the bag over her shoulder. Last, she tucked her radio under her arm and exited the office. Her curiosity and imagination caught fire. She overrode her throttled impulse and called Rich again. This time she left a message.

"Call me, Rich. Let me know that you're okay."

She unlocked her blue Honda, plugged the radio into

the lighter jack, connected her phone to the Bluetooth app, and buckled in. It was normally a ten- to fifteen-minute drive from the *Chronicle* to Portola, but that didn't count traffic jams.

Paying almost full attention to the road, Cindy took every shortcut, ran every yellow light, and when she finally arrived at the crime scene, there was nothing to see but tattered yellow tape.

Something had happened here, but what?

Cops were taking down the tape. Motel guests were pulling out of the parking lot.

She headed to the motel manager's office.

CHAPTER 90

CINDY READ THE nameplate on the counter.

MR. JAKE TUOHY, MANAGER.

Tuohy was broad and balding, and his body language spoke loudly, conveying *What now?* and *Who cares?* But Cindy thought she could turn him to her side. She unzipped her jacket, tossed her hair, and introduced herself.

"I'm Cindy Thomas from the *San Francisco Chronicle*, and I wonder if you could—"

Tuohy interrupted. "Let me see your card."

Cindy handed him one from her jacket pocket. She glanced over his head and saw the framed picture on the wall of a gutted deer hanging head down from a tree, Tuohy standing beside it, grinning.

Cindy zipped up her Windbreaker as he pinned her card to the bulletin board over the coffee station.

He turned around and patted down the flyaway hair in his horseshoe-shaped fringe. His smile was absolutely chilling.

"What do you want to know?" he said.

"Everything. Why don't I just let you tell me what happened here?"

She pulled out her phone, pressed Record, and put it on the counter between them. She said, "Can you spell your name for me?"

He said, "I could, but I won't. Turn that off."

Cindy sighed, then complied.

"Sorry," she said. "It's my job to cover this story."

"Do not use my name. I will deny I ever spoke to you."

"Deal. Let me start over. What can you tell me?"

"There was a guy staying here last night," said Tuohy. "What I heard is that he shoved our cleaning woman down the stairs. We're insured. But her papers are wonky. I don't know for sure. Not my business. Oh. A couple of cops got injured."

"Shot?"

"Shot? No. Who told you that?"

The manager wouldn't give her the name of the cleaning woman or of the man who'd booked the room, or the names of the police officers, saying, "I don't want to lose my job, understand?"

"Of course," Cindy said. "I feel the same way. Thanks for your time."

Cindy shook off the yucky feeling of the last five minutes and walked out to the street, where a couple of uniforms were taking down the tape. She didn't know any of them, but she found one who didn't look like a hard-ass. She was in her thirties, wore a wedding band, and still knew how to smile.

Cindy checked the name on her badge—Officer W. Link—and introduced herself to her, saying that she was head crime writer at the *Chronicle*.

She said, "By chance, do you know Inspector Rich Conklin of Homicide? He's a close friend. Was he involved in the incident?"

The cop said, "Yeah, he responded to the call. He's fine."

Cindy exhaled her relief and asked, "Could you tell me what happened here?"

"I will because your close friend is on the Job, but do not quote me. I'm not authorized to speak to anyone about an open case, let alone the press."

"All right, Officer L-i-n-k."

"Ha-ha. No, I mean it. Really."

"No problem. I promise to keep your name out of the story."

She gave her a stern look.

"I swear."

She extended her hand and they shook on it.

Then Link told her what she had heard. None of it was firsthand, but it was a scoop. Big one.

"It was that guy Barkley, who fired at the cops, I think. And he escaped. The thinking is that he could be one of those drug dealer killers, but I have not heard that officially. 'Unconfirmed, unidentified person says,' right, Ms. Thomas?"

"Exactly."

"Good. Word is that after this incident went down, he stole a squad car and disappeared again. I also heard that he used to be a Navy SEAL."

"Wow, and thanks, Anonymous Source Close to the Police Department."

Link grinned.

"I mean it. Thanks very much."

Cindy groaned through the traffic jam on Highway 101, and after parking her car in the garage across from the *Chronicle*, she headed upstairs and went directly to Tyler's office.

"Got a minute?" she asked.

"For you? Take two minutes."

"Henry, I got a scoop on background."

"Better than the carjack piece?"

Cindy said, "I can do both." Then she laid out what she knew about the incident at the Sleep Well Motel.

"Get going," said Tyler. "You have three hours."

Cindy went to her office and set up her scanner on the windowsill. She'd gathered a lot of information on Barkley since his wife fired on police, giving her husband a chance to escape. She had a research file on the sniper victims, and Link had confirmed what she'd heard—that Barkley had been a Navy SEAL.

At her request McGowan had gathered a stack of research on the SEALs, and now, as if she'd called him up, McGowan was at her door.

"Need help?"

"I'm drafting something," she said. "Tyler wants to see it by six. Now that we're working together, I'd like your input before that."

"Okay, Cindy. I've checked the news feeds. There's nothing about the Sleep Well Motel."

Damn it. She hadn't told him about that. He had police contacts of his own. Or he'd been snooping with his ear to Tyler's office door.

"Good," she said. "Let's hope it stays that way."

She opened her research folder and highlighted portions of the research she'd need. She could do this.

She could do it fast and well.

CHAPTER 91

IT WAS THREE o'clock when Cindy was ready to write.

Headline: POLICE SKIRMISH AT THE SLEEP WELL MOTEL.

Copy: *"Anonymous sources close to the SFPD tell the* Chronicle *that one of the snipers suspected of murdering ten or more people in five cities in under two weeks' time attracted the attention of two SFPD officers today at the Sleep Well Motel in Portola.*

"The suspect, who has not yet been positively identified, was staying at the Sleep Well when the police engaged him. We can't know what he was thinking, but when challenged, the suspect tried to flee. Again, when stopped, the suspect hurled a motel employee down a stairway into the police officers, seriously injuring one of them, and then stole a police vehicle."

Moving now into the body of the piece, Cindy wrote: *"It's been said that the suspect is highly skilled in hand-to-hand combat and cutting-edge weaponry. Anonymous sources close to the SFPD have told the* Chronicle *that the subject is a former Navy SEAL."*

Cindy filled in the background of this elite branch of the military, who were experts in combat diving and land warfare, having trained for five years in weapons and demolition, patrolling and marksmanship and fast rope rappelling, culminating in advanced levels of tactical training.

She noted that the SEALs had come into their own in 1944 during the D-day landings, and highlighted their work in Vietnam, Grenada, Desert Shield and Desert Storm, and the killing of Osama bin Laden.

"If there are active or retired Navy SEALs in this coordinated 'war on drugs,'" Cindy wrote, *"it would explain the precision targeting and the long-distance accuracy of the killings in the early morning."*

She was ready to wind up the story and stopped to consider the kicker. She would love a quote, and Rich had been at the scene. If he even said "No comment" on the record, it would be better than no quote at all.

She called him again, begging the ringing phone, "Come on, Richie. Please pick up."

And her call went to voice mail.

It was quarter to six. Looking through her glass wall, she caught McGowan's eye. She put up a hand so that he didn't barge in, and she sent him a text.

I need another moment.

She lowered her head and fired herself up to write an emotional finale:

"When the first five sniper victims were killed, it was difficult to see a pattern in the shootings or the victims themselves: a celebrity couple, a dentist taking his young son to school, a store owner on his way to work, a professional baseball player in the twilight of his career. It made no sense—until it did. The shootings were not ran-

dom. There was a connection between them. The victims were all involved in dealing drugs.

"Popular opinion was polarized but over the last few days has become weighted in favor of the shooters, cheering them on. One of the shooters, self-identified as Kill Shot, sent an email to this reporter's crime blog, announcing the urgent need for a 'new war on drugs.' That the civilian law-and-order approach had failed to stop the sale of drugs, and that, in fact, more people were dying from drug abuse every year.

"It gives this writer no pleasure to report to the Chronicle's readers that this past week two police officers were killed by sniper vigilantes. This afternoon the unnamed subject of this article disarmed two police officers, and, as reported, they were injured, one of them seriously.

"We call for an end to this vigilante activity.

"It's unlawful, it's dangerous to innocent citizens, and since guilt had not been proven in a court of law, all of these snipers' victims were not guilty.

"It's time for voters and those of us with the power of the pen to take a stand against this criminal movement."

Cindy checked the time. Five to six. No time to double-check it, but that's why she was sending the article to Mc-Gowan. She watched as he read it on his screen, and while he did that, she texted Tyler. *I'm just doing a quick polish*, she wrote. *I need thirty seconds.*

McGowan knocked on her door.

"Well," she said. "What do you think, Jeb?"

"In three words? It's. Not. News."

Cindy said, "Well, I guess we'll see if Henry agrees."

She attached the Sleep Well Motel story to an email and

sent it to Tyler. She turned her back on McGowan and listened to her scanner while she waited, and then her computer pinged. She looked and was elated to see that it was the return mail from Tyler. She couldn't open it fast enough.

Tyler wrote, "It's thin. Wait until the SEAL/shooter, if that's what he is, is in custody. Or until you get a new interview with Kill Shot. Have McGowan keep going with the victim profiles that are confirmed by police."

McGowan held the elevator door for her.

"What did he say?"

Cindy showed him her fist, then rotated it and pointed her thumb down.

The elevator door opened and they got out.

"See you tomorrow," Cindy said.

She didn't wait for a reply.

CHAPTER 92

I LOVE WHAT I do, but these past weeks have made me wish I'd become a schoolteacher, like my mom wanted me to be.

After the Sleep Well Motel witness roundup and the transfer of Randi Barkley to her cozy unjail, I'd collaborated with Conklin on a seven-page report for the brass. Following that, we'd gone to Zuckerberg San Francisco General to check in on Nardone and Healy, as well as Bettina Sennick, the motel housekeeper.

Nardone and Sennick were being released in the morning. Healy was still in the ICU.

Leonard Barkley, damn him, was still at large.

I got home at around eight. Mrs. Rose had fed Julie, but she was still awake, and hungry again. So we split a bowl of leftover noodle soup. Plus a salad. I insisted on greens. Plus a glass of wine for me. Because I deserved it. Plus a cookie for Julie because she demanded it. And one for me, just because.

By nine Julie was sleeping with Martha and Mrs. Mooey Milkington. I was standing in the shower, still streaming adrenaline out to my fingertips. The hot water beat at my bruises, but my mental and muscular tension was unrelenting.

I was occupied with my hydrotherapy and churning thoughts when I heard Joe calling me.

"Lindsayyy. I'm hooome."

I yelled toward the bathroom door. "Don't come in!"

"You're joking."

"I have to prepare you first."

"Prepare me? I'm starting to worry."

"Aw, nuts," I said. "Come on in."

Joe slowly inched the door open, so that by the time he was fully standing in the doorway, I was ready to scream. I parted the curtain just enough to show my face. He stared.

"What happened, Blondie?"

"Can I tell you later? It's not that interesting and I'd rather you go first."

Joe brought a towel over to the shower, pulled back the curtain, turned off the taps, and wrapped me in a white terry-cloth bath sheet. He helped me step over the side of the tub and took me into his arms. His tenderness so moved me that tears welled up and spilled over, and then cry, I did.

"What happened, sweetie?" he said. "Don't tell me you walked into a door."

"I got punched in the face."

"Look at me, Lindsay."

I looked into Joe's eyes and remembered when, not long ago, while he was attempting to rescue people from a bombed glass-and-steel building, a second bomb had gone off. A heavy structure had fallen on his head, and I had thought I would lose him. The operation to relieve the pressure on his brain had been successful. He was as smart and funny as always. His brain was intact, and now he also had a winding scar road from the top of his head to behind his left ear.

"Lindsay?"

I returned to the moment and my dear husband kissed each of my eyes and then my split lip very carefully.

I said, "Please take me to bed."

Joe picked me up as if I were weightless and carried me to our king-size pillow-top mattress. He laid me down and stripped off his clothes. Then he got under the covers and took me into his arms again, this time stroking me while I only wrapped my arms around his neck.

He made love to me tenderly, but I was in a different kind of mood. I was reeling from adrenaline overload. I felt the punch to my face and the one I'd thrown. I was charged up about Barkley—the beating he'd given to Healy and that he'd gotten away, *again*. I was enraged about that and couldn't find relief.

I said, "I need…"

"Tell me."

"I need to push back."

He pinned my wrists to the bed with his big hands and I submitted. Then I got free, turned him onto his back. He gave me what I wanted and more, and I gave him as good as I got. I couldn't remember when making love with my husband had ever been more satisfying, more cleansing, and at such a deep level—and it was because I loved and trusted him entirely.

Afterward we lay on our backs, touching side to side, hands clasped together, and then Joe rolled over and looked into my eyes.

"Who hit you? I want his name and contact information."

I laughed. I laughed some more. And when I was all laughed out, I told him about the saloon fight in a country church cemetery and that the guy who'd hit me was in jail awaiting arraignment.

And I told Joe that I loved him.

He said, "No kidding. I love you, too."

"I know. Put your clothes back on."

He swatted my butt. We dressed, and after we looked in on our little girl, we walked our family dog in the moonlight.

I thanked God that we were all well and together.

I counted my blessings.

CHAPTER 93

THE NEXT MORNING I called Claire's hospital room—again.

Edmund had been keeping me up-to-date on her condition through texts, and I'd sent messages to her through various nurses, who'd passed them on. But Claire hadn't called, and all that I could learn from Edmund was that she was healing from the surgery, walking a little more every day.

I missed her and wanted very much to get my own sense of how she was feeling. I wanted to hear in her own voice how she felt, and I had a couple of tales to tell her.

I called her as I dressed for work—and she actually answered the phone.

There was a moment of stunned silence before I said, "Claire?"

"Who were you expecting?"

"You're awfully fresh. I've been worried out of my mind."

She laughed, and that cheered me up, but I was still feeling both worried and in need of a one-on-one conversation.

"When are they sending you home?"

"I guess that's up to the parole board."

"Yer a riot, Butterfly. Are you free for lunch?"

"You bet I am. I've watched as much Rachael Ray and CNN as I can stand. I need Boxer news."

"Well, I've got some."

"Bring it," she said. "Noontime is good."

I left Julie in her booster seat next to Joe at the breakfast table. I kissed them and Martha good-bye, and once inside my Explorer, I headed toward the Hall. My spirits had transformed overnight. My skin was pleasantly whisker burned, and I had a lunch date with Claire. She hadn't seen my face, and she was going to give me the business. I thought about picking up something she might like. Perfume. A nightie?

My wandering mind was jolted back to the present by my phone buzzing. It was the same buzz as always, but I knew, just knew, that it was Brady.

He said, "There's been another shooting. Actually, a threesome."

I said, "For Christ's sake. A triple homicide—" but he talked over me.

"Outside the jazz center. Northern Station got the call, but you've gotta be there."

I changed course toward that large glass-and-steel building on the corner of Franklin and Fell. I ran my tongue over the chip in my tooth and turned up the scanner. It began crackling like a forest fire with codes that were becoming commonplace: Ambulance requested. CSI. Medical Examiner.

The jazz center is a beautiful building, but today all anyone would notice was the jam-packed area around the base of the building. There were squad cars, unmarked cars, paramedics schmoozing outside their vehicles, the CSI van, and the ME's van just arriving, and they were in the process of closing off the immediate area.

And there was something else, or rather *someone* else, only I would notice.

My good bud, still mad at me, was startled when I pulled the car up to where she stood at the intersection waiting for the light to change. I lightly honked my horn. Spinning around, she recognized my vehicle, then turned her eyes to me.

She came toward the window.

"Oh, man," she said. "Rich said you got punched. I hope your lip doesn't scar."

"Did he tell you I punched back?"

I showed her the cuts on my knuckles and the artistic bruise changing color as it rose up my hand to the wrist.

"Impressive," she said, turning to leave. "Anyway, I gotta go, Linds."

I said, "Wait. Cindy. Do you know anything about the victims?"

She didn't answer.

"Cindy, have you heard any victim names?"

She gave me a hard look that said, *You must have mistaken me for someone who gives tips to cops.*

I sat in the car for a long moment, watching her walk ahead, thinking that this situation totally sucked. Maybe she was in the right. Or maybe she just refused to understand that I couldn't give her unsubstantiated information on an investigation in progress.

Maybe Brady would cut her a break.

I grabbed my phone and I called him.

He didn't wait for me to say hello.

"There were two more hits," he said. "Both in Baltimore. Where are you, Boxer? Clapper is looking for you."

CHAPTER 94

CINDY AND HER college friend, TV reporter Lori Hines, sat up front in the KRON4 sound van.

The front seats were cramped, but the windshield gave them a wide view of the cordoned-off street and the mob of law enforcement on both sides of the tape. Inside the van, behind them, sound equipment and video monitors lined both long sides, where a half dozen video techs edited Lori's interview and maintained contact with production at the studio.

Dead ahead was the jazz center, a modern, nearly transparent corner building. The lobby and café inside it had been open to the public. Until now. The sidewalk outside the open doors was the scene of a triple homicide, a horrific crime.

Upon arrival, law enforcement, both local and FBI, had cleared the teeming lobby. The streets on both sides of the building and all access points were closed to anyone without a badge.

Lori, having squeaked inside before the police perimeter was locked down, had gone live with her report fifteen minutes ago.

By the time Cindy had arrived, police cruisers had been parked across the lanes as barricades, yellow tape and the thin blue line were in place. Cindy felt damned lucky that she'd seen the KRON4 van and that Lori had invited her inside.

Now Lori's cameraman ran the unedited video for Cindy. He had captured thirty seconds of the bodies lying on the sidewalk in front of the jazz center. Cindy had seen many murder scenes, but something about the bodies lying in broad daylight on a public sidewalk was frightening to her.

In the video the camera turned to Lori, who, with her voice catching in her throat, told her audience that guitarist Neil Kreisler had been shot dead with one bullet to his head. This murder had happened just outside the entrance to the jazz center. Kreisler's two bodyguards, names still unverified, had also been brought down by single kill shots to the head.

Lori said to the camera, "There was another person in this group of musician and bodyguards, a minor who was unharmed, and in his best interests this station will not release his name. But I did speak with him before he was taken away by a police escort.

"This witness told me that he didn't see the shooter. One minute he was walking up the stairs near Kreisler. One bodyguard was in the lead. The other was bringing up the rear. According to the young man, the guard behind him was shot first. The leading guard screamed, 'Get

down,' and this young man did get down and that probably saved his life."

Lori went on to say that the witness didn't know anything
about the shootings or why the victims were killed. He had
told her that it all happened super fast, and after the first
shooting he didn't see anything because he was lying on the
pavement with his arms crossed over the back of his neck.
When it was quiet and he looked up, he realized that he was
the only survivor.

"Thank God he was spared," Lori said. "And now the investigation into this terrible crime begins."

Lori gave a hotline number and signed off.

But the Lori of right now was sitting next to Cindy, and
she told Cindy what she couldn't say on air.

"The witness is Kreisler's son, Anton. Security guards
who work for the jazz center heard the shooting, and when
it stopped, they came outside, grabbed the poor kid, and let
him call his mother. The security people saw no sign of the
shooters."

"Thanks for the guided tour," Cindy said. "It's good of you
to share."

"Happy to do it, Cindy. But a shorter version of this video
went live. Every news outlet in the country has the story,
but maybe you can get it onto your blog while it's still warm.
Don't mention the witness's name unless you can get it from
someone you love in the SFPD."

Cindy thought, *That'll be the day.*

She watched through the windshield as CSI unloaded the
halogen lights. They were still taking pictures, but soon the
ME would take the bodies away.

"I have a tidbit for you," Cindy said. "Before I left the office, I heard that two drug dealers were shot in Baltimore."

"Huh. So the war on drugs heads east."

Cindy said, "And that's not all. The Baltimore victims were shot at different times; one at around midnight, the other at about 3 a.m. Plus, those shootings didn't happen at the same time as the jazz center shootings."

"I see what you're saying. The killings weren't synchronized," Lori said. "The MO is changing. Where is Kill Shot when you really need him?"

"I've kept the porch light on," Cindy said, "but Kill Shot has gone dark. Maybe all he wanted was a platform, some limited exposure—and we gave it to him."

"Or maybe," said Lori, "he's dead."

CHAPTER 95

AFTER LEAVING LORI, Cindy drove back to the *Chronicle*, taking a few chances with the speed limit.

She parked in the garage across the street from the newspaper building, made a dash for the entrance against the light, and took the elevator to the second floor.

Once in the newsroom, she stopped at McGowan's cube and filled him in on what she'd learned from Lori.

"I saw the coverage. Pretty gory. That poor kid. I'll bet he was Kreisler's son. I predict he'll be in therapy for about forty years."

"Jeb, have you gotten anywhere with the Baltimore victims?"

"I've got one name. Robert Primo was twenty-nine, killed while walking toward a gay club called Occam's Brain. He was picked off about twenty feet from the entrance, and a bullet fragment cracked the front window. I've got pictures."

He stood beside her and held up his phone, swiped his

thumb across the screen, showing her snapshots of Primo. First one, he was with a group of people his age, and they were all laughing. Next there was a shot of Primo's body lying on the sidewalk outside the club, followed by a close-up of the crack in the front window. The last was a photo of innumerable bottles of Xanax on a tabletop in what looked to be a police station evidence room.

"Tell me this is an exclusive," Cindy said.

"Sorry, Cindy, as fantastic as I am, I got this off the net. The *Baltimore Sun* ran it. But I'll keep trying," he said. "I have faith."

Cindy said, "Hand this off to the new intern. I want you on Kreisler. Everything you can find on him, his family, his greatest hits, and if you can get the names of his body men, that would be a plus.

"If this was a Moving Targets hit, where's the drug connection? This happened in San Francisco. If we work fast, Henry will want this on the front page," she said.

Cindy went to her office and opened her computer. Her email inbox was full. She scrolled from top to bottom, hoping to see an email from Kill Shot, but he still hadn't written to her.

She opened a file and called it "Jazz Center Homicides." Her readers checked her blog several times a day. Accordingly, she started a new thread and planned to update it as news broke. At the same time, it could run as a major story on the *Chronicle*'s front page.

Cindy was off to a fast start with Lori Hines's quotes. She gave attribution to Lori and KRON4, and added incoming notes from McGowan on Neil Kreisler's career.

She asked the question, "If Kreisler's murder was part of the 'new war on drugs,' where are the drugs?"

She let the question hang and then closed the piece with her take on the triple homicide.

She wrote: "*In addition to the execution of Neil Kreisler and two men who worked for him, two men were killed in Baltimore before sunup by the same method. A precision kill shot to the head. No sign of a shooter.*

"The Chronicle *has been running biographies of the previous single-shot victims, and even when the victims were killed in different cities, the times of death were synchronized.*

"*But today's crimes differ.*

"*Item: The men killed in Baltimore were shot at approximately midnight and 3 a.m. The three men killed in San Francisco were executed at some time prior to the morning rush hour.*

"*Are the 'new war on drugs' snipers going rogue? Or has the original pattern changed and is now encompassing a wider area and a looser time frame? If so, what's the battle plan?*

"The San Francisco Chronicle *wants to hear from you.*"

Cindy entered her blog post, wrote a note to Tyler that she and McGowan were on the story. She copied McGowan, too. She packed up to go and was standing at the elevator when her cell phone rang.

Richie said, "You still love me?"

"Why do you ask?"

"Because I love you. I want to take you out to dinner tonight. I need your company while we're both awake."

Cindy said, "Great idea. Stupendous."

The elevator doors opened and Cindy left the building, looking forward to seeing Richie over a restaurant dinner.

She crossed Mission to the garage, walked down the ramp to her spot, and was unlocking her car when Jeb McGowan appeared.

"Everything okay, Cindy?"

"I'm absolutely fine. What about you?" she said.

She organized her bags and the radio on the passenger seat and closed the door. She was walking around the back of her car to the driver's side when McGowan blocked her path.

"What's this?" she said.

McGowan put his hand behind Cindy's neck and pulled her toward him. Then he kissed her.

Cindy could not believe what had happened, but she had to believe it. McGowan had put his lips on hers and stuck his tongue into her mouth, and now he was grinning at her.

He said, "Wow, I've been waiting a long time to do that. Admit it, Cindy. You liked it."

"Let me be clear. If you ever do that again," Cindy hissed, "I will have you fired."

"I don't know what you're talking about," said McGowan. "Are you imagining things, Cindy? Because absolutely nothing happened."

CHAPTER 96

WHEN YUKI OPENED her eyes that morning, she knew that the day she'd been dreading had arrived.

She was still conflicted. The kid was a patsy. But as Parisi had told her at the top of his lungs, it didn't matter what she felt. She had a job to do. *A good prosecutor can prosecute anyone.* And since the defendant had refused to cooperate, she couldn't do anything for him.

So in two hours Yuki would drop the hammer on Clay Warren.

Careful not to wake Brady, Yuki showered, blew out her hair, dressed in a classic blue suit, and stepped into her high-heeled blue suede shoes.

There was a note on the table in the foyer next to her keys that read, "XXX ♥ B." She smiled, pressed her lips to the back of the note, and after returning the lipstick kiss to the table, Yuki gathered her stuff and drove to the Hall.

During the drive Yuki reviewed her prep for the trial.

She'd rehearsed her opening and saw no holes in her

argument. She'd prepared her witness and set up the props, and she liked the jury. And she thought about opposing counsel, her friend Zac Jordan.

Yuki had worked pro bono with Zac at the Defense League and learned a lot from him. He was smart, had a passion for the underdog, and had a gift for connecting with a jury. She'd also learned that Zac lacked a killer instinct.

But even if he sprinkled broken glass on his cereal, his teenage client was facing grand theft auto, possession of a firearm, and holding a kilo of an illegal substance with intent to distribute—to name three.

The really bad news for Clay Warren was that even if he hadn't stolen the car, owned the gun, or possessed the drugs, a cop had been killed during the commission of those felonies. That made Clay just as guilty as the guy in the passenger seat.

The charge was felony murder, and the penalty was twenty-five to life. Yuki had gone way out on a very weak limb for Clay, but her sympathy for him had been wasted.

The kid had brought the hammer down on himself.

Minutes after leaving her car at the All-Day lot across from the Hall, Yuki reached her office with time to spare.

Danusa Freire a recent graduate of Berkeley Law and her second chair, popped out of her cubicle and followed Yuki to her desk.

"Hey, Danusa Anything happening that I need to know?"

Danusa said, "No calls, no walk-ins, and no semaphore signals from sinking ships. I checked your mail ten minutes ago, and there was nothing regarding Clay Warren."

She placed the thick folder of highlighted deposition

transcripts and Yuki's opening statement on her desk and handed her a container of milky coffee.

The young lawyer said, "I just have to tell you, I'm pretty excited. I wish my parents could see this trial."

Yuki smiled at her number two. She sipped coffee without getting any on her suit and picked up the folder.

"Ready, steady, go," she said.

Danusa Freire locked the office door behind them.

CHAPTER 97

YUKI AND DANUSA left the DA's offices and walked fifty yards along the corridor, their heels clacking in time against the terrazzo floor.

Yuki felt her pulse speed up as a court officer opened the door to 6A, and she and her deputy entered the small, oak-paneled courtroom. The gallery was filling as they walked down the center aisle, through the gate, and took their seats at the prosecution table.

Yuki looked across the aisle to where Clay Warren sat beside Zac Jordan at the defense table.

Zac was going over his notes, and Clay—Clay looked as he had the last few times Yuki had met with him. His expression was fixed and hard, wordlessly expressing his decision not to defend himself.

Yuki turned another ninety degrees to check out the spectators. Clay's mother was watching her with drill-bit eyes, boring holes through Yuki. Yuki dipped her head in respect and then took in the rest of the gallery and got an entirely different feeling. Wall-to-wall cops gave her nods of encouragement.

Yuki had just settled back into her seat when Judge Steven Rabinowitz entered the courtroom through his private door behind the bench. Yuki had tried two cases before Rabinowitz. She'd found him fair and even-tempered. You couldn't ask for better than that.

The bailiff stood at the base of the bench and called, "All rise"—and all did.

Rabinowitz took his chair, which was positioned between the Stars and Stripes and the flag of the great state of California. The legal teams and spectators also took their seats with a considerable amount of shuffling and whispering.

The judge exchanged a few words with his clerk and the bailiff. Someone sneezed. A cell phone tinkled a little tune. Rabinowitz said, "No phones. Are we clear? Turn 'em off."

Yuki felt like a young racehorse inside the gate waiting for the bell and the release. She was ready for this trial, prepared and involved and sharp. The jury filed in and took their seats. The bailiff read out the case number and announced that Judge Steven Rabinowitz was presiding.

The judge brought his gavel down, calling the court to order, and greeted the jury. As he began his instructions to them, Yuki thought this case was hers to win.

She would make sure that happened.

CHAPTER 98

JOE WOKE TO morning light slashing across his face, the sheets twisted around his ankles, and the rumbling of Dave's chair rolling across the rough-hewn boards on the floor below. He remembered now, the late-night call from Dave, the drive to Napa.

He heard Dave talking with Jeff the Chef clearly enough to get the gist. They were insulting each other like old friends, going over the menu and getting ready for the day.

Joe had a job, too. Or call it a moral obligation. All he had to do was solve the mystery of Ray Channing's suspicious death without having a badge or any authority at all.

Joe no longer believed that Dave had killed his father.

But he had become convinced that some of Dr. Perkins's hospitalized patients had been murdered. That wasn't enough to bring in the law. There had to be a viable *suspect*. And there had to be *evidence*.

Currently, he didn't even have a *theory*.

Joe kicked off the sheets and thought about the people

he had met over the last couple of weeks: Dr. Perkins himself; Ted Scislowski, who'd slept in the bed next to Ray, who'd been wheeled out of the room, his face covered with a sheet.

He thought about meetings with three of the people who'd lost loved ones—all Perkins's patients—his interviews with night-shift nurses and four people who worked in the winery itself, including the elderly handyman who brought his dogs with him in his truck when he mowed the lawn.

Motive, anyone?

One person rose to the surface of Joe's mind. Not as a suspect but because he felt he hadn't given the man enough attention, hadn't asked enough questions.

Johann Archer, the writer who'd lost his thirty-eight-year-old fiancée, Tansy Mallory, and had written a touching tribute to her in *Great Grapes*. Tansy had been a fit long-distance runner and had shown no signs of cardiovascular disease.

Dr. Daniel Perkins had been the attending doctor the day Tansy Mallory was brought in to Saint John's small ER. The surgeon had treated her for heat exhaustion and ordered her kept overnight for observation. Typical recovery time should have been a matter of hours, but Tansy had died overnight.

What distinguished Tansy from the other two cases was her survivor's take on her death. Archer believed Perkins had killed Tansy through either neglect or intent. Joe hadn't bought the murder plot at that time, but now? Dave Channing and Johann Archer had never met, but Dave had gotten Johann's contact info, and Joe had left him a voice mail last week.

Joe sat up, retrieved his phone from the floor near the bed, and tapped in Archer's number.

"Yes?"

"Johann. It's Joe Molinari. I called you last week? Sorry to call again so early. Do you have time to see me? I'd like to get your thoughts about suspicious deaths at Saint John's Hospital."

"Good. I'm having plenty of them," said Archer. "Something—or rather *someone*—occurred to me, and it might be the guilty party. I need to tell you.

"And I mean you, Joe, specifically."

CHAPTER 99

THE COURTROOM WAS small enough for Yuki to be heard from the counsel table, but she wanted to speak with the jurors face-to-face.

She left her notes on the table, crossed the well to the jury box, introduced herself, and thanked the jurors for serving.

"As an assistant district attorney," she said, "I work for the people of San Francisco. It's my job to tell you about the case you will be deciding and why the defendant has been charged.

"To start, please picture this: At 11:27 on March 15, Officer Todd Morton and his partner, Officer William Scarborough, are driving in the Sunset District on Nineteenth Avenue when a white Chevy Impala speeds through a red light at the intersection of Nineteenth and Taraval.

"Officer Scarborough is at the wheel, and Officer Morton is in the passenger seat. Morton turns on the flashers and sirens, and Scarborough follows the Chevy. Normally, the driver sees the lights and hears the sirens and pulls over.

"But the Chevy's driver speeds up.

"Officer Morton calls it in, and the police dispatcher tells him that the vehicle in question has been reported stolen. Now the Chevy hits Highway 1 South at ninety-plus miles an hour. Cars are going off the road as they see this car running up on them.

"But there is something the driver of the Chevy doesn't expect. The vehicle in front of him doesn't have enough pickup to get out of his way, and now the Chevy is boxed in by the slow-moving car ahead of him and cars streaming past him on both sides.

"Officer Scarborough pulls into the fast lane and makes a hard right in front of the Chevy, road-blocking the lane. The Chevy brakes but skids, hitting the rear compartment of the squad car. Fenders bend, drivers lean on their horns. A simple traffic stop has gone all to hell."

Leaving that image with the jury, Yuki walked back to her table and returned with a large foam-core board. She turned it so that the jurors could see the attached photos of the white Chevy in various degrees of speeding ahead and burning rubber as it was brought to a halt by the patrol car.

Yuki told the jury, "Officer Scarborough will take us through the entire fifteen-second video, but for now we've cut and pasted the relevant frames. See here. This is Officer Morton. He has gotten out of his cruiser with his gun drawn. Officer Scarborough is still behind the wheel. He's calling for backup and making sure that the dash cam is working."

Yuki continued laying out the sequence of events.

"Everything is happening very fast," she said. "The time

between when Officer Morton gets out of the cruiser to approach the Chevy and when he is shot measures only fifteen seconds.

"In that brief gasp a good man, a public servant doing his job, dies. His wife becomes a widow, and his three children, fatherless. And the man who shoots him gets away. The defendant knows the shooter's identity."

Yuki let that last sentence hang in the air.

"But he's not talking."

CHAPTER 100

YUKI WALKED ALONG the rail fronting the jury box, letting the jurors count off the seconds.

Then she asked, "How does the killer get away?

"In the few seconds following the crash and the shooting, the gunman makes a plan. Traffic is now crawling with rubberneckers. The man with the gun steps into the far-right lane, where the driver of a RAV4 is slowing for the accident. The gunman points his weapon at the driver's open window and shouts, 'Get out of the car.'

"The driver of the RAV4 is Mr. Jonas Hunt, seventy years old, and he tells Officer Scarborough later on that he wanted to see seventy-one. He complies with the shooter, gets out of his car. The motor is running. The shooter gets into the car, makes a U-turn across a break in the median strip, avoiding the clotted traffic, and makes his escape.

"The cruiser's dash cam has recorded the Chevy's plate number, and although every law enforcement officer in California looks for the car, they can't find it. The RAV4 is found two days later, abandoned in a junkyard. Mr. Hunt cannot describe the carjacker except to say that he was either white or Hispanic and frightening. Mr. Hunt didn't want to look at his face, and so his description is vague. The carjacker wore gloves, and to date his prints have not been retrieved. The dash-cam view of the shooter is grainy and doesn't ring any bells with law enforcement software.

"Officer Scarborough can't identify the shooter, either. He tried. He looked at mug shots and he spoke with a police artist, but he couldn't make a positive ID. He saw the man from a distance, then he saw him at an angle when he shot Officer Morton, and then when the killer hijacked Mr. Hunt's car, Officer Scarborough saw him with his back turned.

"But one person does know the shooter's identity.

"The driver of the stolen white Chevy at the center of this true story. Officer Scarborough arrests him, and after being futilely interrogated, he is incarcerated in the men's jail. Right now he's sitting with his attorney at the defense counsel table. His name is Clay Warren and he is the defendant."

Yuki stopped speaking for a moment and let the jurors get a good look at the teenager facing a life sentence.

Then Yuki said, "Back at the scene of the crime, Officer Scarborough attends to Officer Morton until the ambulance arrives. Sadly, Officer Morton has already passed away."

Yuki told the jurors that stealing a car is, by law, grand theft of an automobile, a felony.

She said, "The defendant may or may not have known that the car was stolen, or that the shooter had a gun, but guns, licensed or not, must be stored in the trunk or another locked box. This gun was not locked up. It was on the shooter's person. And that felony is charged against the defendant as an accomplice.

"That's not all," Yuki said. "A kilo of high-grade, unadulterated fentanyl was secreted in a suitcase in the trunk of the stolen Chevy—another felony, and another charge against the defendant. As you have seen and I have told you, a police officer making a routine traffic stop was killed during the commission of these crimes. That makes the defendant an accomplice, and just as guilty, under the law, as the shooter.

"Since Officer Morton's death, Mr. Warren has not identified his accomplice, nor has he cooperated with the police or the district attorney. Now he is left to take the weight of justice alone.

"Please find him guilty of felony murder."

CHAPTER 101

JUDGE STEVEN RABINOWITZ turned to the defense table.

"Mr. Jordan. Ready with your opening statement?"

"Yes, Your Honor."

Zac stood, patted his client on the shoulder, and stepped out into the well to address the jurors and the court.

"Your Honor, members of the jury, I'd like to tell you about Mr. Clay Warren, the unfortunate defendant who is also a victim.

"My client is an eighteen-year-old who failed to graduate from high school. Until recently he lived with his mother and twelve-year-old sister, Trina, in Crocker-Amazon, and worked a part-time job not far away at the Shell station on Alemany Boulevard. He does not know his father. His mother, who is here today, works as a housekeeper.

"Money is tight in the Warren household.

"Mr. Warren hasn't told me how he found himself driving a stolen car, running a light, crashing into a patrol car, and witnessing his passenger shoot a police officer to death.

"This young man has never before been charged with any crimes, not even for stealing an apple, before he was involved in the very serious crimes of March 15.

"So what happened on that particular day?"

Zac focused all of his attention on the jurors.

He said, "Let me offer a speculative explanation."

Yuki stole a look at Clay Warren, at his unchanged, masklike expression, then turned back to watch Zac mount his case.

"It's self-evident that the man Mr. Warren was driving in the white Chevy was dangerous," Zac said. "He had a gun, a stolen car, and a million dollars of drugs in the trunk. He killed a police officer in cold blood. Mr. Warren was arrested as an accomplice. I'm going to add 'unwitting.' That he was an unwitting accomplice, and he may have been forced to take part in this criminal endeavor.

"After his arrest my client was locked up in the general population of old-time jail in the Hall of Justice. He recently attempted suicide by hanging. Despite being placed under observation, within days he was attacked by one or more prisoners and stabbed repeatedly to his abdomen with a sharp implement and nearly bled to death.

"Since then Mr. Warren has been held in solitary confinement, under constant watch, so that he isn't murdered and doesn't kill himself for being victimized by the true criminal, and to the eternal grief of his family.

"One could even say that he has been punished and has paid his debt to society.

"Clay's life is now hell, and the only way out is through the good graces of the twelve men and women of this jury."

CHAPTER 102

I WAS TEXTING an apology to Claire for standing her up for yesterday's lunch, when my desk phone rang.

I snatched up the receiver.

"Boxer."

"Sergeant, it's May Hess."

May Hess is a dispatch supervisor who calls herself the Queen of the Batphone. She also works the tip line because she's good at helping people, cutting through the panic and distress.

She said, "I've got something for you, Sergeant. A tourist witnessed the shooting at the jazz center."

"What? Tell me."

"I can do better than that. I've cued up the tape. Listen here."

I heard a recorded voice over my phone.

"Police? Police?"

Hess's voice answered on the tape. "This is the police. Do you have an emergency?"

"No. It's about the shooting yesterday. At the jazz center."

"Okay. And what's your name?"

"Sharon Fogel."

"Spell it for me?"

After the caller spelled it out, Hess said, "What do you know about the shooting, Ms. Fogel?"

"I *saw* it, but I didn't *know* it. I was taking pictures. I'm from Sheboygan. Wisconsin. I'm on vacation. I was going to go to the jazz center, and I took some pictures of the building, and then those men were shot and I ran. I only realized what I had on my phone *this morning*."

"Tell me about the pictures," said Hess.

"It's two pictures, actually. One shows his car. The other shows *him*."

I heard the caller panting, and I was panting a bit myself. Had Sharon Fogel really snapped a photo of the killer?

Hess said, "Ms. Fogel, give me your address. I'll have a police officer come by and get your statement and take a look at the photos while she's there."

I heard a man's voice speaking in Sharon Fogel's room.

Fogel's voice was muffled. I thought she was saying, "Just a minute." Then she was back on the line.

"My husband wants me to stay out of this."

"Ms. Fogel, you won't be involved in any way—"

"I can't."

"You may have something of real value to the ongoing investigation. What about this? Send the pictures to me. I'll forward them to the homicide team."

"Give me your email address," said Fogel.

The voice of the man speaking in Fogel's room was

growing louder. "You've always got to be the star of the show, Sharon."

"Have you got them?" Fogel asked Hess.

"Let me open your email...."

I heard the clatter of the phone hitting the floor. Then the click of the phone disconnecting. The taped call was over, but Hess was there.

"Lindsay. Did you hear all of that?"

I said, "Maybe. Did you get the pictures?"

"Forwarding them to you now. She's staying at the Hilton. I have her cell number."

I told Hess, "Great job."

And then I waited for Hess's email to hit my inbox.

CHAPTER 103

CONKLIN LOOKED OVER the top of his computer and asked, "What was that all about?"

"Roll your chair over."

He pulled his chair around to my desk so that he could see my monitor.

I said, "Hotline thinks we might have a witness to the jazz center shootings. And…the witness sent pictures."

"Let's see."

I opened the email, daring to hope.

The first photo was a glamour shot of the jazz center, the corner view of the building's expanse of glass windows sparkling in morning sunlight. The street was quiet. There was some traffic at the intersection, but this shot had clearly been taken before three people, a semi-well-known guitarist and his two bodyguards, were picked off one shot at a time.

Fogel had said she'd taken a picture of the car.

In the lower right corner of the photo, on the opposite side of the street from the jazz center, was a black Ford Taurus.

I said, "The witness said that the gunman fired from inside a car. Maybe this one. I can read, uh, four numbers on the tag."

"Not a bad line of sight from the car to the entrance of the building."

There were a couple of other cars parked in front of the Taurus, all of which would have to be checked out.

I jotted down the tag numbers as Conklin said, "I'm ready for the next one."

I clicked on the next picture. It had been shot only a few seconds after the first. It showed a man in the driver's seat of the Taurus, his gloved hand on the window frame, pulling the door closed.

"Uh-oh," I said. "So much for his prints."

My partner adjusted the monitor so it faced him square on. "Am I hallucinating? Or is that Barkley without the beard?"

I enlarged the man's face so that it took up most of the screen, but the more enlarged I made it, the more his features went out of focus. I had seen photos of Barkley with and without the beard. But I couldn't be sure that this was him.

I said, "I'll find Stempien. You run the plates."

I called Stempien, but he didn't pick up. It was twenty after twelve. Lunch hour. When I ate out close to the Hall, my cheap eatery of choice was MacBain's. Was it Stempien's go-to joint, too?

Conklin looked up from his computer and said, "The Taurus was reported stolen thirty-six hours ago."

"Could be Barkley stole it before the shooting and still has it," I said, trying out a theory. "Or, Richie. He could've left the car after the shooting and walked off the scene. The car could be right where it was yesterday. The street was closed all day for CSI and until late last night."

"I'll go take a look," he said. "You find Stempien."

I transferred the two pictures to a flash drive and went across the street to MacBain's.

The place was crowded. It always was at lunchtime. True detective that I am, I spotted Stempien at a table by himself, a plate of steak fries, a burger, and an iPad Pro in front of him. I navigated a path through the congested bar and grill, and when our FBI computer guru looked up, I smiled and said, "May I join you?"

He said, "Absolutely," but his look told me that he was checking out my face.

"Fistfight," I said.

"Whoa. You okay?"

"Never better," I said.

Syd came to the table and I ordered what Stempien was having. Once she'd departed, I held up the thumb drive and said, "Mike. You feeling heroic today?"

"Love to be a hero. How can I help?"

"I brought you a snapshot. Can you look and tell me if it's Barkley? If you're not sure, you have to run it through your DeepFace recognition program. ASAP."

"What you call ASAP is what I call normal. As if I've

heard anyone in the past five years say, 'Mike. Take your time.' And I've been waiting."

I laughed. Stempien pushed his plate aside and plugged my thumb drive into his tablet. He stared at his device. He finger-swiped and pressed buttons, but he didn't speak.

I don't think I breathed as I watched him work.

CHAPTER 104

THE JUDGE ASKED Yuki to call her first witness.

She called Officer William Scarborough, and once he'd been sworn in, Yuki told the jury that the witness would run the video and explain what had happened at each moment in time.

Yuki asked the court officer to dim the lights, and then Officer Scarborough pointed the remote at the laptop downloading the digital recording from the cloud.

He said, "First we see the Chevy speeding through the light, and we take off after him."

He stopped the video as the Chevy slowed.

"What's happening here is that the driver is going ninety, and that green minivan in front of him is full of kids and going about forty. For all the horn blowing, the van doesn't speed up."

Scarborough started the film again.

"Now the Chevy is forced to slow down. The van is

crawling in front of him and traffic is flowing on his right and left sides. Here's where it all goes down. I pull into the traffic on the left, speed ahead, and see daylight between the back of the van and front of the Chevy."

Scarborough paused the video to make sure the jurors got a fix on the next move.

Scarborough said, "I make a hard right in front of the Chevy. It's a tight squeeze, but I'm just trying to stop the guy. He T-bones our cruiser, hitting in the rear compartment, and we all come to a stop."

Scarborough explained the action in the last part of the video.

"That's Officer Morton walking over to the driver's side of the Chevy, ordering the driver to step out of the car. But what Morton can't see is that the passenger door opens and a tall man in black clothes gets out.

"I can't see his face," Scarborough said. "I've watched this video so many times, but the crash put our car at an angle to the Chevy, and this guy walks out of the shot. I've got less than a second of his profile. He resembles a dangerous criminal I've seen on FBI posters, but 'resemble' isn't enough for a positive ID."

Scarborough's voice cracked. He cleared his throat and let the video roll.

"He walks around the Chevy to where Todd Morton is standing with his back to him, talking to the driver.

"Here. It's painful to watch. The gunman opens up on Todd. He goes down, and then the son of a bitch fires at the cruiser. At me.

"The dash cam catches me as I get out of the cruiser and

go toward Todd, and I'm calling for an ambulance and traffic is going nuts, and by then the shooter has evicted the old man from his RAV4 and takes off."

Scarborough hit Pause again and said, "At this point Clay Warren gets out of the Chevy with his hands up, and I direct him to put his hands on the roof and not to move. I cuff him. Pat him down. He wasn't armed. The ambulance arrived fast, but Todd was dead from the time he hit the ground."

Yuki asked for the lights to go on. Several people in the gallery were crying, and one person left her seat and pushed open the door.

Yuki said, "I know everyone here feels for you and Todd Morton's family. What can you tell us about your late partner?"

Scarborough sighed and spoke for several emotional moments about Morton, lauding him and stating that neither of them had ever been involved in a shooting before.

"You said you couldn't identify the shooter?"

"His features are regular. He wore sunglasses, and his jacket had a high collar. Mostly, he was on the move, standing away from me or half away from me, and then he was shooting at me. Things were happening fast."

Judge Rabinowitz asked defense counsel if he had any questions for the officer, and Zac Jordan said that he did not. Yuki thanked Officer Scarborough and asked him to step down.

Rabinowitz said, "Ms. Castellano. Please call your next witness."

"We have no other witnesses, Your Honor."

"Mr. Jordan?"

"I have a character witness, Your Honor."

"In that case, let's take a brief recess…uh, a half hour. And then after your witness, Counselor, we'll hear your closing arguments."

CHAPTER 105

I SNATCHED UP the receiver of my ringing phone.

Conklin said, "I'm on Fell Street outside the entrance to the jazz center. You're right again, Boxer."

"We got a break?"

"Black Taurus with a one-eighty-degree view of the entrance to the jazz center and a surprise inside the car."

"Don't make me beg."

"Try not to take all the fun out of this."

"Fine. Pleeease, Richie. Tell me."

"Good enough. I found a shell casing under the gas pedal. I'll stay here until CSI comes with the flatbed. A uni is taking tag numbers up and down the street."

"Good work, Rich."

As I waited impatiently for my partner to return, I looked for Brady. He wasn't in the bullpen. He wasn't in Jacobi's old office on five. His assistant told me he was in a meeting out of the office. And then he walked through the squad room door.

"I was with the ME," Brady said, speaking of Claire's stand-in. "Where's Conklin?"

"Right here," he said, coming through the gate.

Brady said, "Follow me."

Once we were seated in his office, Brady said, "Close the door, will ya?"

Conklin reached behind him and swung it shut.

I was dying to start the meeting with what we knew. A witness to the massacre at the jazz center had come forward. She had taken pictures of the probable shooter. The photo had been vetted by Stempien, who had stated with 95 percent certainty that the man in the picture was Barkley. Conklin had found a shell casing that had gone with the car back to the lab, and the odds were good that it would match the caliber of the rounds in the three dead men.

We'd need prints on Barkley's gun to put these pieces together, but we knew more now than when I woke up this morning.

My gut told me that Barkley was the jazz center killer.

We needed to find him, alive and willing to talk, and we had something to trade. The release of Randi White Barkley.

Brady's expression told me that he had something big to say, so I listened.

"Northern Station got IDs on Kreisler's bodyguards. The one who was walking in front of Kreisler was Bernie Quant, a well-known body man, freelanced for celebrities up and down the coast. The other one is the prize. Name is Antoine Castro, number three on the FBI's Ten Most Wanted."

"*Antoine Castro?* Are you sure?"

Brady passed me Castro's jacket. I saw his mug shot and

his morgue shot dated today. They were a match to his photo on the FBI's Ten Most Wanted bulletin. Also in his jacket was a long list of prior offenses, convictions he'd dodged because of lack of evidence, and the big one: a bank heist in Seattle. Four people died. The gang fled. A survivor identified Castro, absolutely, positively, and that had vaulted him onto the FBI list.

In more recent news, Yuki had told me that before Clay Warren went mute, he'd once mentioned Castro as Todd Morton's killer but had stopped short of positively, then backtracked, and had refused to cooperate ever since.

Now Castro was dead, and I was shocked. After the shootout on Highway 1, I had theorized that Castro had gotten a fresh horse and ridden out of town.

It seemed that he'd been in San Francisco all along.

I said, "Castro is the number one suspect in the killing of Todd Morton. Yuki is trying the kid Castro left twisting in the wind. Brady, don't you and Yuki talk about your cases at home?"

"She never mentioned his name," Brady said.

I said, "Warren is on trial right now. With Castro dead, maybe he'll talk about him, his drug operation, where he lived, you know what I'm saying, Brady? Make himself useful in exchange for a deal."

"Go," he said.

I left the office at a fast clip, leaving Conklin to watch Brady's face when he told him that we had a phone shot of Leonard Barkley getting into a stolen car outside the jazz center, where three people, including Castro, had been killed.

For Clay Warren, Castro's death might be the best thing that could have happened to him.

I ran to the courtroom.

I had to find Yuki before the jury came back with a verdict.

CHAPTER 106

DAVE HAD PARKED his van in the medical center parking lot.

He had reclined the seat back a few degrees so that he could watch the lot and also see Dr. Perkins's second-floor office. At 4 p.m. on the nose Perkins left the building, got into his car, and drove away.

The open bottle of wine rested between Dave's thighs. He lifted it, took a couple of pills along with some fine Channing Cabernet, and waited for his pulse to slow.

Then he made a phone call to the doctor's office.

He recognized her voice.

"Nurse...Atkins?"

"Yes. To whom am I speaking?"

"Uh. It's Dave. Channing."

"What do you want, jackass?"

His words were coming slowly. He took long breaths and exhaled deeply. He said, "I came to, uh, bring something for, uh, the doctor."

"He just left," she snapped. "Don't call here again."

Before she hung up, Dave shouted, "Wait! I brought something. An apology. And a check. For the damage…for what I did, uh, to his car."

"Leave it in the lab pickup box downstairs. I'm hanging up now."

Again Dave yelled, "Wait."

"I have things to do, Dave. You should have your lawyer send the check to the doctor, but I know what you're doing. You're trying to show remorse so that the judge doesn't put your sorry ass away for the full three years—"

"That's not…it. Listen."

"Make it quick."

"I took pills. I don't…have much…time. I wrote…an apology to you, too. And I brought you…a gift. My mother painted a…a small oil. Could be worth…more than… twenty…thousand. My way of saying…I'm sorry."

"What kind of pills did you take?"

Dave's laugh was a croak.

"I took 'em all. Sleep. Heart. BP…"

"Digoxin?"

"Yeah. If he had it, I took it. I barfed some. But he had spares. I'm drinking…Dad's best wine."

"How much of the digoxin?"

"I wasn't, uh, counting."

"How do you feel?"

"I'm…passing…out."

"Where are you?" Atkins asked.

"Out…side. The van. Channing Winery…"

Blinds were cracked open on the second floor. Then Atkins hung up the phone.

Dave watched the lights in Perkins's office go out. He took his phone out of his hip pocket and placed it on the dash. He took another swig of the wine he'd helped grow and bottle.

Then he laid his head back. Waiting. Waiting.

CHAPTER 107

I BADGED THE court officer and he opened the door to courtroom 6A.

There was standing room behind the last row of chairs in the gallery. I took a spot on the aisle and watched Zac Jordan make his closing argument. I was relieved that the case hadn't yet gone to the jury. Maybe I could speak to the judge, hand off the bombshell of Antoine Castro's death, and buy some time for Yuki and Zac to talk to the defendant.

Zac Jordan was wearing red-framed glasses, camel hair over plaid and khaki, finishing with cordovan cap-toes. It was a look that said, *I'm a good guy.* I knew he was.

I listened intently to his closing statement.

He said, "Clay Warren is guilty of trusting someone he didn't know in exchange for an adventure, a road trip, and—just guessing here—a small amount of cash. It turned out to be a catastrophic error, the biggest mistake of his young life.

"It's also possible that the man who shot Officer Morton

put a gun to Clay's head and forced him to drive. We have seen in the video that this killer also aimed his gun at Jonas Hunt and made off with his car.

"I have to answer these questions hypothetically because Mr. Warren won't tell me. He won't tell you, either."

Zac paced a little. His brow was furrowed, and I watched the jurors' rapt expressions as they followed him with their eyes.

Zac stopped and faced the jury, saying, "But when he was first arrested, Clay thought he might know who'd convinced him or forced him or paid him to get into the car. He mentioned the name of a notorious criminal, but he said that he couldn't make a 100 percent ID. And now I know why he wouldn't cooperate or help himself. He was afraid of retribution—and he got it. He was brutally attacked in jail, stabbed multiple times in the gut, and came this close to dying.

"You heard Ridley Sierra, Clay's best friend since grade school, swear under oath that in his opinion Clay is naive and younger than his years. He described Clay as 'gullible.'

"I believe that Mr. Sierra is right."

My heart twisted thinking about Clay Warren, the poor dope, and I wanted to tell him, "Help is on the way."

Zac was wrapping up and time was running out. I saw where Yuki was sitting beyond the railing. I texted her, but she didn't respond. I was desperate to reach her, so I took a chance and crept up the aisle to the bar, reached over, and tapped her on the shoulder.

She spun around, annoyed, but then she read the expression on my face. She mouthed, "What's wrong?"

I stepped on some feet, bumped knees, but I got close enough to Yuki to whisper in her ear.

"Antoine Castro is dead."

She whispered back, "How do you know?"

"He's in a drawer at the ME's office."

Yuki grabbed my hand and squeezed, then stood up.

She said, "Your Honor, Mr. Jordan, I'm sorry to interrupt, but we have new information from the SFPD. If we may approach the bench?"

"This had better be good, Ms. Castellano. It had better be brilliant."

CHAPTER 108

YUKI, ZAC, AND I stood at the bench, looking up at the judge.

Yuki said just above a whisper, "Your Honor, the man who we believe killed Officer Todd Morton has been positively identified by his photo. His fingerprints on his gun matched his prints inside the Chevy and Mr. Hunt's RAV4. I would prefer you hear this information from Sergeant Boxer, who is a homicide investigator with the SFPD."

Judge Rabinowitz looked at Zac.

"Okay with you, Mr. Jordan?"

"Yes, Your Honor."

He said, "If we were on a TV show, I would say, 'This is highly irregular.'"

Irregular or not, the judge called court into recess, and Yuki, Zac, and I followed the judge into his private chambers. He didn't ask us to sit, so we stood around his desk.

Judge Rabinowitz said, "What can you tell me about this individual, Sergeant?"

I said, "The man we believe was the passenger in the stolen white Chevy, the one who shot officer Morton, is a drug dealer by the name of Antoine Castro."

"You have him in custody?"

"He was shot dead yesterday, Your Honor."

"You say the man suspected of shooting Officer Morton is dead?" Rabinowitz said. "And what do you infer from that, Mr. Jordan?"

Zac Jordan said, "As I've told the court, Clay Warren was terrified that the shooter would have him killed or harm his family. Absent the immediate threat, my client may cooperate with the DA. If he tells what he knows about the drugs in the car, if had a working relationship with Castro, we may be able to roll up some major criminal activity."

"Lot of ifs and maybes," Rabinowitz said.

Zac added, "We need a little time, Your Honor. The defense requests a continuance."

"This is highly irregular," said the judge. "But you've got until one week from today."

CHAPTER 109

LEONARD BARKLEY KNOCKED on the back door of a small brown stucco house on Thornton Avenue, two doors down from the nearly identical house where he'd lived with Randi for four years.

His neighbor, friend, and coconspirator, Marty Floyd, opened the door and gave Barkley a wide smile.

"I was worried about you, man," said Floyd. "I never saw so many cop cars as was on TV yesterday. Hey. I've got pork chops and potatoes still hot. Sound good?"

"Fantastic. Got milk?"

"Sure do. And I set up the game. Maybe we can go a few rounds."

"I've walked miles," said Barkley. "I need to wash up, change out of these clothes. And no kidding, I need to sleep."

"Eat first. Shower later. Sleep when you're dead. Sounds like a T-shirt slogan, doesn't it?"

Barkley laughed. He hadn't eaten since yesterday morning. He couldn't remember when he'd last laughed.

"You win, Marty. Eat first."

Marty Floyd—transit cop, political junkie, and full-ranking member of Moving Targets—carefully placed a heaping plate of food in front of his friend Barkley and sat down across from him at the kitchen table.

"Barko," he said. "You're a folk hero. There's going to be ballads written about you someday. How'd it go down?"

Barkley put his phone down next to his plate. A clamshell burner. He sawed off a hunk of pork chop with a steak knife.

"Eat first," he said. "Then talk."

Floyd laughed, got up, and poured Barkley a glass of milk.

Five blocks away Randi White Barkley was riding inside a squad car with her minder, Officer Carol Ma Fullerton.

The dog had been left behind, because as Randi had told Fullerton, she just needed to pick up her electric toothbrush, her own pillows, a box of dog treats, a phone charger, and her personal massager, none of which she'd taken when the police kidnapped her.

Fullerton found Randi quite amusing. She pulled up to the Barkley house on Thornton near the junction with Apollo and parked in the short driveway.

She said, "We should hurry."

"I told you, Officer. Carol. This'll take two minutes. Just wait for me."

"You're in custody, dear," said Fullerton. "Besides, I'm coming too."

"Suit yourself," said Randi, as if she had a choice.

She walked up the three wooden steps to her door, cautioning herself not to look at Marty's house two doors down, where a kerchief had been tied to his car antenna, signaling her that Barkley was there.

The house key was in her hand when she heard Marty Floyd call out to her across two patchy front yards.

"Randi, how's it going?"

"Good, Marty. I have company."

"Yeah, I see. You look rested."

"Later, buddy. Be good," she called out.

Feeling nervous because Leonard was so close and knowing that she wouldn't get to see him, Randi opened the front door.

"Home sweet home," she said without enthusiasm.

Then she went inside with her jailer.

CHAPTER 110

THE *CHRONICLE'S* CITY room was loud and busy, everyone bending their heads over their computers, working toward a six o'clock closing.

Jeb McGowan knocked on the glass wall of Henry Tyler's office, and Tyler motioned him in.

"Sir, I need a minute."

"Anytime. Take a seat."

McGowan chose to stand.

"Mr. Tyler, something happened and I have to tell you about it."

"Go ahead, Jeb. And for Christ's sake, sit down."

Jeb sat on the edge of the leather sofa facing Tyler's desk. He said, "I don't know how to say this."

"Speak, Jeb. Out with it."

"Yes, sir. This is it. Cindy ambushed me in the garage. She kissed me, and clearly she wants more. It's classic sexual harassment, Mr. Tyler. She sees my potential. She wants to sideline the competition."

Tyler picked up his desk phone and called Cindy. "I've got a fire in my office. Can you come down?"

Cindy told him she'd be right there.

She saved her file and, skirting the center of the city room, took the perimeter route, the long way around to Henry's office. His door was open, and after knocking, she went right in.

"Where's the fire?" she asked Tyler.

She saw McGowan sitting on the edge of the sofa but didn't acknowledge him. She sat in the side chair next to her publisher and editor's desk.

"Jeb?" said Tyler. "Tell Cindy what you told me."

McGowan, now red faced, gutted it out.

"You *know* where the fire is, Cindy. I told Mr. Tyler about those unwanted advances you made in the garage, and since you're technically my superior, that's sexual harassment."

Tyler asked, "Cindy? What happened?"

"He sneaked up on me, Henry. He grabbed the back of my neck, so that I couldn't pull away, and stuck his tongue in my mouth. He asked me if I liked it. I told him if he ever did that again, I'd get him fired."

Henry Tyler picked up the phone and punched in some numbers, and when the call was answered, he said, "Marie, Mr. McGowan is leaving our employ. Please do the paperwork. Say his job was downgraded and filled from within. Send security to the city room to take his ID, watch him pack up, and escort him out of the building. Thank you."

Tyler put the receiver down hard and turned back to McGowan.

"Jeb. You're fired. I'm sorry it didn't work out. If it gets back to me that you're bad-mouthing Cindy or me or the *Chronicle*, I'll return the favor. Bookkeeping will direct-deposit your check through the end of the pay period. But I want you out of here. Now."

CHAPTER 111

DAVE WAS DOZING when the side door of the van slid open.

Nurse Carolee Atkins stepped up and sat heavily in the passenger seat. She shook his arm roughly to wake him up.

Dave pressed the button that raised his chair back into an upright position.

"Hi. Nurse Atkins...thanks...for coming."

"What is it that you want, exactly?"

He pointed and said, "Glove...compartment."

Atkins opened the glove box and took out three manila envelopes, one marked with her name, one with Perkins's name. The third one read, "Last Will and Testament."

"Where's the painting you were talking about?" she asked.

"Cargo...compartment. I...crated it up for you. Wrote your name..."

He yawned widely and left the sentence unfinished.

"Dave. Is the cargo compartment open?"

"You mind?" he said, gasping. "Talking to me? My last, uh, day."

Atkins sighed. "Okay, but I have guests coming for dinner, so let's keep it short. What do you want to talk about?"

"Tell me about…Ray. Something you liked. Closing…my eyes. Tell…me."

Atkins said, "I liked your father, a damned sight more than I like you. One time I couldn't leave for lunch because we were shorthanded. He went out and got me a sandwich. And pickles."

Dave Channing was sleeping deeply. Whatever he'd taken—a cocktail of heart medication, blood pressure medication, diazepam, digoxin, which alone could have killed him, and what looked like half a bottle of wine—was shutting him down.

"Dave?"

He groaned.

Atkins opened the envelopes. Yes, there was a check for the doctor, ten thousand dollars. She read the apology from Dave to Dr. Perkins, and it sounded sincere. He said that he'd lost his mind in grief. He hoped the money would cover the cost of repainting the car. He was very sorry for being such a pain in the ass and asked the doctor to please forgive him.

Dave tried to speak.

"What is it, Dave?"

"Pain."

"Sorry. If you'd asked me to help you out, you wouldn't have felt a thing."

"Help me…now."

Atkins ignored him. She lifted the envelope with the words "Last Will and Testament" written on the front. She opened the envelope, took out a piece of typed paper, and started to read. It was a long narrative in which Dave thanked all of his online friends and left his paltry possessions to the staff and the money from the sale of the winery to a children's charity that specialized in helping kids with disabilities. The document had been signed and witnessed by a Jeff Cruz. Nice.

She'd saved the envelope addressed to her for last.

Dear Nurse Atkins,

I apologize for being very disrespectful and making your job harder. I know you did your best for my father, and I'm indebted to you. I've left you a painting my mother named *The Sun Also Rises*, after an Ernest Hemingway novel. It was her favorite painting and all I have to give you. Peace and light.

Good-bye,
Dave Channing

The letter was also signed and witnessed by the same Jeff Cruz.

Atkins knew what Nancy Channing paintings were worth because Dr. Perkins had one. Now she'd have one, too.

Dave sputtered, then asked haltingly, "Was Dad...in pain?"

Atkins sighed. "Yes, yes, he was in pain. I only help the ones who are in pain."

"How?" Dave asked. "How do you...help?"

She said, "Dave, don't bother yourself with details. He wasn't in pain. Like you are. Okay?"

"I'm going...now. For God's sake. Help."

He bent over and, grimacing, wrapped his arms tightly across his abdomen.

"Your father had been sedated, Dave. They're all sedated. I put a little something in the drip line. They're already asleep and they're asleep when they die. Ray felt nothing. He didn't have to suffer like you."

Dave looked up at the tall woman with the cinnamon-colored hair. He could see her hard eyes staring down at him.

"You do that. For them?"

She sighed in disgust, couldn't wait to get away from him.

"I'm a helper. Someone has to do it, and I know how." She clucked her tongue, as if saying, *What a shame you took this into your own hands.*

Then she put her hand on his knee.

"It will be all over soon, Dave. Nothing will bother you again."

CHAPTER 112

NURSE ATKINS LIFTED the half bottle of wine from between Dave's atrophied legs and took a couple of swallows.

It was pretty good. She drank some more and put the rest of the bottle back where she'd found it. Dave Channing was still breathing, but barely. He was wearing a long-sleeved shirt with buttoned cuffs and a turtleneck underneath.

She managed to get a couple of fingers against his wrist. His pulse was slow. His breathing was shallow. She knew what dying looked like. Dave Channing was on his way out.

She said, "I'm getting the painting now, Dave. And thanks for that. I forgive your jackassery. Have a good trip."

Atkins got out of the passenger seat and walked around to the rear doors of the panel truck, hoping to find them unlocked. They were.

She felt a little dizzy as she twisted the handle, pulling the doors open. That was from the wine. She focused on a pile of quilted mover's blankets on the floor of the cargo compartment. She didn't see a crate or a mailing tube or any kind of box at all.

Had Dave's last act been to prank her?

She got into the rear compartment on her hands and knees and felt along the back wall. Nothing. That son of a bitch. She backed out of the van, cursing. Had he forgotten to put the crate in the van? Or had he been so stoned he couldn't lift it?

Getting out of the van was proving to be harder than getting in. There was no light back there, and now she was feeling nauseous. She'd left the papers in the front seat. She had to get them. She carefully backed out of the rear compartment, made for the front door, passenger side—and gasped. Something hard had poked her in the back and was pressing against her spine.

It could only be a gun.

A man's voice said, "Put your hands behind you, Ms. Atkins. I'm taking you into custody."

She recognized the voice but still turned her head to check. It was Dave's friend. Joe something. He was strong. A former football player. She couldn't outrun him, but maybe she could talk him down.

"Dave said he left something for me in the back. You should call an ambulance. He took all of his father's pills. I wanted to call 911, but he wouldn't let me."

Atkins continued to look at the man who was threatening her with a gun. "I've done nothing wrong. You'll see the papers. Dave decided to commit suicide. He wrote it all down."

Carolee Atkins planned her next move. She would leave

the papers and just start walking toward the office. It was only thirty yards to the door. Her key card was in her bag inside the van, but people leaving the building would let her in. Even now the parking lot was coming to life. The sounds of electronic locks opening. Headlights coming on. She heard the purr of a motor. She was taking a chance, but she didn't believe that this Joe guy would shoot her in the back.

She'd taken a few steps toward the medical building when Dave came around the side of the van, maneuvering his chair so that whichever way she walked, he blocked her way.

What was going on? He looked wide awake and fully cognizant. And he, too, held a gun on her. He had his phone in his lap, and he lifted it, pressed a button.

She heard her own voice saying, "Your father had been sedated, Dave. They're all sedated. I put a little something in the drip line. They're already asleep and they're asleep when they die. Ray felt nothing. He didn't have to suffer like you."

Then Dave's voice: "You do that. For them?"

"I'm a helper. Someone has to do it, and I know how."

CHAPTER 113

THE GROUND WAS swimming.

Atkins said to Dave, "What? What's in the wine?"

"Napa Valley's best Cabernet. Nothing more."

Joe Something said, "Do what I told you to do, Ms. Atkins. Put your hands behind your back. You're under arrest."

It was coming to her now. She'd been tricked. Dave had feigned his suicide, every bit of it. And now she was filled with rage. It wasn't legal to tape people without telling them.

She said to Joe, "Arresting me? By what authority, mister?"

"My authority as a citizen. It's quite legal. And if you're thinking a taped telephone conversation can't be used in court, the confession you made to Dave, in person, is allowable, and strong evidence."

Joe forced her arms back and cuffed her wrists. Then he picked her up and gently laid her in the back of the van on the nest of quilted mover's blankets.

"Next stop, police station," Dave called in to her. "We

368

can all give our statements. That goes for Mr. Archer and Mr. Scislowski, who'll meet us there. They saw and heard you in the rooms of the deceased. They know what you did."

"Don't you understand?" she shouted, her voice echoing lazily against the inside walls of the van. "I was doing a good. A good thing. I'm a helper. I was helping people."

Joe said, "You're a serial killer, Carolee. But tell your story to the police. And then you can tell it to the FBI."

He slammed the rear doors shut and locked them. Then he said to Dave, "The SFPD and the Napa sheriff have an arrangement on cases involving the DEA. He'll be handing her off to SFPD."

Dave was grinning so hard it hurt.

"My God, Joe. We *did* it. We *did* it."

"We sure did," Joe said.

The two friends grinned and exchanged a high five, a low five. The kicking from the rear of the van stopped. Joe said, "So what was in the wine?"

"Grapes. But I took a couple of Dad's pills, beta-blockers, to lower my blood pressure, slow down my heart. I needed to make her believe I was checking out. But then she got greedy for our Private Reserve Cab. She's just tipsy."

Joe and Dave laughed for a good long time. And then Dave said, "What a day. I wish I could tell my dad. He went crazy with happiness seeing the two of us together again, Joe. Have I thanked you lately?"

"Yeah. You have. And thank you, Dave."

"For what?"

"For believing in me."

CHAPTER 114

MIKE STEMPIEN WAS in his office at the Hall, remotely hacking into Randi Barkley's computer.

Randi wasn't online, but Leonard Barkley had just signed on from a new location near his house. Piggybacking onto Barkley's screen name, Stempien followed Barkley from his IP address at his new location on Thornton Avenue to an internet café in Gotland to a private home in Budapest to a travel agency in Medellín, working his way layer by layer, ever deeper into the onion layers of the dark web.

He had a pretty good idea that the final location would be Moving Targets. This time Barkley would be his unknowing tour guide.

Stempien wasn't wrong.

After virtually hopscotching around the globe, he watched as Moving Targets' front page slowly came up on his screen, like an image taking form on old-fashioned photo paper inside a tray of fixer.

In the center of the screen was the wheel of fortune. To

the left side was a map of the USA with blinking pin lights marking Detroit and Miami and San Francisco.

Stempien thought those cities were the locations of upcoming hits. "It's part of the Moving Targets program," he said. "Go time, Zero-eight-thirty."

He homed in on the winking city lights and took a series of screen shots, planning to enlarge them later. He might be able to decode names or addresses. He made a mental note that Barkley hadn't spun the wheel.

What Barkley did instead was jump into the chat room, where, using the screen name Kill Shot, he typed, *I'm here.*

Screen names joined Kill Shot in the chat room, and rolling lines of applauding emoticons, yahoos, and fireworks burst onto the screen.

Fellow players urged him to talk, virtually chanting, *Kill Shot. Kill Shot. Kill Shot.*

Tell us about it, Kill Shot. Everything.

Stempien picked up his cell phone and called Brady.

"Lieutenant, this is Mike Stempien with a red alert. I have a physical location on Barkley....Yeah. San Francisco, 430 Thornton. Right now."

CHAPTER 115

IT WAS NEARLY six in the evening when Conklin and I arrived at Silver Terrace.

A uniform standing beside his cruiser at the top of Apollo told us to park in front of the green house, one of dozens just like it, stairstepped down both sides of the sloping avenue.

Conklin drove us down the hill, passing the herd of black armored SWAT and FBI vehicles banked at the curb in front of a brown stucco house that Stempien had identified as belonging to Barkley's Moving Targets comrade Marty Floyd.

We slowed in front of the green house with an overgrown front yard and a stubby, empty driveway and parked as directed. This was the house between the Barkley and Floyd residences, and the interior was dark. The brown house to its left belonged to the Barkleys. Two unoccupied unmarked cars and a cruiser formed a barricade in front of it.

Overhead, an Eyewitness News helicopter chopped at the air, and any minute now the press would attempt to penetrate the scene. They would be barred from this section of the street, but there was every chance that Leonard Barkley would flip the table, set off explosives, and turn this porous residential neighborhood into a shooting gallery.

As I had those thoughts, a pair of black-and-white cruisers parked crosswise on the north and south ends of the 800 block, cordoning off the area, bracketing Floyd's brown house, Barkley's brown house, and the green house in between.

The stage was set.

Richie and I were there mainly to arrest Barkley, and I hoped to God that that would happen without anyone firing a shot. I had an edgy feeling, a cross between high anxiety and disbelief. We'd been looking for Barkley so intently, and he had gotten away so many times, that I could hardly accept that he was trapped, that we would be reading him his rights within minutes or hours.

As I mentally prepared for the unknowable, Conklin spoke on the phone with Paul Chi. I picked up that Chi and McNeil were inside the Barkley house with Randi and her personal cop escort, Officer Carol Ma Fullerton. That Randi and her husband were separated by one twenty-five-foot-wide front yard had to have been planned.

Conklin hung up from his call with Chi and filled me in on the consensus of the cops inside the Barkley house. Based on Randi's nothing-to-lose attitude and escape potential, she'd been locked up inside a windowless back room with cops taking shifts at the door.

It was too bad for Barkley that he'd jumped onto Marty Floyd's computer and logged on to Moving Targets. And I felt bad for Randi, pining for her husband.

But I snapped out of it.

Leonard Barkley didn't deserve sympathy.

He was the number one suspect in the high-profile killings of Paul and Ramona Baron, and the three men who'd been dropped at the jazz center like puppets with cut strings. And it was entirely possible that Barkley had also shot Roger Jennings and other San Francisco drug dealers we didn't know were his victims.

Was Barkley in charge of the entire Moving Targets operation? Was he a soldier taking orders? Could he be charged with any of these killings I had just counted up?

I brought myself back to the imminent Barkley takedown. Barkley was a dead shot, a proficient killer. His neighbor Marty Floyd was a transit cop and so had also been trained in the use of guns. I was glad to see that Brady had called in the FBI to back up our SWAT team. Commander Reg Covington had a high record of success, and he was in charge.

Conklin and I watched from our squad car. SWAT was using the hoods of their vehicles as gun braces. A BearCat ran up on Marty Floyd's lawn, and twelve men in tactical gear swarmed out. Two took positions on either side of the front door. Others took posts near the windows and at the back and side doors.

I radioed Covington.

"It's Boxer," I said. "What can you tell me?"

Covington said, "Barkley's not answering his phone. Neither is the house owner. We're warning them, then going in."

I watched from the relative safety of our squad car as Covington lifted the bullhorn. A high-pitched squeal that felt like an electric current connected every person in the unit as one.

Covington's voice boomed toward the brown house.

"Mr. Barkley, this is Commander Covington, SFPD. We don't want anyone to get hurt. You and Mr. Floyd open the door and show us your hands. Do not do anything stupid."

I watched the door, waiting for it to crack open, for Barkley to step out with his hands above his head. I could almost see him, wearing fatigues and a new beard. Could see him limping from a wartime injury. I waited to hear him say, "Don't shoot."

That's not what happened.

Someone panicked. An officer at the barricade twitched his trigger finger and fired a burst of bullets at the brown house. Automatic gunfire was returned from windows on the second floor.

Conklin and I ducked inside our vehicle as World War III broke out on Thornton Avenue.

CHAPTER 116

THE MISFIRE FROM our side was an epic error that had launched a firefight that could cost dozens of lives. It could continue until every last one of us was dead.

I clapped my hands over my ears and stayed down, actually shaking as I waited for it all to be over. During a brief break in the shooting, I lifted my head from under the dash to scope out the scene and glanced at the Barkley house, ahead and to our right.

I saw a side door open.

Randi Barkley darted out, and despite the recent gunfire, she streaked across her side yard toward the rear of the empty house armed with nothing but ragged jeans and a tank top.

She was trying to get to Barkley.

I knew that because she'd told me she and Barkley had a "pact with death" and that she expected to die with her husband—and clearly she was trying to make that dream come true.

Pointing through the windshield, I said to Conklin, "Look." The BearCat, an armored vehicle resembling a prehistoric reptile, ran up over the curb, crossing the narrow lawn between Floyd's brown house and the green one in front of our car. They were forming a barrier.

I heard Covington shout, "Hold your fire," and the shooting on both sides stopped.

Conklin was out of the car before the bullhorn's echo died. I followed. Predicting Randi's trajectory, Conklin cut her off with a well-timed tackle to her knees. Chi, McNeil, and Fullerton burst from the Barkley house and huddled around us.

In a well-practiced maneuver called a cuff-and-stuff, I got handcuffs on Randi, and Chi and McNeil grabbed her and stuffed her into the BearCat. The driver took off for the outer perimeter, where Randi would be transferred to a patrol car.

Chi was embarrassed by Randi's escape. He said, "There were no doors or windows in that effing room, Boxer."

McNeil said, "However, we didn't do a microscopic inspection of the floor."

I got it. And I didn't doubt that Barkley's entire house was swiss-cheesed with hidden shafts leading to Barkley's beaten path to the Caltrain tunnel that ran under Silver Terrace. But Randi's dash for the Floyd house hadn't done her any good. I watched as Randi, cuffed in the back of a patrol car, cleared the barricades and headed to the Hall of Justice.

I returned to our car in time to hear Covington announce over his mike, "Five seconds. On my go."

The front door split open before Covington had counted to five. The commando to the left of the door kicked it in, cracking it in half. A stout man with blood pouring down his face and arms cried out, "I give up. I give up."

The commando on his right set down his shield, grabbed the stout man's arm, and in one fluid move pulled him to the ground.

That man wasn't Barkley.

I got out of the car again and went up to Covington, who was ordering his men to get the injured man into a police car. I touched Covington's arm.

He said, "Boxer?"

"Let me talk to Barkley."

Covington reached for and opened the closest armored car door. Then he gripped my upper arms, lifted and moved all five feet ten inches of me like I was a doll, until I was behind the hardened-steel door and as shielded as much as possible from oncoming gunfire.

Then he handed me the bullhorn.

I took a breath, then spoke, my voice bouncing off the surrounding houses.

"Mr. Barkley, this is Sergeant Lindsay Boxer. I'm in contact with Randi. Give yourself up, and you can tell her good-bye. Or in three seconds SWAT command is going to cut you down and take you out of that house alive or dead."

I handed off the bullhorn to Covington.

The broken front door clattered apart, and Leonard Barkley emerged holding his hands above his head. I gave him a visual pat-down. Was he holding a weapon? A grenade? He limped out onto the front steps into the open air.

"I surrender," he shouted. "It's over. You should all be proud. The drug dealers win."

CHAPTER 117

YUKI AND OPPOSING counsel Zac Jordan met with district attorney Len Parisi in his office that Friday morning.

Parisi was in a decent mood, and Yuki observed lipstick on his collar. Maybe that had something to do with his sunny, "Hello, you two. Come in."

Zac shook hands with Parisi, and Yuki flung herself onto the couch. She was so emotionally exhausted, she'd dressed in jeans and a blazer this morning. In her mind, it was casual Friday and to hell with anyone who objected.

When Parisi was sitting behind his big-man desk, papers all straight edged and tidy, with the Red Dog clock on the wall showing 8:30 on the dot, Yuki began to explain the situation.

"Len, the death of Antoine Castro robbed the justice system but was a good thing all around. Castro is of no danger to anyone now, but he was an El Chapo wannabe. Some aspiring drug lord is going to pick up his business unless we get out in front of it."

"What do you suggest?"

Zac said, "I've spent a couple of hours with my client, Clay Warren. As you know, he was almost killed in jail, presumably by Castro's crew, who wanted to stop him from talking. He's not a bad kid. I wouldn't call him greedy or psychopathic. He's about average intelligence for a kid his age, but he was smart enough to stop talking when he was arrested."

Zac went on.

"I've got the real story out of Clay, and Yuki can back me up."

Parisi said, "And you want to what? I'm not getting it."

"If you agree with what you hear," said Zac, "we're hoping you'll drop the charges. Because honestly, he's not a criminal and the shanking he got is going to shorten his life. Maybe the judge will see that he's been punished enough. Dismiss the case and get him to a place where Castro's gang can't find him."

"Make it good," Len said. "Right now he's still on the hook for felony murder. Your trial is due to resume early next week."

"Clay is outside," said Yuki. "Let me bring him in so he can tell you himself."

CHAPTER 118

ZAC HELD THE office door for Clay Warren, who leaned heavily on a cane as he came through the entrance.

Parisi stood as Yuki made the introductions, and Clay stretched out his left hand and said, "Thanks for seeing me, sir."

"Hello, Mr. Warren. Have a seat."

The teen was in obvious pain. Zac knew he had bandages wrapping his torso under his orange jumpsuit. He looked for and found a chair with arms, close enough to Parisi's desk.

Zac stood and took a stance he might have used to examine a witness in court.

He said, "Clay, why are you now willing to discuss your relationship with Antoine Castro?"

"Because he's dead, Mr. Jordan. He can't personally hurt me, but I don't feel exactly safe."

"Explain what you mean."

"He's a gangsta, Mr. Jordan. I did nothing to Antoine, but snitches don't live to sing. I didn't say anything, and his crew just about destroyed my whatchacallits…organs. My stomach is punched through in about four places."

"Why did you try to hang yourself, Clay?"

"I was afraid I was going to get killed. And I thought if I offed myself, they wouldn't hurt my mother. My little sister is only twelve. Jesus. I can't stand to think about those animals getting to her."

Tears were falling now.

Yuki walked to the credenza behind Parisi's desk and brought a box of tissues over to Clay. He took a handful and held them to one eye and then the other. His hands shook.

Zac waited for Clay to pull himself together and then said, "Can you tell Mr. Parisi how you came to be involved with Antoine Castro?"

He nodded. "I was his gofer, sir. He gave me money to get him things. Go buy him a box of Ding Dongs at the gas station. Wash his car. That's how it started about a year ago. He'd call and tell me, do this, do that, then he'd give me money, and we needed it. I have a part-time job. Mom makes almost nothing." He sighed and said, "I didn't like Mr. Antoine, but he said he was watching out for me."

Zac said, "Tell Mr. Parisi about the day Officer Morton was killed."

Clay Warren said, "He, Mr. Antoine, needed me to make some deliveries with him."

"Deliveries of what?" Zac asked.

"Drugs. I didn't know what kind. They were in a suitcase. I put that into the trunk for him."

"You knew he was a drug dealer."

"Everyone did."

"Go on," Zac said.

"So he hands me the car keys and tells me, 'First stop, South San Francisco.' He says he'll tell me which way to go. I said okay. I like to drive. And the car handles good. So I'm driving, and this part is all my fault," said Clay Warren. "The light is yellow, but it turns red. No one is coming, so I gun it.

"Mr. Antoine's laughing. Like, *Good job, boy*. Now there are cops following me. And the rest is a blur. Somehow I got locked into traffic. Then the cop car makes us crash. The cop comes over and I don't have a driver's license. I don't have registration. Next thing I know, Mr. Antoine is over on my side of the car and he shoots the cop and steals a car.

"He's gone, and I get arrested for everything."

Yuki asked, "Did you know that Antoine had a gun?"

"I didn't see it, but sure. I knew he had a gun."

"You say you knew he sold drugs. How about the car?"

"It wasn't his. But he didn't tell me it was stolen."

Parisi said, "Mr. Warren, so you knew a lot, but not every-thing. Here's what I need to know now. Do you know where Castro got the drugs?"

"Yes, sir. I know his special source."

"Do you know the names of his customers?"

"Sure. I've driven him before."

"And do you know the names of his crew? People who are also participating in Mr. Castro's criminal enterprise?"

There was a long silence as Clay more or less shut down.

Yuki saw the same expression on his face that she had seen when he'd stopped talking to Zac and to her, when she'd been looking at a slam-dunk conviction for felony murder.

His expression was flat. He didn't make eye contact.

No one was home.

CHAPTER 119

YUKI STOOD IN the center of the room with her hands on her hips, staring at the kid.

"Zac, tell him," she said.

"Clay," Zac said. "If you don't want to go through with our agreement, I'll be happy to take you to jail and say good-bye."

The kid shook his head, looked past Yuki and Zac to the doorway as if he were going to make a run for it, a physical impossibility.

"Sorry, Len," Yuki said. "We won't take up any more of your time."

Clay seemed to understand he'd reached the point of no return. He said, "I could give you a list. Better than that, I have Mr. Antoine's book. I hid it. Everything you want is in there. His allergies are in there. His PIN codes and passwords to his phone. His lists of people and I don't know what all. He was always afraid the government would hack his phone."

"But I have a question. How are you going to stop his crew from killing me and my family?"

Zac said, "Mr. Parisi, I haven't seen the book, but I know where it is. If it's all my client says it is, we need to get him into witness protection."

"Where is it?" Len asked.

"It's in the property desk on the seventh floor."

"What? What are you talking about?"

"Clay, tell Mr. Parisi."

"It was on the seat when the police car made us crash. Fell out of his pocket. Uh...it's only this big."

He showed with his fingers a rectangle about the size of a deck of cards.

Clay Warren looked at his lawyer, who nodded.

"I put it in my jacket, and when I was booked, I handed over all my possessions. The book. Some change. My keys. They put all of it in an envelope with my name."

Parisi said, "Ms. Castellano, please go up to seven and get the book. Mr. Jordan, you and your client please wait outside with Toni. Thank you."

Yuki buzzed out of the office. Zac helped Clay to stand and walked with him to the door. It hadn't quite closed when he heard Parisi's chair squeak as he spun it so that his back was to the entrance.

"Your Honor? It's Len Parisi. I may have some exculpatory evidence to show you before the Clay Warren trial resumes next week."

CHAPTER 120

THE FULL MEMBERSHIP of the Women's Murder Club planned to have dinner at Susie's tonight.

It had been a week or two since Yuki had sung "Margaritaville" in the front room, since Cindy and I had broken bread together, since Claire had given up half a lung, since Yuki's trial had gone backward, which was what she had wanted.

And I had yet to tell how I survived the shootout at the Thornton Avenue corral and, with a lot of help from my friends, brought in the baddest gunman in the West.

We were all excited to catch up, listen, talk, eat with our fingers. Plus I was having a predinner meet-up with Claire. I missed her so much. I had to hear what Dr. Terk had told her, and she felt this wasn't a conversation to be had on the phone or in email.

I said to Joe at breakfast, "Please have dinner without me. This is a major girl catch-up night. Urgent. Vital. Long overdue."

My husband had never looked more handsome. His stay

with Dave Channing had given him a glow. He'd told me all about it, and I admired his ingenuity and his commitment. And that his faith in his friend, and himself, had been renewed.

We'd had a wonderful welcome-home night together, and now he was sitting on a barstool at the kitchen island. I moved in close and stood between his legs, combed his hair with my fingers.

He wrapped his arms around my waist and kissed me, so that I felt a charge down to my toes. He looked at me and said, "You want to go out with your friends, how could I possibly say no? But before you decide to go to Susie's, you have to see this."

"See what?"

Joe got up from the table and opened the freezer, took out a large white paper bag that he'd squeezed in behind the ice cube trays. He brought it back to the counter and said, "Take a look."

I pulled open the bag and peered in at a big, round container, the type commercial ice cream is packed in. This container's lid bore a logo that I remembered well. It was from the French Laundry.

"What is this, Joe? Ice cream?"

"What was your favorite dish?"

"You were my favorite, remember? Don't make me guess. This is so mean."

He laughed.

"I was planning to defrost this for dinner, Linds. Lobster macaroni and cheese. Three Michelin stars. That's the most stars you can get."

I kissed him.

I hugged him. I made sure he knew exactly how crazy I was about him for remembering that, and for scoring a quart of it, too. And then I had to say it.

"How about a rain check, Joe? I need a night out with my girls. We'll always have Napa."

CHAPTER 121

CLAIRE AND I got to Susie's before five o'clock and took a small table in the front room, which housed the long bar and the little stage for the steel band.

"Weird seeing this place in daylight," Claire said.

"Nothing's cooking," I said. "Literally."

Afternoon sunlight lit up the ocher-colored, sponge-painted walls and street paintings of a marketplace in Jamaica. The steel band often played a tune about that marketplace. I softly sang, "'Ackee rice, salt fish are nice. And the rum is fine any time of year.'"

Claire didn't join in, but she signaled to the bartender. He went by the name of Fireman, and that was name enough.

He called out, "What can I get for you, ladies?"

Claire called back, "Vodka, rocks."

I said, "Anchor Steam. And we need chips."

I assessed how Claire looked and sounded, and determined

that she was tired and sad and sobered by her medical experience.

She said, "I know what you're thinking. But it's not as bad as I look."

"Tell me," I said.

We had to wait for Fireman to set down the drinks and the bowl of chips, and after he'd said, "Can I get you anything else?" we shook our heads no in unison.

"Are you in pain?" I asked her.

"Not like you'd expect," she said. "And I'm half a lung lighter, can you tell?"

I forced a grin. It was hard to do.

Claire sipped her drink, commented that they'd given her no alcohol at the hospital. She crunched on some chips as I tried to find a way to ask her, *What's the prognosis, girlfriend? What's the deal?*

"Have you met my replacement?" she asked. "Mary Dugan?"

"Temporary replacement. She's nice."

"Qualified, too," Claire said.

"I'm going to kill you now," I said. "If you don't talk, this fork is the last thing you'll ever see."

She laughed, and God, it was a great sound. She looked happy for a couple of seconds and my heart expanded. Was she going to take her job back from the blonde in the ME's office? Was she going to go to Napa with Edmund and have another life-changing meal at the French Laundry? Or was Claire stalling? Was she looking for a way to tell me very bad news?

"You know how much I like Mitchell Terk?"

"Dr. Terk. Yeah. I know."

I swear I couldn't help it. I was gripping the fork so hard my knuckles were white.

"He says the margins are clean."

"This is true? You're telling me the truth."

She gave me a look like, *This is me. I don't lie to you.*

"There's a little more," she said.

"Don't stop now."

"Put down the fork, Sergeant. Keep your hands where I can see them."

I laughed, hard.

Then I said, "Will you please frickin' tell me, Butterfly? Speak and don't stop until I say so."

She took a pause to sigh, then said, "Cancer's a bastard, Linds. I'm good right now. But I have to go in for a checkup every three months for a while. Then every six months. And I have to take doctor's orders. No problem. Terk said I'll dance at my daughter's wedding. He'll be dancing, too."

I stood up, reached across the table, and put my arms around Claire's neck. It was not the most graceful hug in the world, but I couldn't let go. Claire got an arm around me and patted my back and said, "I love you, Lindsay."

I told her that I loved her, too, bent to kiss her cheek, and rocked the table, knocked over the drinks, soaked the chips, listened to the beer bottle hitting the floor.

"Oh, man."

Fireman called from the bar, "Set you up again, ladies?"

"Please and thank you," I said. "This time double chips and I'm having what she's having. With a bow on top."

CHAPTER 122

FIREMAN SAID, "YOUR table is ready."

That was great news. Claire and I made our way through the bar, which was filling up rapidly, passed the pickup window, and crossed into the back room. We slipped into the red leatherette booth we considered our own and sat opposite each other.

Lorraine checked in with us and brought sparkling water, and within a couple of minutes Yuki arrived, looking like she'd had a full-body massage and a mani-pedi.

"So damned great to see you," she said to Claire, sliding in beside her. "What's it been? Couple of decades?"

"Couple of weeks, Yuki, dear. All's well. I was just telling Lindsay it's checkups for a while, but Dr. Terk blew the all-clear whistle and said I'm free to go."

Yuki hugged Claire and said, "We missed you. When are you coming back to work?"

"Soon. Going to try something new. Sleep late. Play with

my little girl. Listen to music. I told the powers that be not to expect to see my shadow until Groundhog Day."

Ha. Groundhog Day had passed, but never mind the details.

Yuki asked where Cindy was, and to be honest, I wasn't sure she was coming. And if she came, were we buddies again?

I said, "Why don't I go first. Cindy knows all about the firefight in Silver Terrace."

"You go, girl," said Claire.

I filled my friends in on the whole fandango, condensing a bit so that Susie's didn't close up for the night while I was still talking. Yuki was following so closely, it was like she was taking notes.

"Does Barkley have a lawyer?" she asked.

"All I know is that he asked for one. And he made no statement at all."

"That's too bad," said Claire. "How're you gonna pin any of those murders on him? No witnesses. No forensics. What?"

"Guy by the name of Marty Floyd," I said. "He's not military. He says he never shot anyone, but he knows Moving Targets like the back of his dog."

I explained that Randi was in the women's jail, not talking, but Marty Floyd had spent eight consecutive hours with Mike Stempien, who now could decode Moving Targets.

"When Stempien goes back to the FBI next week, he's going to be the man of the hour, the week, and maybe the year," I said. "Here's hoping there's going to be a clean sweep of Moving Target shooters on both coasts."

I ducked my head and whispered, "We gave Cindy the exclusive story. Here she comes."

CHAPTER 123

CINDY SAILED INTO the back room with a big grin, a police scanner under her arm and a computer bag over her shoulder.

She scooted in next to me, put her radio on the table, and said, "Claire." All she said was "Claire."

"I'm gonna be fine," said Claire. "That's your headline and your bottom line, and I don't know when I'm going back to work. Maybe when I get enough of being home all day with Edmund and Rosie."

"Yahoo," said Cindy. "All caps. Above the fold."

Claire grinned.

Cindy had questions, of course, but when she was assured that Claire was on the right road, she linked her arm into mine. She said, "Damn it, Lindsay. That was awfully good of you."

"To?"

"To hand me the finale on the Kill Shot series. Holy cow, I've been struggling to keep up, let alone get a good front-row seat on these killings, but that interview with Brady ahead of the FBI announcement gave me a seat on the stage."

"Great, Cindy. I'm glad it turned out that way. And when Stempien's back with the FBI, I think they're going to shut down the whole Moving Targets operation."

"It's going to be hard," Cindy said. "Killing drug dealers really caught fire with the populace. They liked it. They cheered every time a drug dealer bit the dust. But the good guys won. Oh. Before I forget, I got a *raise*."

Yuki said, "And that means…"

"Dinner's on me," Cindy said.

We lifted our glasses and ordered our dinners, and I swear it was like starlight was beaming down on the four of us. And as our meals were served, Yuki had a few things to say.

"I picked this up on the ADA grapevine," she said. "Lindsay, Joe was mentioned."

"My Joe?"

"The very one."

Yuki told us what she'd heard about Carolee Atkins, RN, who was some kind of angel of death.

"The DA's office here will be prosecuting her. Two murders have been charged to her so far, but I have a feeling about this. More bodies are going to turn up. When old men with heart disease die in a hospital, nobody is alarmed. But I think the alarm has just sounded. I see autopsies in the near future looking for a medication that just plain stops your heart."

Claire said to Yuki, "Last I heard you were trying a case of a kid wheelman in the wrong place at the wrong time."

Yuki said, "Sorry to say, I cannot tell you more, but that young man disappeared with his family, and we're about to roll up a lot of drug dealers without firing a single shot."

We ate with our fingers, got a little sauced, and reveled in our camaraderie. Before we refused to let Cindy take the check, she asked me to come with her to the ladies' room.

"Hey. Linds. I'm sorry I was such a pill. I was wrong to push you where you couldn't go."

"You were doing your job, Cindy."

"And you were doing yours, Sergeant. I really cannot express how much I admire you."

I thought of the many times Cindy had been instrumental in solving crimes with her press card, by being the dogged bulldog she is. I remembered her taking a bullet and bringing down an armed killer on the block where I lived.

I said, "I feel the same way about you, Cin. You're the best."

Back at the table, we made a coffee toast to the Women's Murder Club, and to how lucky we all were in our jobs, and our friendships.

Claire said, "I'm gonna add some heavy cream to that."

She creamed her coffee, and then all of us, even those who hadn't had real cream in years, dosed our java.

I looked around at my three friends and thought how we didn't take our luck for granted. We never did.

We split the check and, soon after, went home to the men and children we loved.

May it always be so.

ACKNOWLEDGMENTS

With thanks to top attorneys Phil Hoffman and Steven Rabinowitz, partners at Pryor Cashman, LLP, in New York for their wise counsel, and, at the Bureau of Criminal Investigations, Stamford, Connecticut, Police Department, the real Captain Richard Conklin and tech wiz Mike Stempien.

We also wish to thank Mitchell Terk, MD, of Jacksonville, Florida, who advised us in the care of Claire Washburn, and thanks, too, to Michael A. Cizmar, Special Agent, FBI (retired), PMC *(private military contractor)*, Afghanistan.

And our admiration for Mary Jordan, who keeps innumerable plates in the air without dropping a one, to our gifted researcher, Ingrid Taylar, West Coast, USA, and to Team Patterson at Little, Brown. You are #1.

ABOUT THE AUTHORS

JAMES PATTERSON is the world's bestselling author and most trusted storyteller. He has created many enduring fictional characters and series, including Alex Cross, the Women's Murder Club, Michael Bennett, Maximum Ride, Middle School, and I Funny. Among his notable literary collaborations are *The President Is Missing*, with President Bill Clinton, and the Max Einstein series, produced in partnership with the Albert Einstein estate. Patterson's writing career is characterized by a single mission: to prove that there is no such thing as a person who "doesn't like to read," only people who haven't found the right book. He's given over three million books to schoolkids and the military, donated more than seventy million dollars to support education, and endowed over five thousand college scholarships for teachers. The National Book Foundation recently presented Patterson with the Literarian Award for Outstanding Service to the American Literary Community, and he is also the recipient of an Edgar Award and six Emmy Awards. He lives in Florida with his family.

MAXINE PAETRO is a novelist who has collaborated with James Patterson on more than two-dozen thrillers, including the bestselling Women's Murder Club, Private, and Confessions series; *Woman of God;* and other stand-alone novels. She lives with her husband, John, in New York.

READ ON FOR AN EXCERPT
FROM THE NEXT
WOMEN'S MURDER CLUB THRILLER...

CHAPTER 1

CINDY WAS AT work in her office at the *San Francisco Chronicle* when she heard a woman calling her name.

More accurately, she was screaming it.

"Cinnn-dyyyyyyy."

Cindy lifted her eyes from her laptop, looked through her glass office wall that faced the newsroom and saw a tall, nimble woman zig-zagging through the maze of cubicles. She was taking the corners with the deftness of a polo pony as a security guard with a truck-size spare tire chased her—and he was falling behind.

As a reporter Cindy had a sharp eye for details. The woman shrieking her name wore yoga pants and a Bruins sweatshirt, a knit cap over chin-length black hair, and had mascara bleeding down her cheeks. She looked determined—and deranged. The woman didn't slow as she raced toward Cindy's open door, but a moment later, the lanky woman was inside Cindy's office, both hands planted on her desk, black-rimmed red eyes fastened on hers.

She shouted at Cindy, "I'm Kath-leen Wyatt. K.Y. You remember now?"

"Your screen name."

Wyatt said, "I posted on your crime blog this morning. My daughter, Linda, and her little baby girl are missing, and her husband killed them."

Security guard Rafe Bailey pulled up to the doorway, panting. "I'm sorry, Ms. Thomas. You," he said to the woman who was leaning over the desk. "You come with me. Now."

Cindy said, "Kathleen, are you armed?"

"Be serious."

"Stand by, Rafe," Cindy said. "Kathleen. Sit down."

The guard said that he would be right outside the door and took a position a few feet away. Cindy turned her attention back to the woman now sitting in the chair across from her desk and ignored the inquiring eyes of writers in the newsroom peering through her office wall.

Cindy said, "I remember you now. Kathleen, I had to take down your post from my blog."

"He beats her. They're gone."

Cindy's boss, Henry Tyler, leaned into her office. "Everything okay, Cindy?"

"Thanks, Henry. We're fine."

He nodded, then, tapped the face of his watch.

Cindy nodded acknowledgment of the six o'clock closing. Her story was in the polish phase and it was half-past five. Henry had a word with Rafe and then closed the door.

Cindy turned back to Kathleen Wyatt saying, "You accused a man of murder and used his name. The rules are right there on the site. No vulgarity, name-calling, or personal attacks. He could sue you for defamation. He could keep the *Chronicle* in court until the next ice age."

Wyatt said, "You come across as such a nice person, Cindy. But, like everyone else, you're all about the money."

"You're doing it again, Kathleen. I'm going to have to ask you to leave."

The woman folded her arms over Cindy's desk, dropped her head, and sobbed. Cindy thought Kathleen Wyatt was out of her mind with fear.

Cindy said, "Kathleen. Kathleen, do you know for a fact that this man, Lucas, abducted Linda and your granddaughter?"

She lifted her head and shook it, "No."

Cindy said, "Another question. Have you called the police?"

This time when Kathleen Wyatt raised her head, she said, "Yes. Yes, yes, yes, but have they found the baby? No."

CHAPTER 2

WHILE KATHLEEN WYATT dried her eyes with her sweatshirt Cindy retrieved the post she'd deleted this morning and read it again.

Kathleen had written about her son-in-law, Lucas Burke, using ALL CAPS to shout in print that Burke had abused Kathleen's daughter, Linda, and that he had even been violent with their one-year-old baby, Lorrie. Kathleen had written that she was terrified for them both, and even though the two had only been missing for a couple of hours, she trusted her gut.

Cindy had seen the post a few minutes after Kathleen had submitted it. The screaming capital letters, the many misspellings, and the nature of the post unloaded on a newspaper blog made the poster sound crazy. Or else, it had been someone's idea of fun.

Now that Wyatt had broken into the newsroom and told the story to her face, her credibility had risen. But, damn it. Cindy couldn't know if Kathleen was paranoid or in an understandable panic that her loved ones could be in danger—or worse. Her fear was relatable and the idea of a murderous husband plausible. It happened too often. And that it may have happened since Kathleen posted her cri de coeur this morning made Cindy feel awful and guilty. And still, there was nothing she could do to help.

Kathleen slapped the desk to draw Cindy's attention.

Her voice was rough from yelling, but she said, "I called the police as soon as I couldn't locate Linda. She has run away with the baby before. She's twenty now. An adult. And after you call the police once or three times, you have to beg them to pay attention. But I did it. The cops called in the K-9 unit, put out an Amber Alert. Or so they say. I don't know for sure."

Cindy said, "When there's a missing baby, what'd you say, she's a year old?"

"Closer to a year and a half."

"They're looking for her."

Kathleen reached into her fanny pack and pulled out a picture of mother and child. They both looked very young. "Lorrie is fourteen months to be exact. And you're right. Anytime a baby is missing, they're supposed to go all out. That baby could be dead already. If you'd run this picture in the paper six hours ago…"

"I'm a reporter, Kathleen. I need confirmation, you must know that. But, still, I feel sorry—"

"Don't you dare tell me how sorry you are. Sorry won't help my daughter. Sorry won't help her baby girl."

"Sit tight," Cindy said. She reviewed her story about the shooting in the Tenderloin, changed a few words and then rewrote the "kicker," the last line. She addressed an email to Tyler, attached her story and pressed "send."

Kathleen Wyatt watched.

When Cindy saw that the email had launched, she said to Wyatt, "No promises. Let me see what I can do."

CHAPTER 3

CINDY SPEED-DIALED the number, then drummed her fingers on her desk until Lindsay picked up.

"Boxer."

"Linds, I need some advice. It's important."

"What's wrong?"

"No, I'm fine. Can you give a couple of moments to a woman with a missing daughter and grandchild?"

"Me?"

"Thanks, Linds. I'm putting you on speaker. Lindsay, this is Kathleen Wyatt. I'll let her tell you. Kathleen, this is Sergeant Boxer of Homicide."

Lindsay said, "Kathleen. What happened?"

"They've disappeared into a black hole."

"Say again?"

Kathleen said, "My daughter, Linda, and her baby disappeared this morning, and her husband has threatened to kill them."

"You say they disappeared. Is there any indication that they were hurt?"

"My daughter won't answer the phone. She is always home all day with the baby. I went over there. The house is empty. Her car is gone. I've called her and called her, and we always, always speak in the morning after Lucas has gone to work."

"He's the husband?"

"Linda has told me I don't know many times that he's said that he hates her. He wishes Lorrie had never been born. He's hit her, but not so it shows. And yes, I've called the police."

Lindsay asked, "Had Linda taken out a restraining order on Lucas?"

"She wouldn't do it. She's only twenty. She doesn't work. She was afraid of him, and also, oh God help her. She loves him. She's too young. Too dumb. Too needy."

Horns honked over the phone line. Lindsay was in her car. She raised her voice over the clamor and asked Kathleen, "What was the police response?"

"Today? They say they talked to Lucas, but he had an alibi. His girlfriend, probably. You should see him. Smooth as ice. Lucas. He denies threatening her, them, of course. They have some units searching and they have dogs now in the vicinity of his house. And drones. And they say Linda will come home. And Lindsay—if I may call you that? This time I really think he means to kill them. Or what I really think? It may be too late."

The words "too late" tailed up into a heart-wrenching howl. The security guard reached for the door, but Cindy put up her hand and shook her head.

Lindsay said, finally, "Go on."

Kathleen said, "Linda told me his girlfriend is another dummy, younger than she is. He meets these girls where he teaches—"

"Who was the officer who took your complaint?"

"I don't remember his name. I left his number in my car."

"Is he a uniformed officer?"

"Yes. I flagged him down. Oh. Bernard. Officer Bernard."

"Kathleen," Lindsay said. "I'll check with Officer Bernard. Give Cindy your number and I'll get back to you. I agree that if Linda has run away before, she may have done it again. But if a baby has been missing since eight this morning, that's a police matter. Call the SFPD, major crimes division and ask for Sergeant Murray. Keep your phone charged."

"I've met him. Renny Murray. He doesn't take me seriously."

"I'll call him, too," said Lindsay. "See how the investigation—Sorry, I've to go."

Cindy said goodbye to Lindsay, watched Kathleen write down her phone number with a shaking hand as she muttered, "You should help me, Cindy. Lorrie is dead. I feel it in my heart."

Kathleen was crying as if she was sure they were dead. As if she knew.

Cindy said, "It's almost dark. Go home and call the police again. Did you call Linda's friends? What about her neighbors? If you hear anything at all, let me know. Wait. Give me that picture."

Kathleen handed the picture of Linda and Lorrie to

Cindy who snapped it with her phone. She told Kathleen that she could run it with a request for information as to the whereabouts without mentioning Lucas Burke.

Tugging at her watch cap, Kathleen muttered a thank you and Cindy walked her out to the elevator. Cindy went back to her office wondering why Kathleen Wyatt had come to her. Was going to a newspaper her way of getting ahead of suspicion? Was she right about her son-in-law? Or was Kathleen Wyatt a paranoid schizophrenic?

She'd talk to Richie when she got home tonight.

And then she'd call Lindsay.

CHAPTER 4

I'D BEEN AT my desk since seven a.m.

It was now eight-thirty on Tuesday morning. Brady had called a meeting for nine, all hands, and I had to get some answers for Kathleen Wyatt before the meeting.

My partner, Inspector Rich Conklin, and I sit at facing desks at the front of the dull gray homicide bullpen. He'd just arrived, heard me talking to Sergeant Renny Murray over the phone and went to the break room to get coffee.

He knew I was doing a favor for Cindy, his live-in love and my friend. When he got back to his desk, I thanked Murray and hung up as Conklin pushed a fresh mug of mud over to my desk. It was black, three sugars, just how I like it.

He asked, "What did Murray say?"

"He said that Lucas Burke is a bad dude, but he doesn't think he's a killer."

"How bad?"

I blew on my coffee, then referred to my notes.

"Lucas threatened a female motorist after a fender

13

bender, grabbed her shoulders, called her names, and shook her. He was charged with assault and battery, but the motorist didn't press charges. Same year, Lucas took a chain saw to a neighbor's tree he claimed was on his property. It was the neighbor's tree. He got fined. Looks like eight hundred dollars. End of that. Then, Kathleen reported him for domestic abuse of her daughter, but Linda denied it, said her mother is nuts. Kathleen is a little loosely wrapped, Richie. And that makes her hard to read, but also true, abused women often deny the abuse. Anyway, that's Lucas Burke's record. He's at least combative. Sounds like he's got an anger disorder."

Rich said, "While you were on the phone, I checked with missing persons. Missus and baby Burke are still missing. I hope to God Linda really did run away."

"It's reasonable to hope," I said. "Her phone, wallet, and car are gone. She hasn't used her credit card, but that's not proof. She could have a boyfriend picking up the tab on their way out of town to—I don't know, name a place, Cancun."

I called Cindy and sipped coffee while Rich walked over to Cappy's desk, sat on the edge of it, and traded what-ifs with him and Chi. I could hear them opining on the upcoming meeting, but there was little controversy. We were all of the same opinion. Brady was going to announce his future plans, and we all would be affected by it. But what had he decided to do?

The root of the matter was the scandal that had devastated the Southern Station, our station, not long ago. Ted Swanson, lieutenant of Robbery, had conceived a get-rich plan that involved enlisting two teams of bad cops who had successfully knocked off drug dealers and a number of payday loan joints.

A shooting war broke out between a ruthless drug kingpin and the cops. Eighteen people died in several shootouts and even Swanson took enough lead to kill him two or three times over. But he survived his injuries and was now serving out the rest of his worthless life at Chino, a maximum-security prison downstate.

Warren Jacobi, our friend, my former partner, and at that time chief of police, had to take the fall for Swanson's dirty, illegal, drug war that had gone on under his nose. He was retired out and Jackson Brady, our good lieutenant, picked up the slack for Jacobi, running Homicide and the Southern Station at the same time.

Brady farmed out most of the robbery and narcotics crimes to different police divisions and still, managing so many cops, so many issues, was too much for one man, even if the man was Jackson Brady. When asked to choose which job he wanted, he'd put off the decision. Maybe he took too long. Lately, rumor had it that the Mayor was having talks with Stefan Rowan, a heavyweight organized crime commander from New York, to replace Jacobi. That meant Brady would stay in homicide and report to the new man.

The bets heavily favored the New York top cop to become our boss of bosses.

I looked past Conklin and saw Brady leave his office in the back corner of the squad room. He put on his jacket and headed up the center aisle toward the front of the room.

Conklin got up from Cappy's desk as Brady passed and joined me at our desks.

Brady took the floor, his blond-white hair pulled back in a pony, his denim shirt tucked in, his dark jacket unbuttoned.

I couldn't read his expression, but I loved working for Brady. He was smart. He never asked anyone to do anything he wouldn't do. He was brave. And he was loyal to the people who reported to him.

What scared me most is that the rumor might be wrong. That Brady was going to step up to become chief of police, and the hard ass New Yorker would replace him as Homicide C.O.

Maybe a promotion would be good for Brady, but speaking for myself, it would break my heart.

For a complete list of books by
JAMES PATTERSON

VISIT
JamesPatterson.com

 Follow James Patterson on Facebook
@JamesPatterson

 Follow James Patterson on Twitter
@JP_Books

 Follow James Patterson on Instagram
@jamespattersonbooks

COMING SOON